# Aqueous

Shyback, Jade, 1973- author.
Aqueous : a novel

2023
33305253894665
ca      06/12/23

# Aqueous

. . .

a novel

Jade Shyback

**XENO**

Book design by Mark E. Cull

Library of Congress Cataloging-in-Publication Data

Names: Shyback, Jade, 1973– author.
Title: Aqueous: a novel / Jade Shyback.
Description: First edition. | Pasadena, CA: Xeno, 2023.
Identifiers: LCCN 2022019365 (print) | LCCN 2022019366 (ebook) | ISBN
    9781939096098 (paperback) | ISBN 9781939096104 (ebook)
Subjects: CYAC: Undersea colonies—Fiction. | Survival—Fiction. |
    Environmental degradation—Fiction. | Science fiction. | LCGFT: Science
    fiction. | Bildungsromans. | Novels.
Classification: LCC PZ7.1.S51873 Aq 2023 (print) | LCC PZ7.1.S51873
    (ebook) | DDC [Fic]—dc23
LC record available at https://lccn.loc.gov/2022019365
LC ebook record available at https://lccn.loc.gov/2022019366

The National Endowment for the Arts, the Los Angeles County Arts Commission,
the Ahmanson Foundation, the Dwight Stuart Youth Fund, the Max Factor Family
Foundation, the Pasadena Tournament of Roses Foundation, the Pasadena Arts &
Culture Commission and the City of Pasadena Cultural Affairs Division, the City
of Los Angeles Department of Cultural Affairs, the Audrey & Sydney Irmas Char-
itable Foundation, the Kinder Morgan Foundation, the Meta & George Rosenberg
Foundation, the Albert and Elaine Borchard Foundation, the Adams Family Foundation, the Riordan Foundation, Amazon Literary Partnership, the Sam Francis
Foundation, and the Mara W. Breech Foundation partially support Red Hen Press.

First Edition
Published by Xeno Books
An imprint of Red Hen Press
Pasadena, CA
www.redhen.org

# Aqueous

CHAPTER ONE

I missed the sun. I missed its warmth on a breeze that tickled my skin, and the blinding effect of its stare. I dreamt of running beneath it, breathless, chased by the laughter of sun-kissed siblings. Bleached locks and tan skin were the fleeting recollections of my terrestrial childhood lost, but the ocean created amazement too. It orchestrated new memories that I was thankful for, and the view from my pod was unarguably magnificent—a vast seafloor aglow with life. A place where fantastic creatures floated by, winding their way through the waving gardens our botanists had engineered. New species discovered us as we discovered them, curiously approaching the glass to observe humankind, or what was left of it.

I was a lucky one, one of the few who remained, and I was trained to understand that there was no benefit in longing for a time that had perished in the sun. Besides, my subterranean plant taxonomy catalogue wasn't going to log itself. It was time to snap out of the past and into to the present, so I pivoted my chair away from the glass, back toward my desk.

I've lived most of my life two and a half kilometers below sea level in subterranean merstation number three, also known as Aqueous—an underwater utopia created during an ecological coup to save the human race. The mini-pod that I occupy is standard-issue for a trainee my age, and acts as my floating, spherical bedroom underneath the sea. Made of syntactic foam and borosilicate glass, it has translucency for privacy and transparency for optimal environmental observation. Tethered above a common corridor and uniquely designed, mini-pods seal with a bottom airlock so that in the event of an emergency, not that we have ever had one, they could automatically detach, allowing the pod and its inhabitant to drift upward and become, in theory, a one-way ticket to the surface, not that anyone would want to go there.

The shell of each mini-pod contains identical furnishings. My pod, MP124, has the all-important learning nook complete with desk, chair, keypad, and monitor. There are two bookshelves located above the desk that, for the most part, are never used because the educational manuscripts and essays studied by trainees are stored on the shared drive. I keep, however, a small yellowed satchel of beads on the lower shelf. It's the only item that I own.

My berth, positioned above the nook, is a starry planetarium of twinkling station lights. It's an observatory of departments towering high above my pod where the corridors and gathering spaces of Aqueous stand at attention, illuminating the surrounding water. As a comforting nightlight, it's breathtaking, and I mean that quite literally. Outside of the glass, I would not be able to breathe.

My clothes hang aligned, hooked to the side of the nook. The few outfits I have are standard-issue based on rank and will be surrendered when my rank changes. Currently, I am ranked Y10 and have been allocated Standard-Issue Dress (SID) to reflect this. Like all Y10s, I have daytime SIDs, athletic SIDs, dinner SIDs, formal SIDs, casual SIDs, and sleeping SIDs. The residents of Aqueous are valued equally, making uniformity paramount.

Behind the nook is the lav, containing only the essentials: a sink, a washlet, a shower, and the tiniest mirror imaginable because while cleanliness is necessary, vanity is not. I am given one small towel per week, never any paper, and the all-in-one cleanser is restocked sparingly. To make matters worse, minimal water consumption is expected. Showers are not only timed, they're infrequent. Washing thoroughly, quickly, is imperative because beneath the floor of each pod is an elimination chamber designed to recycle all waste. Reusing the water too soon increases the likelihood of becoming very, very sick.

In stark contrast to the ocean beyond, everything in a mini-pod is bright white. I was taught that this, in conjunction with applied photonics, counteracted the negative psychological effects of life in the dark, but our superiors liked to jest that the all-bright-white eliminated the mess associated with teenage bedrooms. It was difficult to imagine mess in the absence of possessions.

I was staring absentmindedly at my taxonomy catalogue.

*Ugh.*

I pivoted back to the glass once again, abandoning my log to return to the magic of the undersea. The minimalistic design of my mini-pod did not extend beyond the glass. The waters of Monterey Canyon provided a spectacle of habitats to delight any young observer. From cavernous walls, to rocky outcroppings, and sandy seafloor, it was an aquatic playground of magnificent proportion. Pink, pompom anemones waved at comb jellies as fangtooth fish swam by. Tiny flapjack octopi propelled themselves through the saline as the ominous anglerfish searched for its next snack. It was a seafloor performance of endless entertainment until it was interrupted by my AI Assistant.

"ATTENTION. ATTENTION. Empyreal Blaise has identified at your airlock," it alerted.

I quickly tapped the release, allowing an elegant woman to ascend. Irrefutably the most beautiful resident on Aqueous, I never tired of her pleasant face. Wide-eyed with high cheekbones and a long golden mane, she was effortlessly regal and every inch the admiral's wife. Her hair was routinely knotted at the nape of her neck, emphasizing her height, and her lean frame allowed her SIDs to drape favorably over a heart true and pure. She was heaven personified. Intelligent and poised, her counsel was sought by many, making her an unofficial ambassador of the station, and a wave of calm washed over me as her expression relaxed into a loving smile.

"Oh Marisol, you have the look of a lost little lamb. Are you still hard at work?" she asked, floating toward me with outstretched arms to gather me into her familiar embrace.

*A lamb . . . What did a lamb look like again?*

There were too many marine species to catalogue to consider the characteristics of a lamb. I disentangled myself from her long limbs.

"I'm stressed. I have no idea how I am going to get everything done before graduation. I've got to finish my taxonomy report, curate bacteria samples, review my labs on carbon cycling, finish the assigned code review, and log a few more hours of simulated dives. My thesis is nowhere near completion and grad is a week away, followed immediately by the anniversary."

"But you'll have a chance to relax at your party."

"I appreciate that you want to celebrate my birthday, but could we postpone it? Or better yet, skip it altogether? I have no time for a frivolous party."

"There's always time for a party when you're turning sixteen. You're growing up too quickly for my liking," she said, stepping back slightly to scrutinize my overall well-being. Her visual analysis always made me uncomfortable because we did not look alike. My small stature was shadowed by her towering height and my hair had browned during a decade in the dark.

She glanced around the room.

"You'll have your new pod and assignment soon. I'm so proud of you, Marisol. You've accomplished so much in ten short years, but many of those same accomplishments will be celebrated collectively by the Y10s at graduation, and I want to showcase *you*. Just you. You deserve the spotlight before we celebrate scholastic achievements with your peers, followed by station successes with all of the residents during the anniversary. I know you'll enjoy it, and I'll be sure to schedule it after the trials, once the pressure is off. You'll have time to get everything done, so don't fret."

Despite my heightened anxiety, I was relieved to talk of celebrations, not assignments. She was masterful at making me feel better and had always been my biggest supporter. My savior, in fact. I wouldn't disappoint her by admitting that my nightmares were back, or that my thoughts often drifted to the past. To do so would dilute her role in my upbringing, diminishing the joy she associated with my unavoidable milestone birthday.

"Come on. Let's get out of here. You need a break."

"I can't spare the time," I argued in futility.

"I know best, and I won't take no for an answer. Besides, you're not allowed to refuse your mother."

She extended a long, dainty finger to gently tap me on the nose before turning to glide toward the airlock. She expected me to follow, but I stood motionless behind her. Unknowingly, she had tapped into something painful. Something that had lingered for ten long years. No matter how much I appreciated her, or how much I loved and admired her, she wasn't my mother. We had left my mother under the warmth of the sun.

## CHAPTER TWO

It was dawn, but we were not high enough.

"You must climb, Sunniva. We cannot stop. Not yet," said my mother.

It was hot and we were dirty. More dirty than usual. Our hands had torn and bruised black from crawling along the jagged hillside, but we needed to traverse the barren slope before the sun rose. The large rocks and caves of the mountains above would shadow us from the midday sun.

We had heard of a fortified, alpine village that was rumored to have rations. It was possibly the last food source in the area, making it well worth the climb, but we were not alone, and there would not be enough. Dozens of displaced families were making the same desperate ascent. Hopeless, defeated, empty, and silent, we snaked upward, together, to plead with those at the top.

The end of the world had arrived too quickly, and as many had predicted, rising temperatures melted the ice caps, flooding coastal cities. As the sun relentlessly cranked up the heat, we witnessed the largest global human migration ever recorded. People moved inland, placing a tremendous strain on food supplies.

What didn't flood, burned, and viable farmland diminished. Crops turned to dust, fresh water dried up, and food supplies dwindled. Then our power grids overheated and failed, and without sufficient renewable technologies we lost air conditioners, lights, gas stations, internet, plumbing, and telephones.

No electricity meant no refrigeration, so what little food could be grown, spoiled. Farmer's herds perished, as did wild animals and birds, making ground insects and roots a primary source of nutrition for those still alive.

We had angered the sun so greatly that it ceased being our regulator, our rejuvenator, and retaliated against our greed by scorching Earth in blistering reprehension for our disobedience and abuse. Stripping our biome to expose our fragility, the sun doled out a punishment so severe that most people died, and those left suffered perpetually burnt skin, cracked lips, and hunger as the indelible reminders of its wrath. Our only hope existed in the lower temperatures of higher altitudes, so we climbed.

As temperatures climbed, so did the topography of our planet. Alpine areas, formerly too cold to sustain vegetation, greened. The hippies in these areas, living off-the-grid, were initially the least affected. Ecologically minded, outdoor enthusiasts, they had purchased inexpensive properties, installing photovoltaic modules, cisterns, and wind turbines to power their modest retreats, but as prices skyrocketed for sustainable homes, many were convinced to sell. Enticed by fat offers from the wealthy and powerful, alpine homesteads changed hands quickly to the detriment of sellers, who were late to grasp the ephemerality of currency. Soon there was nothing left to buy and nowhere safe to go. Then the walls went up, fortifying alpine compounds where the rich could survive.

My mother had not been rich, but she had outshined, outlasted them all. She had been a housekeeper until there were none left to keep, and now her heat soaked hair lay tangled around her glistening face. It was the beauty of the vagabond life I knew. Her beauty, and I loved it. Her thick matted locks would fall to her shoulders when there was nothing to tie them back. They framed her face like a picture, and I liked to twirl them between my fingers while her inquisitive eyes inspected me.

In dire times we still found joy. She enjoyed playing tricks, like convincing me that my foot size had doubled and I would have no shoes, before revealing an extraordinary pair that she had recovered during our pilgrimage. She would laugh wholeheartedly at my surprise, throwing her head back in delight to let the notes of her happiness ring true. She was small, but resourceful, and her strength had endured, even under a merciless sun.

It is remarkable what the human body can endure when given no alternative. My mother would not surrender. She would adapt. She moved us at night to conserve energy because daytime temperatures were too hot. We scavenged for dwindling nourishment along the way, and though we were running out of resources, I was not aware. Her focus had shifted to keeping me content until it was no longer possible.

I was exhausted and had stopped climbing again.

"Look here, Sunniva. You are a lucky one. I have found some magic story beads for you."

Her eyes twinkled with excitement.

"What are they, Mommy?"

I stared down at the crisp pine needles in the palm of her hand.

"Each of these beads will grant you one fantastic story, full of bountiful treasure and gigantic beasts, but as a princess you will have to be brave."

I grabbed every bead as fast as I could and looked up into her wise, hazel eyes.

"I am brave."

"Yes, Sunniva, I think that you are, but have you ever seen a dragon?"

"No, Mommy. Have you?"

She looked from side to side, slowly, deliberately, in a manner not to be overheard, despite a lack of listeners, before whispering, "Give me one bead and I will tell you all about the king and queen who captured it."

I passed her the best pine needle that I had, careful not to drop a single one, for I would need them during our adventures ahead. That's when I would prove to her how brave I could be.

She accepted the bead and resumed moving slowly up the hillside, and I, clutching my precious beads tightly in my small battered hand, eagerly followed.

• • •

I was an accident. Conceived beyond the failure of existence, long after couples knew their offspring would perish, I was remarkably celebrated as a gift from the sun. I was Sunniva, the youngest and only daughter of my parent's three children, and I was spoiled. Not in the conventional way, with expensive toys and sweets, but with my father and two brothers vying to be my favorite. They kept me blissfully unaware of the peril we faced.

My father, Senan, was a mechanic. He could fix anything, but he was especially good at making dolls. I had a village of stick people, fastened with wire and clothed in trash and dry grasses. We named them together and created an adventure for each one. It was unusual behavior for a rugged, burly man, but he had a soft side he reserved for his girls: his daughter and his wife. He taught his sons to care for me as though I were porcelain, in the same manner he cared for my mother. Theirs was a love story that could not be clouded by smoke-filled air, and together they would curate our remaining days with imaginary adventure.

We danced and sang, made forts and played games well beyond the fires that forced us to abandon our home, and I was too small to understand our circumstances. It was never discussed. My fantastical education was rooted in whatever tale they told me. I never went to school.

My father and brothers were excellent storytellers. I travelled to the moon and back on the shoulders of Colm, my eldest brother. He was the tallest of our vertically challenged clan, with a gentle and agreeable demeanor. I would dig my hands into his thick, wavy hair as I rode on his back, racing through the galaxy, narrowly escaping the clutches of the black hole that wanted to pull us into its infinite abyss. My younger brother, Lorcan, played the black hole or the monster or the shark. He was whatever nemesis was trying to get us that day, but we always escaped and inevitably convinced him to join us, choosing good over evil.

My father had given each of us a nickname. With the responsibility of an adult and the playful antics of a child, Colm became the chameleon. I liked his nickname much more than mine. I was the ant. It wasn't impressive at first, and the attempts of my brothers to stifle their laughter each time my father used it, failed, but he assured me that the little ant was far more powerful than it appeared. According to my father, ants were clever little creatures that could enslave other ants to do their work. He made it sound impressive, so I became fond of it. I was the fierce little ant that could control the entire family, and I loved it.

Lorcan was the dingo. Cunning and agile, he was a ferocious predator. Noisy too. He was loyal to his pack, but dominant toward others. It suited him. My mother was the raven. Exceedingly intelligent and opportunistic, my father explained that folklore credited the dark, feathered raven with dropping a rock into the ocean to form the first land. She liked it, and it pleased our father, who had nicknamed himself the eagle.

Combining the first initials of our nicknames, my father decided that we were the Crusaders of Adventure, Daydreams, and Rainbows Evermore (CADRE). A small group of people united and trained for a specific purpose, our cadre's purpose was survival, but our bird-brained parents were trained and dedicated to the escalation of fun. Combining limited resources with an endless landscape of imagination, CADRE was determined to enjoy each moment of our expiring union. For example, I had never seen a real rainbow, it never rained, but I had crested one a hundred times on my journey to the Jungle of Judgement, where I would condemn the naughty giant to save the flyaway fairies. Lorcan was always the giant, I was the winged wizard, Colm and Dad played the fairies, and Mom was the judge. Befitting.

The Crusaders of Adventure, Daydreams, and Rainbows Evermore made every moment count, and the amusement of our actions stamped out heat stroke and hunger like firefighters stamped out flames, but the joys of our exploits could not sustain us, and my brothers ultimately died. We lost Lorcan first. He collapsed as we searched for elusive Aztec gold. My father told me that he would be taken by their gods to a sacred temple, and that we would find him at the end of the game. I was satisfied with that and our pilgrimage continued. Then Colm couldn't stand up. I was told that Colm had been put to sleep by the spell of an evil sorceress and had to wait for true love's kiss to wake up. But we would see him afterward, so we continued on without him.

I did not see my parents mourn the loss of their sons. They stroked their hair and folded their arms across their chests before giving each of them a prolonged hug, but in their determination not to upset me, not a single tear was shed. They simply walked me away. Until it was my father's turn. His death was different. He was conscious, but could not stand or speak, and motioned with a shaking hand for my mother and me to leave. I was confused, as he was usually the leader of the game, but my mother told me that he needed to wait quietly for the queen of the butterflies to transport him to Mystical Cocoon, where Lorcan and Colm had started an enchanted game of hide and seek. If she saw us, he wouldn't get to go, so my mother kissed him goodbye and we walked off, content. In fact, we walked past many people that day. Lifeless families drying up in the sun.

• • •

The king and queen were still searching for the dragon when we reached impassible gates at the base of the summit. The sun had begun to whip its unrelenting rays across our weary shoulders, so we tucked ourselves behind some rocks, in shade unclaimed by the other survivors mulling about. Upset and frustrated, they jostled for priority before the iron gates inscribed with the name *Nebulous*. I believed it was the fortress of the most royal nobility in the land, and I was disappointed that I could not immediately enter to tell them that I was a princess.

A curious hum resounded from within—electricity. The village had power that had not been extended to those suffering, and this discovery enraged the people trying to enter. Their anger turned to violence as the growing mob banged fists and hurled rocks at the heavy doors. Hours of unsuccessful attempts to scale the entrance led to scouts surveying the perimeter, which led to digging, which led to sobs and finally silence. There was no way in. The occupants were well prepared for our arrival. Their fortress was impenetrable.

I did not know that this stronghold had been my mother's last hope, but defeat was visible in her eyes. There would be no food or water for us, and the shadows near the fortress walls were teeming with violent people. To remain as we were would result in injury, so she gathered me into her arms and carried me safely away from the others. Walking away from the gates, we settled into a nearby ditch where she cradled me in her lap.

"You've earned your beauty sleep, my princess. You were a strong, brave girl today."

She stroked my cheek with her cold, unsteady hand as the color drained from her face. Unaware, I circled my left arm around her neck, letting my heavy head sink onto her shoulder.

"I'm thirsty, Momma."

"Sleep first, my darling. We'll sleep under this dazzling sun until we can continue our adventure this evening. That's when you'll hear the best story yet."

Clutching my magic story beads in my right hand, my eyes grew heavy to the faint drumming of her heart. I wanted the story now, but I was too tired to stay awake.

# CHAPTER THREE

I opened my eyes as the ground around us shook. I may never have woken were it not for those vibrations. It was getting dark and I was nauseated, struggling to bring my vision into focus. This night was different. The blistering daytime sun demanded silence. It sucked up sounds like we had lapped up dew drops before moisture disappeared, but in the sun's dusky absence, people stirred. They scavenged like mice searching for crumbs in a dark kitchen, but the sounds of this evening exceeded the grumblings of hungry souls searching for food. It muffled the commotion of the survivors who, united, could not produce an equivalent force. This was loud, and my head pounded from the noise.

A mechanical orchestra, the deafening forte continued to build with each of my unsteady breaths, and great plumes of dust began rising high above the fortress, into the evening air. Then, in an instant, as if someone had summoned the sun, the village was illuminated in bright white light. The fortress had awoken like a gigantic beast, and its dusty breath began billowing over the walls. Spilling upon us, choking us out, the mob scattered in search of air.

I attempted to stand, but I would not run after the others. I could not leave my mother.

"Momma! Wake up!"

I tugged frantically at her threadbare tunic, but she was lifeless.

"Quickly, Momma! Wake up!"

I began to cough on the dust. It had filled my lungs, drying them, and creating a sound equivalent to a bark. It was this sound that caused my mother to move. First her eyes, then a hand. She reached up to me, confused.

"What is it, Sunniva? What is happening?"

"I don't know, but I'm scared."

At that word my mother became alert, focused, and looked at me with complete calm.

"Scared? How can you be scared? Let me see . . ."

Her eyes scanned the situation before us.

"Oh, yes. This is it. This is what we've been waiting for."

She slowly rose to her feet as the thunderous groans continued to bang forth from behind the Nebulous gates.

An alarm sounded. The scattering survivors paused to look back, and raising their arms to shield themselves from the bright lights atop the walls they could see that the iron doors were moving.

"ATTENTION. ATTENTION. To avoid injury, please stand clear of the doors."

It was an automated safety message broadcasted outward for our benefit. It continued to loop, but did nothing to prevent the swarm of people outside from rushing to the gates and into the village above.

My mother and I did not move. We stood together, frozen in astonishment, as survivors raced in and an armored military brigade rolled out. Countless vehicles drove past us, climbing over the uneven terrain from which we came, disappearing into the night. My mother would have recognized this as an organized retreat. An abandonment of the fortress for a more viable solution elsewhere. We were at the wrong destination. Wherever the convoy was heading was where we needed to be, and any resources that had sustained the occupants of the fortress were almost certainly depleted.

My mother's shoulders hunched forward and her head dropped. She used her fingers to rub her forehead as she tried to formulate a new plan. Any relief found within the gates would be short-lived and she needed a solution. Then, like an answer to an unspoken question, a Humvee stopped directly in front of us, and a broad-shouldered, uniformed man exited the vehicle. He turned back to assist a pretty woman tactfully descending behind him.

They stood before us as my mother looked around. With the entrance to the fortress now deserted, they could only be looking at us, and despite my mother's fatigue, her posture straightened as the man and woman looked from her to me and back to her again. I knew something big was happening. The moment seemed significant.

*Is this what we'd been searching for? Were they the king and queen? Where were the princes and princesses? Did they know I was a princess too?*

I did not hear what the uniformed man said to the pretty woman, but she squared her shoulders directly with his before making a clear reply.

"She is the one."

Without hesitation my mother sank to her knees, to my height. She gripped my shoulders firmly and looked directly into my eyes. Whatever was happening was important to her, and I would not let her down. I would be brave.

I had never seen her cry, and although she was smiling there were tears on both her cheeks. I sensed her relief and sadness as I raised my free hand to wipe them away. Then, armed with her tears in one hand and my story beads in the other, she uttered a last sentence.

"Sunniva, it's time to find your dragon."

## CHAPTER FOUR

"Have you ever ridden in a Humvee?"

The broad-shouldered uniformed man was looking down at me, waiting for my answer, so I shook my head from side to side in a negative response.

"Well, today is your lucky day."

He winked at me, and, grabbing me under the arms, hoisted me up to a waiting officer.

"We have delicate cargo, Commander Hark. Please take good care."

He was most certainly the king because Hark did as he instructed, placing me on a backseat before clambering through to the front. He would change seats with the king to navigate beside an additional officer, a driver, who smiled at me quickly before refocusing on the controls.

I was able to look out the window to see the queen comforting my sobbing mother. Something was not right, and I began to feel the same anxiety that had overtaken me when the ground shook. It was fear.

The interior of the vehicle was dark and air-conditioned. It felt good in comparison to the jarring lights and heat outside, but I began to shiver as the king and queen reentered. The queen lifted me onto her lap, and then slid over, behind Hark, to make space for the king. She put her arms around me, making me uncomfortable, but I did not resist.

Hark indicated that we were clear to move, and then the Humvee lurched forward, accelerating quickly. I realized that I needed the queen's arms to hold me in place. It was rough, and I was not used to motorized transportation.

I wanted to wiggle around, to get comfortable, and to ask why my mother was not with us, but I knew that I would not do either. My throat was dry, with a lump in it, and my intuition told me that I did not want the answer anyway. I remained perfectly still and silent.

"Would you like some water, my darling? Oh, my apologies. Your hand is full. Will you tell me what you are holding?"

She had noticed my clenched fist, but I could not answer. A single tear rolled down my cheek, giving my response.

"I bet it's very important. Should we wrap up your treasure in here? To keep it safe."

She unfolded a clean cloth.

I nodded and opened my hand. The pine needles, given to me by my mother earlier that day, were crushed inside.

"These look to be precious, indeed. I promise that I will not lose them."

I handed my story beads to her, and once they were safely bundled away, I took the bottle of water and had a long, cold drink.

Clean air and water did wonders to make me feel better. They were items that had not existed in my world, but were easily obtained here. My mother must have known this, for she would have wanted me to have these things. I started to relax. I would see her soon.

The Humvee soldiered on, and the queen produced a beautiful ball in the color of the setting sun.

"Have you ever tasted an orange?" She began to unravel it. "This will be one of the last ones we see until our crops are harvested again. Until then it'll be dried fruit only."

She was nice, but I did not know what she was talking about, so I gave no indication either way.

"Oranges used to grow on trees, but with their decline we engineered a method to grow them on vines. Like growing them on a string. It's slightly more complicated than that, but highly efficient, and they are the most delicious fruit. Would you like to try a piece?"

She offered me peeled segments on the palm of her hand.

I inspected them. For as long as I could remember my diet had consisted of bark, roots, and bugs. Edible weeds and succulents, when found, were a blessing, and water was only available when it could be dug. I put an orange segment in my mouth and winced in pain as my glands reacted to the sour fruit. I held my hands to my cheeks, making the queen giggle.

"Well, that was quite a reaction. What do you think?"

It hurt, but I wanted more, so I accepted the remaining segments from her and finished it off.

I couldn't recall being able to eat and drink freely. For the first time, I had consumed as much as my frame would allow, and I was satisfied. It was remarkable. The life of a king and queen was everything I had imagined, and I pondered what other treasures they must have as the huge wheels of the Humvee bounced over the rocky terrain. We were descending rapidly down the steep hillside, and despite newfound nutrition, my head began to pound and my ears began to pop. I felt unwell.

*Are we there yet?*

The motion of the vehicle churned the contents of my stomach, and I began to sweat. My mouth began salivating, but not because of a new taste. I tried to breathe deeply, to quell the nausea growing in my tummy, but then I gagged and vomited on myself and the queen.

I was embarrassed and expected a strong reaction, like surprised disgust, or horror, but the three men didn't notice. They were preoccupied with maneuvering the vehicle and communicating with the convoy ahead. The queen remained calm, unfazed.

"Oh, you poor dear. This must be a lot to take in. Not to worry. I'll wipe us down and we'll be as good as new."

She produced another bottle of water and a clean cloth, instantly, and dampened the cloth before gently wiping off my face and hands. She tapped the shoulder of the king, motioned for him to pass her something, and he produced a soft blanket that she placed over her chest. Then, pulling me close, she wrapped me in it and folded her arms around me once again. I was clean and warm, and despite the separation from my mother, feeling safe. I liked the queen, and I allowed myself to relax against her as I grew accustomed to the motion of the Humvee. Then I drifted back to sleep.

• • •

I awoke to a loud, clear voice.

"Admiral Blaise, I have confirmation that the launch is proceeding as planned. We should be arriving shortly," stated the young driver.

*Admiral Blaise? Why is he calling him that? I thought he was the king.*

I propped myself up on the queen and listened intently.

"Thank you, Lieutenant Fischer," replied the admiral. Then he turned back toward us. "Ladies, we're here. Right on time. It will be a busy and exciting morning, so I'm glad you got some sleep. You'll need all the stamina you can gather for the long day ahead. Are you ready?"

The queen, or whom I thought was the queen, nodded at him as the vehicle stopped. Commander Hark exited the vehicle while Lieutenant Fischer remained in place to power it off. I was passed into the arms of Admiral Blaise, who then carried me on his hip, as my father used to do, out of the vehicle and into the hot wind. It hit my face, causing my eyes to water, and I shielded my eyes with my left arm while my right arm steadied myself against his shoulder.

I tried to register the scene before us. We were at the beach, where hundreds of military vehicles had assembled in tidy rows before the sea. Officers poured out, lugging bags and trunks filled with what I presumed to be the last useful treasures of humankind. Their spouses and children followed. It was organized, somewhat. A choreographed mass movement. An exodus.

Lieutenant Fischer joined us and busied himself with the organization of the Blaises' belongings.

"Admiral, sir, I believe that your possessions are in order. Requesting relief, sir," shouted the Lieutenant. It was noisy and chaotic, but I got the impression that he always spoke in an overly loud, concise manner.

"Oh yes, Fischer, you need to sort out your little brother, don't you?" It was a rhetorical comment to which the admiral did not wait for a response. "We'll be fine here. Go and gather your charge, and we'll meet again below. Thank you for your assistance. You did a splendid job today."

The lieutenant saluted before hurrying off, into the crowd.

The admiral, his wife, and I had been left near a long, floating pier, stretching hundreds of meters into the ocean. The pier itself was dark, but the water below was aglow with activity. Between us and the pier was a security checkpoint, where a thick queue of navy personnel and their families had formed. We were waiting for Commander Hark, who had gone to search for his clan. They had travelled in a separate vehicle, a tank, and would join us before we proceeded to the checkpoint.

Although the sun was down, the temperature remained arduously hot, and I missed the climate control I had temporarily enjoyed in the Humvee. The air was less clean at sea level, and I coughed a few times while we waited for the Harks.

I watched as men and women moved forward, slowly progressing to present their identification. The pier was restricted by a fence. There were few children and no elderly.

A middle-aged man approached the guard and presented his identification. The guard used a handheld scanning device to verify it, but the scanner turned red. It was the first time I had seen red. It had turned green for the individuals proceeding him.

"Please step aside, sir. Your access has been denied," said the guard.

"Denied? That's impossible. Scan it again," said the man.

The guard obliged and raised the scanner to the man's identification. Red.

"I'm sorry, sir, but you are not authorized to pass. Step aside."

"But there must be some mistake. I am supposed to go. I'm the lead engineer that built that thing."

The guard ignored him, motioning for the next person to step forward for scanning.

"This cannot be right. You've made an error! What do you expect me to do now?" he yelled, but no one was helping him. In fact, most of the people nearby stared at the ground, refusing to make eye contact with him, choosing instead to pray they wouldn't be the next one refused access to the pier.

He caught me staring at him, then looked to see who was accompanying me, and recognized the admiral.

"Admiral Blaise! Admiral Blaise! Oh, thank goodness. You must sort this out. There has been some sort of mistake, and my access has been denied, but I know you can fix it . . ." he trailed off and stopped.

The admiral had turned his back on him, looking toward the crowd for the commander, as if nothing uncomfortable was happening. The admiral's wife bent down to tend to me, straightening my ragged, dirty clothing. She too was avoiding the situation by avoiding eye contact with the man.

"Is this how we will be treated? We build you a haven before being cast aside to die?" he screamed.

Additional guards emerged from the crowd to drag him off as the crowd watched silently. Anxiety was high.

"Where is Hark?" barked the admiral as the sweaty commander emerged with his wife and daughter.

"I'm here, sir. Sorry for the delay. My daughter's rabbit escaped, and we had a heck of a time catching it."

He was gasping for breath.

"That little sucker's fast," he proudly stated, before noticing the admiral's annoyance. "It won't happen again, sir. We're ready to board."

The admiral rolled his eyes. It was not an ideal time for the queue to hear that Miss Hark would be permitted to take her rabbit.

I was unsure why we had waited for the Harks because Blaise was clearly in charge. I would later learn that he bent rules for his wife. It had been at her request that we waited for them. She had hoped that the commander's daughter, who appeared to be about the same age as I, would quell any fears I had.

I looked at the commander's daughter. She had fiery red hair and an inquisitive, freckled face that was looking right back at me. Her eyes surveyed my tattered dress and hole-ridden shoes, and as she got closer she winced and turned her head to the side. It was the barf. I stunk.

"Ew! Does something stink around here? Any chance you threw up on the way down?"

"Naviah Hark, you behave yourself right now!" her mother demanded. "Empyreal, I am so sorry for that. Please forgive my daughter's lack of manners."

"It's fine, Duanra. They're kids, and kids are honest."

To her mother's horror, Naviah continued, "Because I almost barfed too. It was way too bumpy and uncomfortable in there, wasn't it? What's your name, and how old are you?"

I liked her, and wanted to reply, but instead I looked at the ground and said nothing. Empyreal responded for me.

"Her name is Marisol."

I looked up at her with a perplexed expression while she continued to explain, turning to look at me as she spoke.

"Her name is Marisol Blaise, and she is our daughter." She stated it calmly, like it was nothing new, before turning back toward Naviah and adding, "Marisol has had quite a big day today, and the heat is making her tired, but I'm sure you'll be the best of friends in no time at all."

Satisfied, Naviah looked back at me.

"Do you want some of my clean clothes? I hear we get new uniforms anyway. Right after the launch."

Again, I did not answer as I was still processing Empyreal's comment: I was their daughter. I hoped she knew that could only last until my mother joined us because then I would be her daughter again.

We followed Commander Hark as he led us to the guard at the front of the line.

"Commander, welcome. I see you have your family, the admiral, his wife, and . . ." His words trailed off as his eyes fell upon me while he scanned the five identification cards that had been presented to him.

The admiral approached him and lowered his voice.

"I would like to introduce you to our daughter, Marisol," he said, patting my head. "An erroneous action on our part, we packed her identification in our bags, and it has been forwarded below with our things. I will send it back up for scanning when we're unpacked."

"Ah, very good, sir," said the guard, uneasily. "Please proceed to your pod. You can skip the vitals."

There was a medic taking the temperature of everyone who passed the checkpoint, but we walked by him, onto the pier, without hesitation. The water beneath us was growing more intense, with shifting light and rolling bubbles. It appeared to be boiling, but surely it was not that hot. As I waited for some inclination of what was to happen next, a large glass ship emerged from the sea.

I looked to the Blaises for clarification, and the admiral gave the same smile and wink he'd given me before, when I'd been lifted into the Humvee.

"Have you ever ridden in a pod?"

CHAPTER FIVE

She led me away from MP124, along the MP corridor toward the labs, but not for more training, I hoped. She had promised me a break.

As we walked beneath the airlocks we could see the ocean dancing beyond. The subterranean world of Aqueous was shimmering beneath the daytime lighting, mimicking daylight hours above. Our engineers had leveraged this healthy ecosystem at the bottom of the sea. It was a last stand for humankind.

The rapid decline of Earth brought with it the realization that our space program would fail. High costs and slow progress forced new leaders to terminate celestial solutions in search of homeland alternatives for human survival. Space was abandoned for the depths of the sea, with clandestine leaders directing all resources toward the development of a sustainable marine existence.

Seconding the world's most talented scientists and engineers, three separate merstations were initiated: Sihai Longwang was the first to be erected, and was located in the deepest waters of the Mariana Trench; the second was Morskaia Derevnia, and was built in the Kuril-Kamchatka Trench; merstation number three, called Aqueous, was assembled off the coast of California.

Utilizing military and navy personnel from across the globe, highly classified Operation Nereids enlisted the brightest minds to save our race, and ultimately unite our species. Abandoning patriotism, experts from various countries and creed raced against the sun to develop technologies equipped to withstand the unforgiving characteristics of the deep ocean, but our collaboration built more than stations, it solidified our tolerance for human diversity.

The world found harmony in our unified goal. We found peace through death. The desperation to survive fuelled optimal efficiency because being integral to the planning and execution of merstation development secured the lives of those involved, and the ones they loved. It was the motivator that spurred the creation of our elaborate sea cities, that decades before would have been deemed impossible.

"Let's stroll down memory lane," said my mother as we walked toward the training labs. "I want to remember these past ten years with you. The best years of my life."

She tucked her arm under mine to pull me a little closer. It was an emotional time for her. She would witness the graduation of her only child with joy and sadness. The child she was unable to conceive, but received as a miraculous gift amid unthinkable tragedy, was almost independent.

We continued walking. Aqueous was huge and spanned many levels. There were exterior components resting on the seafloor, and interior departments stacked on carbon piles. It consisted of four floors: the sub level, the main level, the atrium level, and the observation deck. We were approaching the training labs located on the main level at one end of the MP corridor. Their location allowed trainees to expeditiously move from their mini-pods to class.

The MP corridor, for trainees between the ages of eleven to sixteen, was a boarding school for residents-in-training. It was a first step toward independence in a microscale world. At the other end of the MP corridor was the FUNdamental Learning Centre for SUBteen Scientists and the Sea Turtle's Nursery for Kinetic Residents. Both of which were connected to the FP corridor, where their parents and younger siblings were housed in family-pods.

Trainees living independently were assigned mini-pods in age clusters. For example, the mini-pods of Y6s were grouped at the far end of the MP corridor, furthest from the labs, next to the Y7s, and then there were the Y8s, the Y9s, with the Y10s situated adjacent to the labs.

Upon graduation, trainees received their assignments and moved into larger pods with specific design capabilities suited to their new roles. I was excited and anxious to discover what my assignment would be. I enjoyed seafloor exploration the most, but an assignment in Robotics & Automation or Manufacturing & Technology could be interesting. I loathed Proteins & Cloning, and Biosolids & Compost had an awful smell. Botany was downright boring, and albeit beautiful, I couldn't commit to a lifetime of torment in the arboretum.

Thankfully, we continued past the labs where I could see my cohorts intently focused on their monitors reviewing insect incubation, mechanics, sanitation, human biology, physics, pressure, light refraction, solar power, hydrothermal vents, coding, cloning, diving, and a myriad of other things in preparation for our final assessments. It was intense, like most things in the hydrosphere, and although I liked the challenge, I was happy to take a small break. In hindsight, space exploration may have been easier.

For psychological and physical safety, Aqueous was designed as a never-ending series of common areas and passageways engineered to feel as though one could traverse the compound indefinitely. To my knowledge, there were no dead-ends. Each area of the station could be accessed by multiple hatchways, with each hatch possessing the structural integrity to completely seal, instantly and autonomously, in the event of depressurization. The hatches could save lives which was paramount in a society where so few lived.

We intuitively stopped talking as we neared the administrative offices of Matriculated Marine Life Sciences and Subterranean Exploration (MMLSSE). It was where our professors concocted lesson plans. Trainees called it Malice, due to the overwhelming workload and expectations of those overseeing our education; however, an assignment to this department was significant. They were our experts, laying the foundation for each new idea. They armed us with knowledge necessary for human sustainability, and in a submarine society based on math and science, they were the mentors of our new world order.

To avoid detection, we crept past MMLSSE. Being caught gallivanting during the crucial hours before exams would be harshly frowned upon, and even Empyreal, highly ranked and respected, would be chided for her misguidance.

We burst into laughter once we were clear, nearing the infirmary.

"It feels good to be naughty," she joked.

"Who's naughty?" asked Leop, emerging from the stairs.

Leop was a fellow Y10, and like myself, should have been studying. He was surprised by the sight of my mother.

"Mrs. Blaise, excuse me. I didn't realise it was you."

"Leop, I was asking *you* if it feels good to be naughty. I'm surprised that you've chosen to break from your studies at this pivotal moment in your developmental journey. Did you use the officers' staircase?"

The officers' staircase connected the OP corridor and Command to the dining hall, the infirmary, Robotics & Automation, and Mass Landing. They were the essential areas needed by all officers, and the designated staircase made their utilization of the station more efficient.

"I w-was just gr-grabbing a drink from the dining hall after observing the nodule fields on the monitors in Mining & Minerals. I w-was light-headed," he stammered. "I haven't had time to sleep lately, and this route was shorter."

Leop was interested in mining for resources through deep water drilling, but had commenced compiling the necessary data to support his thesis on advanced robotic snake boring far too late. Sleeping was not an option for him.

"I think it's best that you return to the labs and refocus on securing your future."

"Of course, Mrs. Blaise."

Leop shot me a worried look as he hurried past, back toward the labs and out of earshot.

"That was a tad excessive. Not to mention, sneaky," I scolded.

"True, but it's in his best interest. He's unlikely to leave the labs again."

I followed her up the officers' staircase. Leop shouldn't have used it, but Empyreal Blaise could. Until, that is, we heard voices descending toward us.

"Quick! Over here."

She exited at the atrium level, and I followed her into the dining hall where rows of long white tables stood in salute, ready to serve. It was a versatile space that could function as a simple, maritime canteen or be transformed into an elaborate ballroom. When draped in swaying textiles and flooded with festive lighting we could be convincingly transported to Europe, Asia, Africa or Australia. Celebrations big and small were enjoyed here, and undoubtedly, this space would be utilized for the Y10 graduation ceremony and the ten-year station anniversary. It was an exciting time for residents.

Beside the dining hall was the kitchen. It was the centralized area for all meal preparation on Aqueous. Unfortunately, despite a myriad of ingredients, our kitchen staff predominantly prepared seafood, and after ten years onboard I still hadn't developed an appetite for it.

We did not enter the kitchen, but continued instead toward the grand pavilion. A true masterpiece, the biodome served as a gathering space to observe marine life descending from above or marvel at the superstructure below. There were comfortable chairs and sofas paired with tables of varying size so that residents could congregate in groups or seek solitude. Soft pillows and throws were found throughout, giving the impression of opulence in an environment that demanded frugality.

Subset into the glossy white floor was a meandering boardwalk, winding its way through a wondrous thicket of trees. Discovery gardens of varying climates showcased native terrestrial blossoms and genetically enhanced species, like the magnificent magnolia in continuous bloom. Observation ponds, aerated by an enormous rain wall, housed exotic sea life and the countless hybrids of submergent and planmergent flora developed by Aqueous botanists. Hydroponics, large and small, added beauty and oxygen to the wondrous retreat. It was a place of relaxation and rejuvenation, showcasing the ingenuity of our residents.

The grand pavilion also served as a shrine to our former healthy planet, before it flooded and burned. Floor to ceiling digital life-walls, separating the grand pavilion from the dining hall and the bethel, had been erected to project the geography and hobbies people had enjoyed during terrestrial life. Each day reflected a new theme, distracting us from the confines of the sea. They were a constant motion picture of memories to some, and things unknown to others, fulfilling a responsibility to educate youth about the activities and animals they would never know. The life-walls of the grand pavilion created an escape from the station, and an appreciation for days gone by. They provided informal learning in an environment where constant learning was critical.

My friend, Yarrow, created life-wall videos showcasing animals in their natural habitats. Today's loop was a montage of the Amazon, seen from the vantage of a colorful macaw. The bird zipped past monkeys, armadillos, capybaras, and sloths as it transported us through a thriving rainforest. It was a lush, green paradise we would never experience firsthand, reminding us that we should never take more than we can use.

"Mrs. Blaise, Marisol, how nice to see you."

It was Amley, another Y10 who was not in the labs.

"Amley, what a surprise that *you*, out of all of the Y10 trainees, are

not holed up in the labs utilizing every last moment to maximize your assignment success."

The statement was unusually sharp, putting Amley on the defensive.

"I'm journaling the light production of the plants I introduced to luciferin, Mrs. Blaise."

"Well, we won't keep you then."

Amley watched, perplexed, as we continued on our way. She had campaigned for grand pavilion plantings to glow at night and was monitoring her trials. She had been utilizing her time appropriately.

Once we were out of earshot I said, "That was unnecessary."

"It was. Just a little farther."

Secular by preference, my mother avoided the bethel. It was a place of worship for any seafaring faith. Aqueous did not have a designated minister, but residents worshipped singularly or in self-formed groups. Hard cover copies of religious publications, the only tangible books on Aqueous, were provided, in addition to digital materials.

My visits to the bethel, fleeting and infrequent, had been primarily limited to weddings and christenings. I had paid respects to the departed, but rarely. Death was scarce at the bottom of the sea, especially in the absence of elderly and communicable disease. The few who had passed, like Tadi Nerak and Junith Nahk, had died suddenly of undiagnosed, hereditary defects. They had been incinerated immediately.

Funerals were quiet and modest. There were no lifeless bodies on display, as I had seen so often on the surface. Residents were encouraged to reflect on happy memories, and consult Dr. Pryor, our psychologist, in the event grief guidance was necessary.

"Regardless of where we are going, I feel like you're taking the long way around," I said.

"I'm trying to avoid detection, remember?"

"And failing miserably at that."

She giggled in agreement as she entered the grand staircase.

*Were we going to her pod?*

Located on the observation deck, officer-pods were special. Limited in number, they were reserved for the highest in command and had unique characteristics. For starters, all OPs were mobile. They could maneuver independently and travel long distances. They were also much larger. While the bedrooms and bathrooms were similar to an FP, most OPs required a receiving room for guests. They also needed a secure office, with bio-authentication access.

My father, Admiral Blaise, holds the highest rank on Aqueous, and therefore, has the most sophisticated pod. His admiral-pod, known as AP1, has a situation room that can accommodate his immediate staff. It also has dual docking, with direct airlocks to both the OP corridor and Command, because that's where interstation communications and overall undersea operations are coordinated.

We finished climbing the grand staircase, a column spanning four floors, to enter the OP corridor. AP1 was at the end of the corridor, suspended beneath it, next to Command.

"Is that it? You're taking me to the pod? I'm here all the time."

"Well, to be honest, you're never here anymore, and no, I'm not taking you to the pod. We're taking the pod someplace else."

A mischievous grin grew along her lips as we descended the large airlock together.

"We're going cruising in AP1? Seriously? Did you get consent for this? I mean, this must have required at least a dozen stamps."

"Stamps? Have you even seen a stamp?"

"We learned about fountain pens and ink in a recent communications lecture. Stamps, envelopes, and post were mentioned fleetingly. It was a joke."

"Well, joking aside, desperate times call for desperate measures. I'm losing my baby soon which means that I am emotionally fragile and unstable. I will be forgiven for stealing AP1."

With that said she sat down before the instrument panel, disengaged AP1 from Aqueous, and allowed the pod to sink slightly before pulling safely away from the station.

*Losing her baby? Where else could I go?*

I was surprised by her emotional state. My mother was formidable. Other than our first few days together, almost ten years ago, she was cool and collected, emotions always in check, but if her heightened anxiety was driving this AP1 escapade, I was all for it. This temporary escape was exhilarating. Even engineering marvels, such as Aqueous, staled after a while.

Tethered to the seafloor, the station sprawled outward below us, creating a labyrinth of corridors, common areas, and pods. My mother manipulated our speed and depth, piloting to the outermost edge of Aqueous before diving downward to the seafloor, and admittedly, I was feeling better. Near the carbon supports she steered the pod under Manufacturing & Technology, zig-zagging AP1 through tubing and cables like a sea creature chasing its prey.

"Any chance we'll be attacked by a giant squid?"

"I hope not, Marisol, but you never know."

Humboldt squid had invaded the canyon decades earlier. Adept survivors, the giant squid successfully inhabited the most inhospitable places in the ocean, and, with seemingly minimal intelligence, could thrive in light or darkness and adjust to extreme changes in pressure and temperature. They had endured an ice age and global warming, which spurred the question: was great intelligence or fluid adaptation more important for survival? Humans, the superior thinkers, were on the verge of extinction while the giant squid swam on, unfazed.

The squid were aggressive predators. Measuring up to fifteen meters in length, with sharp, strong beaks, they weren't able to pierce the shell of a pod, but they could bump our craft or scratch the glass with their barb-covered arms. As a child, waking up to the eyeball of a salivating squid pressed against the glass of my pod had been ter-rifying, but inevitably it would leave, choosing to feast on something less difficult to catch.

Speaking of feasting, the squid had become a food source for Aqueous residents. We learned to bait and trap them, and they made excellent calamari, even though I found it disgusting.

We passed a pile of abandoned ships, left behind by a sinking pop-ulation. It made an ideal reef for the introduction of edible sea life, especially after our mining engineers directionally drilled target spe-cific hydrothermal vents. The vents created chemoautotrophic bac-teria, providing energy and nutrients to nearby species without the need for sunlight. In combination with our reef, the bacteria created an ideal ecosystem for sea fauna like crabs, clams, giant tubeworms, and slugs.

The vents also provided heat and emitted mineral-like sulfates, sulfides, and quartz. They were rich in oxygen, combating anoxia, and spewed valuable commodities like lead, iron, zinc, copper, silver, and gold. These metals solidified in the chimney nodules above the vents, making them available for station use.

I enjoyed watching mineral-laden fluid bubble from the earth's core, but my mother would never pilot AP1 over the vents near the sta-tion. It was too dangerous. Death by melting would be very, very bad.

Travelling slightly above the seafloor, I noted the various edible plants that I had been tasked to catalogue. Developed by our marine botanists from Aquatic Horticulture & Research, they were remotely sown and harvested by our robotics teams, near the vent-warmed water. Combining these marine garden vegetables with the gelati-nous sea creatures nearby, our culinary team could create limitless combinations of ceviche salad, all of which were disgusting.

I too had been taught how to dive, but only in simulation. I found it thrilling nonetheless, and couldn't get enough. It was the freedom and adventure that I needed. The ultimate underwater escape.

We cautiously approached one of the turbine grids suspended between the canyon walls. Geophysical research had taught us that turbidity currents had carved away the seafloor to create the stunning valley before us. The study of hydrodynamics had allowed us to harness energy from these currents to create power for the station. Essentially, we could counteract one of our greatest challenges, darkness, with the utilization of seawater movement. Ocean currents flowed through the turbines, turning the blades, which then turned the shafts they were connected to. The shafts connected to generators inside the mechanical room, and the generators connected to an electrical substation that acted as the central hub of electricity within the station. Distribution of electricity throughout the station was conducted by wires, similar to the power lines formerly used on land. For safety, there were grates covering the turbines so that we couldn't collide with the rotating blades.

Diverting AP1 before colliding with the turbines, my mother appeared to be circumnavigating the station. I still had no idea where we would end up, but I was happy to inspect the canyon walls and dynamic seafloor; it was a field study of the scientific processes I had been learning about during the last ten years.

The power created underwater was augmented with floating photovoltaic modules on the ocean's surface. Dubbed Sunshine Isle, Aqueous engineers had amassed football fields of the floating solar panels, positioned and connected to the station. Power from the isle was directed downward to the mechanical room in water resilient power lines.

We carefully avoided the lines and pipes that connected our life below with our former life above.

Inevitably, thick, ashy surface air would obliterate the rays of the sun, making our transition to hydrogen-powered fuel cells, which utilized hydrogen from the hydrothermal vents, critical. I was unaware of our present dependence on Sunshine Isle and made note to inquire about this with my professors.

We passed a large vertical pipeline also connected to the surface. Previously serving as oxygen intake, it's only purpose now was to expel exhaust; however, our ability to efficiently recycle and reuse gases had improved so dramatically that these too were almost redundant.

After passing under Robotics & Automation my mother slowed AP1 to a hover and pivoted to face the station. We were several floors beneath our starting point at Command.

"This looks familiar," I said. "Mass Landing?"

"The most significant part of the station, my love. The place where we became a family."

Allowing the pod to rise slightly, she positioned it at the height of sub level, in front of the giant dock where Aqueous residents had met their salvation ten years prior. It was utilized far less now that all souls were onboard, mainly serving to receive visitors from the other two merstations throughout the year.

Reaching down beside her, my mother grabbed a bundle of fabric and passed it to me. I unfolded it on my lap.

"My dress? My sandals? You kept them all these years?"

The moment when we met came flooding back through the texture of the cloth. I raised the dress to my face to inhale the highs and lows of that day from the scent on the thread. There had been sunlight and darkness, hot and cold, pain and relief. My mother was relinquishing my childhood. Her job was complete.

"Marisol, that was the greatest day of my life. It was the day that I found you and you became mine. I have been thankful for you every day since, and with your birthday coming up, then graduation and your assignment, I needed to tell you that. I need you to know that despite how it happened, it was the greatest gift to myself and your father . . ." she trailed off. Something else was bothering her. "Whatever happens next, please remember that."

"Oh Mom, you're being so dramatic. It's not like I'm moving back to the surface to recolonize a despondent planet. I'm merely moving to a corridor a little farther from the corridor where I live now, which isn't that far from yours. Hopefully it's near Robotics, in case you want to put in a word for me, because after today I'm absolutely convinced that I want to be a cuvier."

"I had hoped you would become interested in something else. It can be dangerous, Marisol, and lonely. They've never chosen a woman before."

"But it's the only assignment I'm passionate about."

She stiffened, and her eyes shifted from mine to the ocean beyond the cockpit.

The cuviers comprised the elite diving team on Aqueous. They were our seafloor soldiers, and when circumstances prevented Aqueous engineers from completing tasks remotely, they stood ready to deploy at the discretion of the admiral. The cuviers were the only residents regularly authorized to leave the station. As a special operational unit of Aqueous, working independently on undisclosed activities, it was surmised that their primary responsibilities included robot retraction, perimeter checks, complicated repairs, and ferrying services. They were our maritime knights of the round station, well-mannered, fearless, and exclusively male.

"Why would gender stop me? You've always taught me to pursue my goals, and that I am as capable as any man."

"I have."

"You know, you're cute when you're overly weak and emotional. You should let this side out more often, Mom."

I threw my arms around her, but my words and my hug were not reciprocated. I pulled back from her. She was nodding distractedly, looking down at her hands. Then she changed the subject.

"I know you've continued to have nightmares. The AI Assistant generates a weekly parental report on trainee biometrics, including sleep patterns."

*My AI Assistant was spying on me? I should have assumed that.*

"And your professors tell me that sometimes you are someplace else, lost in your thoughts. I know you get distracted by the memories of your biological mother."

We had never spoken of the family that I had lost, but over time I had understood that they were never coming back.

"What happened above was a tragedy, Marisol. A tragedy that we can talk about when you're ready. If you want to. About your loss and pain. I want you to know that I would change it all in a heartbeat for you, if I could."

Despite the nightmares and flashbacks, I was truly thankful for her and the second life I was given. It had been instant, life-altering, without my consent, but many on Aqueous had been separated from their loved ones during that initial descent. It was the best of a bad situation.

I reached over and grabbed her hands. "You turned out to be alright, you know. What if Duanra had chosen me?"

She laughed. "She's such a nice woman. Be extra kind to her. She was cursed with Naviah, after all."

We looked once more at the giant dock before us. With Aqueous looming overhead, what was foreign to me once, was now my happy home. A warm familiar space filled with residents I loved and admired. A watery womb rebirthing our race.

"I guess I should get you back to your work. Let's face it, this break was more about me than it was about you, Marisol."

"You'll always be my mom, Mom."

She patted my hand appreciatively and then inflated the ballasts, allowing the pod to rise until we were once again level with Command. It had been a nice retreat. Exactly what we needed. I had released some pressure, which allowed me to consider someone else. My mom had fears also, and we needed to communicate them.

Birthdays, graduations, and assignments were not the end of the world. We already lived through that, and the soft worn fibers of my dress proved it. It was a reminder of our fragility, and a symbol of great strength. There had been so much loss, and by now, with certainty, what had remained of the tattered population above would have faded like the fabric. I was at a crossroads, another new beginning, and it was time to bury my life above to enjoy my life below.

## CHAPTER SIX

I was pulled forward by the hand because my legs would not move. I was too focused on comprehending what I was seeing to be able to move my legs at the same time. It was some sort of round, glass contraption that they kept calling a pod, but most of it remained hidden beneath the churning water. Whatever it was, there must have been many of them to transport the hundreds of people readying themselves for departure.

A large clear periscope, like on the submarines my brothers had talked about, but bigger, extended upward from the top of the vessel, and we focused our attention on the loading officer.

"Approach the airlock with caution. One at a time, and watch your step. Stand in the center of the marked circle. You will descend slowly. Small children must be accompanied by a parent. Keep your head, arms, and legs clear of the seal as it closes above you."

She repeated her words matter-of-factly, directing people onto the pods that kept emerging from the sea as if nothing was out of the ordinary.

Naviah and her mother stepped off the pier and onto a gangplank beside the airlock.

"Wow, this is cool! Right, Marisol? Don't you love it?" exclaimed Naviah. "We're going down with the fishes, and we can be mermaids together!" she squealed as she descended into the pod by her mother's side. As her face disappeared I heard her shout, "My red hair is the perfect color for this!"

The airlock returned, empty, and Empyreal moved toward it. Holding my hand, encouraging me to follow her, we stepped onto the circle as instructed and waited for it to move. The sea was surging from the movement of other vessels surfacing along the pier, but our airlock descent was smooth.

As we moved downward I could begin to see the interior of the craft. Duanra and Naviah had taken seats mid-ship and were adjusting their safety restraints. There were two chairs at the front of the pod, before the instruments, where a pilot was seated. He turned and greeted us.

"Good evening, Mrs. Blaise."

"Good evening, Keel. Let me introduce to you my daughter, Marisol."

I assessed him from head to toe. He was clean, friendly, and appeared to be happy. It was a good sign. If he wasn't worried, we must be safe.

"Well, hello there, young lady," he chirped. "Are you excited to see your new home under the sea?"

He was barely able to contain his excitement, but I stared back blankly, processing the information.

*Was that the plan? I was going to live under the ocean? Was that even possible? Was I supposed to be worried?*

Everyone was calm, even eager to be going to a place that I presumed was dangerous. My brothers had told me about sharks and currents. It was deep and dark, and I didn't know how to swim.

"Did you bring the items I requested?" Empyreal asked.

"Yes. Here you are, ma'am. As requested."

"Oh, how wonderful. Thank you for this. Marisol, please come with me."

We walked toward the back of the pod, past Naviah and her

mother as they argued over how she should wear her harness. Naviah wanted it around her waist so that she could move her shoulders and arms freely, while Duanra insisted that it was also meant to be secured over her shoulders.

Unlike everyone else, Duanra was not calm.

"Naviah, you must sit still and let me tighten your safety belt."

"It's too tight! I can't breathe! And how do you expect me to touch stuff if I can't move my arms?"

I continued past them, following Empyreal into a separate room at the back of the pod. There was a bed with a side table and a small desk with a chair, and there was a bathroom behind the wall at the back of the bed. Empyreal shut the door to the bedroom and sat down on the bed. She began opening the package the pilot had given her.

"Marisol, come and look."

She waved me over and unfolded clothing that looked to be approximately my size.

"I didn't know exactly what size to get you, so I guessed. I hope it will fit."

She held up a white cotton sweatshirt. It was embroidered with a circular blue crest that I could not read, and there were matching blue cotton pants. There were also socks and athletic shoes that she had set beside her on the bed.

"Would you like to try them on? I think Naviah will be quite surprised to see you model the latest standard-issue clothing for your age group. What do you say?"

I nodded. I was dirty and had become cold in the air-conditioning of the ship. I wanted to snuggle into the warmth of the soft fabric, so I picked up the clothes and walked to the bathroom to change. I struggled to tie my new shoes, but the clothes fit, and as I righted myself in my new outfit I caught a glimpse of my reflection in the mirror. My clothes were new, but I was not. It felt like a costume.

The thought continued as I carried my soiled dress and sandals back to Empyreal and hesitantly surrendered my identity into her lap. Sensing my misgivings, she did not request my opinion on the comfort or the fit of my new clothes, and after adjusting my laces we silently returned to the lounge as Commander Hark descended the airlock with the carrier holding the rabbit.

We took our seats across from Naviah and her mother.

"Buckingham! I missed you! I'd come and let you out of your cage, but I'm imprisoned in this damn chair!" declared Naviah.

Duanra closed her eyes and did not reopen them. She did not attempt to respond to or reprimand her daughter. She had reached her limit. Sensing her frustration and fear, Commander Hark addressed his disobedient child.

"Naviah Hark, you are no longer permitted to speak. You may not utter another word. You have worn out your mother and she needs silence from you. You shall remain silent until after we dock, and that's an order. Do you understand me?"

His tone implied that there would be no further discussion.

Naviah let out a massive huff and crossed her arms over her chest. Her eyes, unblinking and unyielding, had locked with her father's in a last show of defiance, but understanding that he would be victorious she conceded and mumbled through tightly closed lips, "Yes, sir."

"Wonderful," replied Hark, and happily clasping his hands together he said, "I believe it's time to get on with this adventure. Please remain seated as our diver, Lieutenant Commander Keel, initiates our descent."

"Initiating descent, Commander Hark," said Keel.

The pod began to vibrate as the ballast tanks filled with water, allowing the ship to sink. Empyreal and I buckled ourselves into our seats. There was a table between us and Naviah and her mother, but each seat could swivel toward the glass if we wanted to view the ocean. The commander seated himself beside Keel, and the admiral stood behind them.

It was almost dawn, but the water was still dark.

"I'm afraid there won't be much to see this morning," commented Hark. "Even if the sun were high, we'd likely only benefit from its glow for the first two hundred meters. Beyond that, only small amounts of sunlight penetrate the water, with absolutely no sunlight penetrating the aphotic zone located eleven hundred meters below the surface."

He was surprisingly enthusiastic.

"Do you know what creatures abide in the deepest, darkest parts of the ocean?"

He'd forgotten that he had forbade his daughter to speak, and she scowled fiercely at him.

"There are elephant seals, Cuvier's beaked whales, sperm whales, and giant squid!"

An alarmed squeak escaped the pursed lips of his closed-eyed wife, but the commander continued with his educational monologue as we made our long descent.

Satisfied with the ship's instrument readings, the admiral took a seat next to Hark as the pilot continued to dive lower, toward our amphibious destination. All three officers appeared familiar with the pod and the journey.

Naviah eventually nodded off, but Duanra did not sleep. The white-knuckled grip she exerted on the arms of her chair gave the impression that she was not as comfortable as her daughter or husband.

"How about a snack?" asked Empyreal as she unbuckled her restraint and rose from her chair. She crossed the lounge to access cabinets on the partition next to the bedroom and returned with a tray containing items that I had not seen before.

"These are vegetables," she said. "Carrots, cauliflower, and cucumber."

The colors were so vibrant that it was hard to imagine that the items arranged on the tray could be eaten.

"And this is an apple."

She pointed to the items, encouraging me to choose something, so I grabbed a carrot.

"There's more water also."

Provisions were abundant in this new world, and I was delighted by the new flavors and textures in my mouth. To be able to drink until I had had enough . . . That had never happened before.

I ate my snack slowly, while looking through the glass. I was sure I would see a whale if I examined the blackness long enough, and then all at once it wasn't black anymore. I didn't see a whale, but there was light spreading outward beneath us as though someone had torn a hole in the bottom of the world to let the sunshine pour in.

*Were we upside down?*

I straightened myself in my seat to get a better view as the interior of our pod filled with light. Not a single sea creature the commander had explained had shown up for our arrival, but my disappointment subsided when I spied the faint outline of a castle. It was an underwater palace that grew bigger and brighter until it shone brightly before us, with an aquamarine aura rising proudly from the seafloor. Its massive, multi-domed exterior emitted silver rays of hope to an influx of terrestrial refugees, and the fortunate families already docked could be seen familiarizing themselves with new surroundings, navigating their way through the transparent corridors of their new frontier. It was more magnificent than any of the imaginary places I had visited in the past, and now I understood why my mother had sent me.

Our pod slowed and hovered in place before a large docking area. Equipped to receive multiple pods, it would soon be our turn to enter the mouth of the giant. I hadn't noticed when the commander had stopped speaking, but our pod had been silenced by the presence of the beast. After several moments the admiral stood and cleared his throat.

"Marisol, it is my great honor to present to you, Aqueous." Then, with less confidence, he asked, "What do you think?"

I looked beyond the glass to assess the mammoth, saltwater city anchored in front of the pod. Never in my wildest dreams could I have invented such a magical place. Then I looked back at the admiral and his wife. They were watching me, waiting, hopeful for a positive reaction. I liked them, and it was so comfortable here. I could tell that there was less suffering.

"It's wonderful," I replied.

Empyreal raised her hand to her mouth as she let out a small gasp of relief. She rose from her chair as the admiral moved beside her, wrapping his arm around her shoulders. They looked at each other lovingly, and then down at me and smiled.

Those were my first words as Marisol Blaise. They were the words that confirmed that I had been reborn with the acceptance of my new life. They were the words that indicated that I would be alright, and undoubtedly, words of relief for my new guardians, who had made a spontaneous, life-altering commitment earlier that day.

I smiled back at them, and they each extended a hand toward mine. In that moment we became an unsinkable team. We became a family. They would be my parents until my mother arrived.

CHAPTER SEVEN

After placing my childhood clothing on the shelf above my beads, I walked directly to the lab, arriving in time to see Murphy Stout singe off his eyebrows in an overzealous attempt to ignite the combustible carbon pellets he had created in his poorly designed carbon utilization kit. It was a thesis far beyond his capabilities that should have been abandoned weeks ago. Yes, the station had a mandate to prioritize the removal of carbon from the $CO_2$ in the station, but Murphy was never going to be the man to do it.

Murphy was a fellow Y10, and he was kind and pleasant. He always tried his best. Popular with his peers, he had a great sense of humor and didn't take himself too seriously. Unfortunately, his love of food led to an insatiable appetite that, combined with his complete lack of agility, increased his likelihood of sustaining accident-related injuries during the advanced lab work in year ten. With significant hours spent in the infirmary, Murphy had missed the majority of his classes, causing him to unintentionally struggle with straightforward tasks.

"Dude, you idiot! Look at your face," mocked Felix Nyrmac, a skinny boy who skirted his studies to focus on optimizing the misery of others. "You were supposed to burn the pellets with the blow torch, not conduct clinical trials on facial hair removal."

Murphy walked to the sink to look at his reflection in the mirror.

Brushing it off, as if his burns were nothing, he stated, "I think I look fairly handsome. This shade of soot is trending right now."

"Mr. Stout, go to the clinic at once and have that checked out. Despite your theatrics, it must be painful," instructed our chemistry mentor, Professor Eseer.

Murphy nodded and quickly left the lab, looking relieved to be dismissed.

"Let's reacquaint ourselves with the fire extinguishers beneath our desks, shall we? We do not want to create a scenario by which our fire brigade must rescue us," continued Eseer. "Need I remind you that the safety of all residents is paramount on Aqueous? We work together, in harmony, to find solutions to sustain the human race. We do not laugh or take pleasure in the suffering or misfortune of others, Mr. Nyrmac."

The professor resumed the marking he had been working on before Murphy exceeded the melting point of his eyebrows.

"Boring old man. He's so stale. I think we could find mold growing on his skin," whispered Felix.

"What was that, Mr. Nyrmac?" asked Eseer.

"Pardon me, sir. I said, 'Murphy looked pale. I think we should notify next of kin,'" lied Felix, effortlessly.

"And I'm saying what a tale. I think you've committed a sin," replied Eseer. "Leave your desk at once, Felix, and proceed to Biosolids & Compost. I will notify them that you've kindly volunteered to clean the sludge tank, and that you will be arriving shortly."

"Dammit," seethed Felix, dropping his tablet on his desk and pushing himself forcibly backward, causing the legs of his chair to screech loudly across the floor.

Insidious giggles erupted from Creedan, another immature Y10, who was unsurprisingly bent over an unlit Bunsen burner, pretending to work. Felix cuffed him across the back of his head as he strode past toward the exit.

"If you ever want to borrow my game controller again, you better wash those poopy hands when you're done," said Creedan.

Felix spun around, saluting him with devil horns and an outstretched tongue before vanishing through the hatch.

"Never a dull moment, right, Marisol?" Naviah, my ocean-floor bestie, approached and perched herself on the side of my table. "Where've you been?" she asked, not waiting for my answer. "There's so much drama at the bottom of the sea. Who could have predicted we'd rival *The Really Fabulous Housewives of Beverly Hills*, right?"

"I usually don't get your references, Naviah, but I'm pretty sure that was not the title of that show."

"Well, if you would stop studying for one second, you would be overjoyed to learn that beyond the assigned reading on the shared drives, there's a perfectly good underwater internet still sitting there, waiting to be your friend."

Yes, Li-Fi was still there, transmitting via LED flashes of light, but it was worthless to me if it only improved my knowledge of the pop culture of yesteryear. Besides, with the world population based on three tiny merstations, there was hardly any new content.

"I can't spare the time. It's becoming common knowledge that I want to become the first female cuvier, so that means that I'll need to be better than the boys. They will beat me in the physical trial, so I will need to excel in other areas. Knowledge could be the thing that sets me apart."

"If you say so."

"We can celebrate by binge watching reruns once we are happily assigned. Alright?"

"Very well. Your wish is my command. I shall be your loyal supporter until we can have fun again. Unless of course you have a change of heart and choose a life less motivated. Take me, for instance. I am happy to coast by with marginal knowledge, securing an assignment in the slightly less dangerous, but oh so glamourous, world of Atelier. Utilizing limited science, I will transform old fabric into new, irresistible fashions loved by all, and, if that weren't enough, I will design and install the most remarkable dining hall decorations ever witnessed. Transforming the space into a spectacle of amusements; making all of our dreams come true."

Her eyes were wide, cast upward in symmetry with her outstretched arms. Lost in a trance, she gazed past me, imagining the future assignment she had just described.

"Earth to Naviah, can you hear me? It's reality calling."

"Oh boy, I got a little carried away for a second. I need to sit down."

Naviah's enthusiasm for life had never faded. A decade older, she was as vibrant and jubilant as the first day we met. Vertically challenged, her bright green eyes and award-winning smile compensated for her limited height, making her larger than life. She had embraced her curly, red hair, often adorning it with flowers and allowing it to twist and bounce wildly as she skipped through the hallways of Aqueous. She modified her standard-issue clothing by cinching her top with electrical cord or applying a feathery applique to her shoes. One-of-a-kind, she was the darling of the ship. A free spirit loved by all, but she loved me the best. I was thankful to have her by my side. She was the wind in my sails. Figuratively speaking, of course. We no longer had wind.

There was a swish behind me as the hatchway slid open and closed again. The scent of mandarin wafted past, and my heart filled with dread. Lilith Brizo had entered the lab. This I was certain of, before even laying eyes on her.

Lilith boasted of steeping valuable mandarin blossoms in her all-in-one cleanser. A trick that was sure to attract the limited number of cute, young bachelors on the station. I hated her, and I wanted to be exactly like her, at the same time. She had a dark, razor cut bob that accentuated her long neck and sharp jawline. She moved like a cat, or at least what I anticipated a cat moved like, and her words were spoken slowly so that her audience could hang on them. She was captivating and clever, brazen and bewitching, and I stared at her always for way too long while trying not to look as though I was staring at her at all. It was so pathetic.

I watched Lilith saunter across the lab to establish her place next to Creighton Kress. Creighton was our unofficial Y10 leader. Handsome and well-mannered, he was popular amongst his peers and adults alike. His outward beauty was only shadowed by his inward kindness. Fair-minded and calm, Creighton was the automatic authority to quell disputes within the classroom or on the athletics pitch. He could see the goodness in all, and preferred inner beauty to external facades, but despite this, he was just as stupid. He was blinded by the charms of Lilith, like all of the idiot Y10 boys. It was sickening.

"You should stop staring now," said Naviah. "You're starting to look like a stalker."

"How can he be into her? Can't he smell the death of oranges on her skin? It is utterly unjust that the few remaining members of the human race will suffer a scurvy demise so that Y10 boys can inhale the intoxicating aroma of her hair."

"Holy bull shark, you like him!" she emphatically whispered. "You have developed a crush on Creighton. When did this happen?"

"I do not have a crush on Creighton. It's her. She gets under my skin."

"No, I don't believe you. Something has changed. We've been together for ten years, all of us, and I've never seen you bothered by her to this degree, so the only thing that could be different now is that your feelings for Creighton changed. I get it. He's magnificent, his physical prowess is unmatched, and the two of you would make a darling pair. The captain's son with the admiral's daughter. We couldn't ask for anything more Charles and Diana if we tried."

"Who?"

"I named my rabbit after their palace. Anyway, Buckingham

would obviously be the ring bearer. I'd string a pretty ribbon on his little hind leg, and the rings would jingle down the aisle as he happily jumped . . ."

"Stop it. Keep your voice down and ceasefire. You're being ridiculous," I scolded, but secretly I liked the idea of incorporating her adorable rabbit into my marriage ceremony to Creighton. "I don't have time for boys, and especially not one that is enamored with a self-engrossed, statuesque, opportunistic freeloader, who is freakishly smart and talented. It's so irritating."

"And her voice is divine. Don't forget that. She'll be performing at the anniversary. I can't wait to hear what pieces she has prepared."

I shot Naviah a look to remind her that she was my best friend, not Lilith's.

"But I'm sure she'll be pitchy and bloated with some sort of incurable, dermatological breakout. Don't worry."

At that moment, Lilith threw her head back and laughed loud enough that everyone would hear and look over. Creighton was smiling, clearly enjoying her attention, so much so that he was unaware that Lilith was glancing at his tablet and copying his calculations on Bernoulli's principle. Then she invited him to join her at her table where she proceeded to feign ignorance until he ultimately completed the lab work on Pascal's law for her. Obviously, there were two ways to get ahead in life: hard work and determination, or opportunity and deceit.

*Sickening.*

Sensing my frustration, Naviah tried to shift my focus away from them.

"What are you working on today?"

It was a good question. In the final countdown to graduation, the Y10s were given free time to complete various projects and prepare for the trials. There were many assignments that we could be completing at any given time.

"I want to finish the surface science study on the long-term stations effects of solid-to-liquid interfacial tension so that I can work on my thesis. I'm improving the aquadynamics of long-range pods to reduce drag, thereby increasing the range of battery cells. I'm hoping that my new designs will be instrumental in securing my assignment as a cuvier."

In the year of graduation each Y10 was asked to formulate a hypothesis in their area of interest, and subsequently find a way to prove or disprove their theory. I knew Naviah's thesis had involved working with textiles, but she hadn't divulged exactly what she was doing.

"You've been close-lipped about your project, Naviah. What are you working on?"

"I'm so glad you asked. Months ago I began collaborating with the culinary minds on Aqueous to create new from old. Think ink. Squid to be exact. It's the most glorious midnight blue, and it makes an effective textile dye, so I combined the precious ink with unused, discarded fabric. Atelier has mounds of trimmings that they've swept under the rug, so to speak. Collected right from the floor and stored for future use, I convinced them to give me some scraps that I could weave into usable swatches and dye. I then used my newly-created, midnight blue swatches to create a gown. It's a masterpiece, like the ones we used to find on the internet and dreamt of someday wearing. It's so beautiful. You will love it."

"Wow. That's amazing. You're certain to get an Atelier assignment with that, and here I thought you were still learning how to sew. When will you wear it? There aren't a lot of opportunities to runway new fashions when all of us dress the same."

"That's the best part. The time has come for my big reveal, and the dress is for you! You're going to wear it when we celebrate your birthday. Eek!"

She clasped her hands together under her chin while jumping up and down in front of me.

"What? Me? No. That's not possible. I don't think that's a good idea. Get Lilith to wear it. She's perfect, and she's taller, so it will drape nicely. She can wear it for her performance during the anniversary."

"No way, Marisol Blaise," she snapped, using my assumed last name for emphasis. "You're not getting out of this. I spent hours and hours on that dress, in addition to the years I have given to this friendship, and you are going to wear it even if it makes you uncomfortable. Even if you have to endure the entire merstation staring at you, with envy. You are the most perfectly shaped, brilliant young woman that I know, and you are going to be my muse on your birthday whether you like it or not, and that's final."

She slammed the palm of her hand loudly on the table before storming out of the lab. It was a side of Naviah that I had never experienced before. Yes, she could be headstrong, but never toward me. I preferred the old Naviah. The one I knew five minutes ago.

The lab became quiet. I looked down at the wave tank I was using, wishing that no one around us had witnessed her outburst. Confrontation was something that I dreaded. I am, before anything else, a pleaser, and scandal and attention were things that I avoided, always. It was true that I was highly competitive, but I enjoyed quiet, unassuming success.

"Hey Marisol," said a male voice beside me. "How many waves does it take before Aqueous tips over?"

It was Creighton. I hadn't noticed as he and Lilith approached my table. He grinned as he studied my model, politely avoided the obvious by refraining from asking about Naviah's outburst, but his intense interest in my demonstration increased my heartrate. He was so good-looking. He reminded me of the lifeguards we'd seen on reruns of *Bondi Rescue*. They were ripped, with strong shoulders and quads, running toward the surf, determined to rescue the swimmers caught in the rip.

*Dreamy.*

Lilith positioned herself closely beside him, suggesting situational ownership.

"Hello, Creighton, Lilith. How's it going?"

"We're making progress," he said. "But seriously, how were you able to replicate the exact impact of subterranean currents on the structural integrity of the station?"

His hand moved upward to cradle his chin as he dropped his head to study my work while waiting for my answer, but not wanting to offer any explanation to Lilith, who had proven herself to be an intellectually paratrophic opportunist, I dodged his question.

"Just lucky, I guess. I hope the profs will be satisfied."

"You're almost done. We had some trouble simulating complete anoxia for one of the segments in Lilith's demonstration on the varying characteristics of deep water, but I think we've sorted it out."

He gave Lilith a satisfied nod, but I was distracted by the observation that he had had a growth spurt. His voice was deeper and his shoulders had broadened. Gone was the cute little boy who had been afraid to leave his mother's side. He had been replaced by a handsome young man with calm strength and a confident voice. His blond tousled hair gave off a relaxed vibe in juxtaposition to his inquisitive, deep-set eyes. Hands thrust in pockets, Creighton stood inoffensively next to Lilith, whose arms crisscrossed her body in closed hostility. To redirect the attention back to herself, she began pivoting, back and forth, as she peered down her perfect nose at my project, smiling her wicked, determined-to-win-at-all-costs smile.

"We're calling it a day and changing for dinner," he said. "I think almost everyone has gone up. Kyro left earlier, so he should be there already."

Kyro was claustrophobic, which prevented him from occupying a small mini-pod. He always left early to ensure that he had enough time to return to his parent's family-pod to change before dinner.

I looked across the lab. There were only a handful of trainees left:

Felton's fingers were frantically programming; Mason was refurbishing the rotating sponge on a derelict submersible cleaning drone, also called a scrub; and Yarrow was shaping large decorative bowls from melted seafloor trash.

"So we'll see you in the dining hall?"

"Maybe, Creighton. I'm not that hungry, but you never know. I may head up there if I get this done. I'm not sure."

It was like I had forgotten how to speak.

"Well, you're welcome to join us if you come up."

He turned to leave, pausing chivalrously to let Lilith go through the hatchway first, before vanishing down the corridor.

I needed to eat, and Aqueous had strict mealtime policies. Dinnertime for my cohort had almost expired.

Dinner was served from 17:00–22:00 with staggered seating times. Small children to Y5s were given priority from 17:00–19:00, Y6s through Y10s were permitted to dine between 18:00–20:00, and adults (those who had received their assignments) were permitted to eat anytime from 17:00–22:00, thereby allowing families to eat together or adults to dine in peace. Leftover meals were available around the clock for those working nightshifts.

To promote hygiene and reduce the risk of infectious disease, all residents were required to wash and change for dinner. Daytime SIDs were exchanged for stiff dinner attire because dinner was not only about eating. It was a gathering where triumphs were discussed and obstacles were reconsidered. It was our daily ceremony of subterranean civility.

All Aqueous SIDs were emblazoned with the same blue, double-ringed, circular crest that I first saw as a child. At the center, *AQUEOUS* was embroidered in bold uppercase. Circling this, between a double ring, was the phrase: *Submerging Together To Where We Began*. It was our slogan. A contract. An agreement to reinstate life on Earth from the depths of its origin, and no matter how bad our day had been, if we had disagreed or quarreled, dinner was a time to regroup. Remembering this, I decided that it was time to leave the lab and go to dinner.

I tidied up my workspace by logging off of my monitor and returning my equipment to the storage cupboards. I pushed in my chair, and proceeded to exit the lab to return to MP124 and change, and as I passed through the hatchway I was startled by a familiar voice.

"Exactly who I wanted to speak with," said my father.

*Busted.*

There would be no avoiding interrogation. I stopped and turned around to see him approaching with Captain Kress, Creighton's father.

"Hello, Dad. Good evening, Captain Kress. How are you?"

"We had an interesting day watching AP1 circle the station. Were you part of that?"

"It was Mom's idea, and I was taken hostage. It won't happen again."

Captain Kress, always motionless and impossible to read, stood perfectly erect with his hands clasped behind his back. Like most officers, he was a formidable opponent, not to be wagered against. His hair was exceedingly short, graying on the sides, but this did not soften his demeanor. He was a seriously straight, no-nonsense type. Hyperefficient, black and white, and his small piercing eyes were burning holes into the side of my head as he watched me speak to my father. Undoubtedly, he was comparing my words to my body language to determine if I was lying.

I started to perspire.

"Ah, I see. Well, if your mother needed to use it then I assume that there was a good reason. Let's hope that no one in Robotics & Automation, or anyone else for that matter, noticed."

It was a warning not to speak of it to others.

*Noted.*

He knew that I would not disobey him, and I knew that he would never question my mother. She would not have to explain her reasoning for piloting AP1 without his consent. Despite her poised, almost submissive persona, there was a strength residing in my mother that was unyielding. From my perspective, my father understood that she was his superior. Empyreal Blaise was the true admiral of Aqueous.

"Command commented, but I took care of that. I told them that I had tasked the cuviers with AP1 system checks and a station perimeter drill. No questions asked. That's why it's cool to be the admiral."

Captain Kress looked at the ground, embarrassed for him, but I was used to my father's lame jokes.

"Were you with the cuviers today?"

He knew that I loved diving and was intrigued by their unit. It was the assignment I coveted most. There could be nothing more thrilling than projects and adventure outside of the station. Becoming a cuvier meant acquiring a new vantage point, and a worthy purpose. It was acknowledgement for being one of the best onboard. Legendary, in fact. They were the defenders of modern maritime exploration. Heroes, if needed, possessing mathematical agility and physical prowess. Cuviers were trained to tackle dangerous aquatic conditions. Maybe my father mentioned me to them. I hope he remembered to remind them that the admiral's daughter was graduating shortly.

"You'll be disappointed to know that I was not with them today. Do you still find them interesting, Marisol?"

He was joking again. Pretending to forget that it was my childhood dream to join them.

"My interest has never wavered."

"That's my girl. Setting her sights on the top."

My father's pride caused the captain to shift uneasily on his feet before stating, "Becoming an aquatic diver is a demanding assignment with limitless risk. The professors have told me that you are a proficient study, with the potential to be placed in any department, but wouldn't you prefer something more feminine? It's not the place for a young lady."

My father's expression fell as he said, "We'll have to wait and see how it all works out. The Aqueous Assignment Committee has excellent succession planners onboard, and there are lots of great projects to work on in any department, not to mention lots of great talent to place. Sweetheart, I'm sure you'll be assigned appropriately to something that you will become passionate about. Trust the process."

I did not like what I was hearing. I was at the top of my class both academically and physically, outperforming all of the Y10 boys. A misguided, chauvinistic comment from an apathetic captain would not be enough to sideline me. He was not even part of the decision-making process and would be better suited keeping his poisonous thoughts to himself.

"With all due respect, Captain Kress, I wish to become the first female to join the team, and I have been preparing for this for as long as I can remember. I believe that I will have the scores and physical aptitude to qualify, and my thesis on pod range maximization, by way of advanced aquadynamics, will benefit the cuviers. Now if you'll excuse me, I am going to change so that I may join my peers for dinner."

I nodded a quick farewell, and stepped sure-footedly away from them to quell my overwhelming doubt.

## CHAPTER EIGHT

The dining hall was bustling when I arrived. It was an ordinary gathering of happy families, reuniting after a fruitful workday to eagerly exchange updates on their projects and activities. There was no additional adornment today. The aroma of culinary creativity garnished the room, but the remarks of Captain Kress had curbed my appetite.

I noted friends greeting each other as they carried their trays to empty chairs, and small children, having finished their portions, running around in playful games of tag. Laughter floated on the air, making it much more than a meal. It was a theatre of thankfulness, an auditorium of appreciation, and I loved it.

I smelled the spicy scent of creole. By my summation, our mess chef extraordinaire, Sergeant Reginald Eirome, had whipped up his special seaweed and shrimp dish. Maybe I would eat after all. I had become a timorous eater. The knowledge that I wouldn't starve had made me picky, but I could stomach shrimp, especially after it had been drowned in spices.

Sergeant Eirome was a conduit of comfort. He knew the names and favorite dishes of every soul onboard, and would try his best to prepare individualized, "home-cooked" meals for those having a tough day. His exceptional culinary training and gastronomic ingenuity utilized unusual seafloor ingredients to create mouth-watering (in my case eye-watering) recipes, but it was his demeanor that solidified his status. His loud, bellowing voice conveyed encouragement and enthusiasm. His laughter was melodic, uncontrollable, contagious, and often accompanied by jubilant tears. He played Santa at Christmas, the bunny at Easter, and Superman at Halloween. During Eid, Diwali, Hanukkah, Chinese and Russian New Year, Sergeant Eirome taught tolerance through taste. He celebrated them all by capturing the essence of cultural cuisine and educating each of us on the festivities of humanity. We felt better after he fed us, having been unified by his ubiquitous utensils.

By the time supper was served, the Sergeant segued from cuisinier to maître d', greeting diners as they arrived. Most nights were general seating, so as honorary host he extended handshakes, hugs, and high fives.

"Is that my Marisol? Our dream girl from the deep blue sea, poised to take on Poseidon himself. How are you doing today, young lady?"

He greeted me with his signature fist bump, jellyfish move.

"Fine, Reggie. Much better now that I'm here with you and out of the labs. How are you today? Dinner smells great, as always."

I half-lied. It did smell good today, but it didn't always smell like this. There were things that I detested and avoided. I had endured many "skinny" dinners, when my stomach would growl in duress after my nose told my throat to refuse to swallow the sea creature that my brain refused to identify as food. It was a standoff of my organs well beyond my control.

"I hear you're giving those boys a run for their sea bucks this year. You go, girl! I'm banking with you."

"I'm trying my best."

"You crush them in the trials like 240,000 standard atmosphere. Do you hear me?"

"Yes, I hear you. Thanks for your support, Reg."

He was so huge and cute. I felt like a superstar every time I talked to him.

"Marisol!"

I heard my name yelled from across the hall.

"Marisol! Over here!" it shouted again.

I looked past Reggie to find the source, and I spied a large group of Y10s at a table near the back of the room. Some were standing, some were sitting, and many had their hands in the air waving me over toward them. I started in their direction, greeting familiar adults and children along the way, until my path was blocked by Starren, Julip's younger sister.

"Marisol, when are you gonna play with me?" she asked, yanking downward on my arm.

"Starren, every time I see you you've grown. What are they feeding you?"

Leaning forward I used the same arm she was yanking on to tickle her, causing her to giggle loudly.

"I can play with you after the trials are done. Will you be free?"

"Yes, I will, and I can show you my headstand! Here, hold Lucky," she demanded, thrusting a jar containing her pet cricket into my hands and running off toward another friend. "Raven! Marisol's gonna watch me headstand!"

I watched as she grabbed Raven's hand and led her away toward a grouping of Y1s.

*Adorable.*

Amley approached.

"Marisol, Creighton told us to save you the seat beside him. The one to the left of Yarrow," she said as she walked past. "Lilith was sitting there, but she went to rehearsal."

"Sounds good," I lied. As if I wanted to be wanted because Lilith left. "Aren't you staying?"

"Taking mine to go. I need to utilize every last moment to maximize my assignment success, remember?"

*Burn. Note to Empyreal: be less abrasive during our next covert mission.*

Amley was a motivated student. She used her time wisely, prioritizing studies over social alleviations. She was diligent, usually less sassy, and I liked her. We shared a similar work ethic, but our interests were polar opposites. She was not a risk-taker and found happiness in horticulture.

I walked toward the table and took the seat she told me to utilize. Everyone was there except Lilith and Creighton. He probably walked her to rehearsal. The situation was far worse than I thought.

"Hey, Elsby. Can you pass this to Julip?"

I leaned over Creighton's empty seat to hand her the jar containing Lucky.

"It's Starren's pet cricket," I explained.

"Oh, bless. Julip, you are so lucky to have a little sister. My parents finally told me to stop asking for one."

Elsby passed the jar across the table to Julip.

"I'm lucky, but she's so brazen. I don't know where she gets it."

Julip was cripplingly indecisive and preferred tasks involving detailed directives. I had tried to tutor her, but she would need an assignment not requiring deduction. She peered inside the jar at Lucky.

"Her crickets have it rough. This jar is a death sentence. I secretly replace them before she realizes they aren't asleep. She has no idea they're a foodstuff."

The pitiful plight of pet crickets was something I had never considered, but either way, they were all eaten in the end.

Our conversation was interrupted by the hysterical screams of Purity, a self-professed germophobe who was easily pranked.

"You are childish and disgusting!"

Felix and Etan were laughing uncontrollably.

"Too bad she didn't eat it," howled Etan. "That would have been even more hilarious."

Etan was a buffoon. Physically mature, his sense of humor was stunted. He took pleasure in the mockery of others, and his jokes

were insulting, often cringeworthy. At the moment, he was torment-
ing a tiny defenseless fish.

"Everybody up!" directed Crimson. "Shrieking isn't doing him
any good. Help me save him. I need a dish or a mug with clean water
so that we can rinse him off and dump him back into the observation pond."

Sugar, a trainee on exchange from Sihai Longwang, offered her
water glass to Crimson, who scooped up what appeared to be a distressed fish from Purity's bowl of creole. The creole was ruined, but
the fish would be fine.

"Yarrow, come with me to release it," said Crimson.

"As long as I don't have to touch it," he replied.

"How do you normally transition the aquatic species from one
pond to another?"

"I have a scooper thingy. I love creating beautiful pondscapes, but
I don't touch any of the stuff, like, with my hands. Yuck."

Crimson shrugged, and they left for the grand pavilion as Sugar
scolded Etan.

"You wasted a full portion, Etan."

"And you're beyond your station, so mind your own business," he
shot back.

"Etan, did you just whip a zinger that made sense? I'm impressed,
buddy," said Creedan.

Etan cast him a hollow stare.

"And just like that, mind-blanking Etan is back," said Elsby, shaking her head in an I'm-not-surprised sort of way.

Creighton reappeared to reclaim his empty seat, and Lilith was
delightfully not with him.

"What's going on here? Seems tense," he said.

"On the way back from the labs Creedan dared Felix to prank Purity, so Felix got Etan to steal a minnow from the grand pavilion and
toss it into Purity's bowl," explained Joen. "It's been a panic ever since."

Creedan smiled. With his hands relaxed in his pockets, he rocked back and forth, heel to toe, enjoying the chaos that he had created.

"I would have jumped into Purity's bowl willingly. Anything to get away from Felix and Etan," declared Creighton. Then, looking to Felix and shaking his head, he said, "Man, if Nesme finds out you endangered one of her babies you'll be cleaning that sludge tank for life."

Felix smiled and shrugged his shoulders. "Someone's got to keep it spicy around here. Besides, I know you'll appreciate me someday. You've just got to lighten up a bit first."

Creighton crossed his arms in disagreement, as Felix looked over to me and winked. He grew more shameless each day. He got up, motioning for Creedan to join him, and they sauntered away with Etan following desperately behind.

Creighton leaned toward me. "Have you eaten today, Marisol?"

"Not yet. Where were you?"

My question sounded completely insecure and controlling.

"I went to poach extra dessert. It's lemon squares tonight, and you know they're our favorite. I was determined to find extra for us both," he said, proudly unfolding a napkin containing half a dozen tarts. "Marisol, I give you the mother lode."

Survival on Aqueous was dependent on sustainability, so mealtime planning was critical. Dietary Analysts were assigned to develop portion suitability for every age and gender. They calculated the nutritional requirements for each resident, and then collaborated with the arboretum, Habitat Hatchery, Aquatic Horticulture & Research, Poultry Production, Proteins & Cloning, and the kitchen culinary teams to develop appropriate weekly menus in consideration of harvest schedules and the weekly catch. What was farmed and fished was compared to what was cooked and consumed. Leftovers resulted in a reduction of next day portions because we could not afford to waste what was cooked. It was a daily endeavor to ensure that individual portions were nutritionally optimal and waste-free.

I was not surprised by Creighton's gift of lemon squares. It was yet another reason why he was so well-liked. He knew how to make his friends happy. He had noted our shared love for the tart treats years ago.

"You were able to find that many residents willing to give up their dessert?"

"Not exactly. Reggie's a pro. He knows what we prefer, so I knew he would have made extra portions of this meal. It's a favorite, and everyone will want it two days in a row. I went to him directly and begged for extras."

Despite not yet having eaten my own creole portion, I grabbed one of the squares and started devouring it.

"Oh, these are so good. Thanks for sharing," I said as the crumbs got stuck on my face, fell all over the table, and then onto my lap. I was a mess.

"I've always shared my lemon squares with you, Marisol," he said softly so that the others could not hear him. Then, leaning in closer to me, he added, "And I always will."

My heart stopped beating, and I was floating, but I wasn't literally floating because I was still in my seat. As I looked up for clarity, into his smoldering eyes, I became quite certain that I was no longer breathing, and I was also conscious of the crumbs all over my mouth, chin, shirt, and hands. There were crumbs everywhere, and my mouth was hanging open with mushy lemon filling inside of it, but crumbs aside, Creighton Kress had announced that he intended to share his dessert with me, forever, in a way that suggested that he meant more than dessert.

*Wow.*

"You'll want to be sure to brush your teeth extra carefully tonight," Anit warned. "The sugar in those squares can chew right through your enamel."

*Way to ruin the moment, Anit.*

Anit, another Y10, was across from me and overly interested in oral hygiene. I ignored him, averted my eyes from Creighton's, and remembered to shut my mouth. I also tried not to choke, but not choking meant that I was still breathing, which was a good sign, and my heart was beating again, also good, although wildly and mainly in my ears as though I was in danger. Whatever, I was still alive.

As I tried to brush the crumbs off, my eyes met Naviah's. She was farther down, across the table, sitting next to Murphy. Sensing that I needed an immediate rescue, she reached for Murphy's elbow and tugged it toward her, tipping his algae sweet tea onto her dinner SIDs tunic.

"Murphy! Look what you've done! Can you please be more careful?" she scolded with unnecessary emphasis. "Now I will have to go and change. You cannot expect me to stay like this," she argued, even though Murphy had said nothing.

"Marisol, will you come with me please? I am so upset, and I should not be alone right now," she continued, in a manner far too dramatic for empathy.

"Of course not, you poor thing. Ah, let me a-assist you in your dampened state by walking you to your p-pod," I stammered, getting up and fleeing the dining hall ahead of her.

We looked like a couple of weirdos.

"Don't forget to floss!" Anit yelled behind us.

Once we were through the hatch, away from the group, she asked, "What happened back there, Marisol? Hopefully something significant because I took eight ounces of algae for you, and it might stain."

"Creighton told me that he'll always share his lemon squares with me."

It sounded much less significant saying it aloud, and rarely speechless, Naviah responded with raised eyebrows and confusion while gesturing to the wet mark setting on her top.

"It was the *way* he said it. It went well beyond lemon squares, and it was accompanied by a softer tone and an intense look."

"News flash, Marisol, he always looks intense. He's hotter than the superheated water spewing from those submarine geysers we're always learning about. He's packing heat and coming in hot, twenty-four-seven. It's an everyday occurrence in the life of Creighton Kress."

"Yeah, I don't think that's what packing heat means. Do you think I misunderstood?"

She let out an empathetic sigh before saying, "I'm afraid so, little one. Sharing portions is commonplace. Like, do you actually think that Murphy's just big-boned?

She had a point.

"You're under a lot of pressure at the moment, so it is understandable that you jumped the gun on this one. Once we've submitted our theses, and completed the trials, you'll feel better. Let's spend tonight prepping anything you choose. What should we work on next? Stain removal?"

"No, fitness. Let's go to Athletics Development. We can run away from this embarrassing day. Besides, I've got to keep my training up if I want to slay the dragon."

She looked perplexed.

"Huh?"

"It's nothing," I said.

"I hear they have dragons on Sihai Longwang."

"Not literally, Naviah."

"Really? Well, it's irrelevant anyway. Empyreal insisted that we would be best friends, so you're stuck here with us. Lucky for you, I enjoy it."

"And I appreciate that."

"Onward to Athletics Development, Miss Blaise. I'm exhausted already."

## CHAPTER NINE

The Aqueous routine began immediately for many. Pod assignments were received upon boarding, with additional, specific instructions being transmitted by AI Assistants after initial airlock descent. Despite the early hour, each resident was expected to shower and don their appropriate SIDs before immediately making their way to their assigned departments. They would be introduced to colleagues and familiarized with their new working environment before any meals were served.

Team-building would follow, as time permitted, but the urgent concern was ensuring a smooth station start. To successfully salvage our terrestrial society, Aqueous needed to positively respond to the several thousand residents stepping aboard. Humanity had arrived at the point of no return, and the implacable nature of the deep sea would be impetuously crushing if her conditions were not met.

For children and youth, and there were not many, expectations were different. The youngsters of the sea, with one designated parent, received a week of leniency from educational activities and station-critical jobs. Together, they were encouraged to explore their new marine habitat and make new friends.

It was late morning by the time we arrived at our family-pod. FP1 was a last minute alternative to AP1, due to my unexpected presence. Empyreal had decided that it was in my best interest to be surrounded by other children, near my school, rather than reside near the offi-cers, high above in Command.

I wasn't tired when we arrived. The extensive changes I was wit-nessing had fueled my curiosity, so Empyreal decided that we could venture down the corridor for a brief introduction to my new teach-ers before having breakfast and a nap.

Hand in hand, we walked along the unfamiliar passageways that would eventually feel like home. We explored the station interior and exterior alike, for the glass shell that incubated us also exposed the new frontier we'd claimed. It was a vast, cavernous valley flooded with water and light.

Aqueous engineers had synced the station's exterior lighting with the twenty-four-hour cycle of the sun, mimicking the daylight hours of the terrestrial life we had abandoned. Bright lighting was currently illuminating the surrounding infrastructure, but at night the lights would be dimmed to create a sleeping routine.

We walked passed the Sea Turtle's Nursery for Kinetic Residents. It was an area devoted to educating the smallest members of Aqueous, fondly known as the little stinkers, and it looked marvelous. I could see toys and games scattered on a soft, colorful floor. The walls were covered in a shimmering tiled mosaic of multi-colored fish swim-ming through beautiful aquatic plants. The ceiling was covered in large upside-down domes that looked like bubbles, and there was music playing. I could see children seated at small tables and chairs, doing crafts.

"I want to go in there," I said, pulling on her hand in an attempt to make her stop.

Empyreal laughed, joyfully, and said, "Yes, we can go in there, but not yet. We need to go to your school first and meet the children your age."

*School? Why was I was going to go to school?*

I had played CADRE school with my brothers, but I had never gone to one.

"I thought we didn't need school anymore."

"That was the situation for many people, for many years, but now that we live on Aqueous we need school more than ever. We need to learn more about the ocean so that the land can rest and Earth can become healthy again."

We passed through the hatchway of the FUNdamental Learning Centre for SUBteen Scientists. It was my school where I would be known as a fleck. It was less colorful, and there were no fish on the walls. The flat, aquamarine-colored ceiling was illuminated in moving white light that looked like ripples on water, but that was where the creativity stopped. The hard floor was a dull, muted gray, and the walls were plain white. Numbers and letters had replaced the fish, and there was no music playing in the background. It was not as good as the stinker's school.

"I don't like this one. I want to go to the other school."

"Let's give it a chance. I bet there are some wonderful surprises here that you haven't discovered yet. Besides, the other school is for smaller children, and I can tell you're way too smart for it already."

An older, pleasant-looking woman approached us.

"Good morning, Empyreal. It's always nice to see you. Who do we have here? I didn't know that you had a daughter."

She bent forward to shake my hand. She had short graying hair, glasses, and a warm smile. I liked her immediately.

"Why yes, I do have a daughter, Mrs. Brightly. This is Marisol."

"Marisol Blaise, how are you today? And what do you think of this amazing station? Have you seen your new pod yet?"

I nodded my response as I looked around the room.

"Are you excited about becoming a fleck?"

I cast my eyes downward and shrugged. It wasn't that exciting.

"I'd like to show you something that I think you may like. Can you tap your foot over there?"

Mrs. Brightly motioned to a circular section of the floor that became flooded in pink light as I neared. At the edge of the circle, I tapped lightly with my right foot, and it burst into a grid of colorful squares that swirled into a vibrant shade of green. Digital grass began to grow, then flowers bloomed and trees appeared as a multitude of baby animals scurried forward from a growing forest. It was amazing.

"Do you know what that is?"

I shook my head.

"That's called spring. Here, try another one."

I followed Mrs. Brightly around the room until I had discovered all four seasons. I was starting to like the idea of becoming a fleck. My school was way better than the stinker school.

"I want to save some of the surprises for another day, but I will say this, Marisol, you're going to love what the walls can do."

*Mrs. Brightly was a wizard, for sure.*

On that particular morning the walls remained silent and white, but I started to take a keen interest in the rest of the space. It was enormous. There were multiple classrooms beside the common area, each containing interesting artifacts, and farther back the floor was carpeted by plush shag in various shades of teal, purple, and gold. It looked soft, and I wanted to lay on my back and slide across it, but I decided to show my manners instead. There were blue sofas and enormous floor pillows positioned atop the rug, and I made note to flop on a pillow as soon as we were done with the tour.

Along the back wall, and much to my delight, was a playground with navy monkey bars and a set of light blue swings. There was a wall where a few children were climbing on little secured handles, and there was a pirate ship perfect for a rambunctious game of tag. School was way better than my brothers had described.

"Do you want to go and play with the children?" asked Mrs. Brightly.

I nodded. It was sensory overload and too much effort to speak.

"I'm sorry, Marisol, but I don't think so. We've been up most of the night, and it's going to be a big day," reminded Empyreal. "We can't stay."

"Everyone is tired. Let me get Marisol checked in. If she doesn't make new friends this morning, she can come back anytime."

We followed her back to her workspace, near the entrance, where she logged into the system and began asking Empyreal questions about me.

"Height and weight?"

"Ah, I think she's about . . ."

Empyreal was stumped, and stopped speaking.

Mrs. Brightly looked at me and then back to Empyreal.

"No problem. Swing by the infirmary sometime this week and submit it to me later."

"Thank you, Mrs. Brightly. I will be sure to do that."

"Blood type?"

Empyreal paused again, then shook her head.

"How about a birth date?"

Mrs. Brightly was becoming aware that Empyreal knew nothing about me.

"No, I don't know that either."

Having not anticipated the questions, Empyreal had not prepared the answers, and it was blatantly clear that I was not her child. She appeared to be on the brink of tears.

Mrs. Brightly stopped typing and looked up from her monitor.

"Well now, now. Don't be sad. No one ever said that families have to be biological. Choosing to be together is equally important, and as for your date of birth, Marisol, birthdates are not about getting older. No, no, no. Birthdays are a celebration of life. They mark the anniversary of a new addition to the family, and I believe that we have a new addition to celebrate today."

In a heartwarming gesture, she turned to the children around the room and announced, "Attention, everyone! I have a happy announcement to make. Today is Marisol Blaise's sixth birthday. Isn't that wonderful news?"

Excited chatter echoed back to us.

"And because it's so wonderful, I will inform the kitchen that we need a cake!"

Louder cheers erupted as the children began to twirl and chant, "Cake! Cake! Cake!"

Empyreal placed her hands on her heart and smiled appreciatively at Mrs. Brightly as the merry cheers for cake continued to ring through the room. She let out a small laugh before putting her arm around my shoulder in a display of our union. There was nothing to be ashamed of and everything to celebrate. April twenty-second had become my birthdate, and we would get cake. I was excited about it, even though I had no idea what cake was.

As the cheers subsided, a sad-looking boy arrived with his father, and they approached Mrs. Brightly to check in.

"Good morning, Mrs. Brightly, Empyreal," greeted the tidy, middle-aged man. He was studious looking in his glasses and long, white jacket. His SIDs also included a navy, V-neck sweater, layered over a light blue, collared shirt, and gray trousers. He wore spongy white sport shoes on his feet. "I hate to burden you, but I am late to the infirmary to familiarize my assignees with the facility. Can I leave Felix in your care until I can return?"

His question was delivered in a rhetorically flat tone. He did not expect refusal.

"Daddy, don't leave me," cried the little boy. "I can help you. Let me come with you this time."

"No, Felix. A medical facility is no place for a child, and today will be exceptionally busy. You're better off here, making new friends."

"Daddy, no. Please," pleaded the boy.

"I should be able to return this evening, Mrs. Brightly. If things run smoothly, that is. If not, I see comfortable sofas back there. They'll make an acceptable bed."

"Take me with you, Daddy!"

"I will be back as soon as I can," his father said, patting him awkwardly on the head. "Empyreal, I will see you in my practice this week?"

She made no indication of answering him, and he left abruptly, not needing it. His son, Felix, covered his face with his tiny arms and threw himself on the nearest sofa, sobbing. He was exhausted and alone in an unknown place.

• • •

Dr. Nathaniel Nyrmac had convinced himself that the demands of his occupation would prevent him from having a family. The world was in chaos, and he would ensure the medical well-being of those chosen to serve. He refused romantic distractions until a love so efficacious injected his heart, making him immune to detachment. He married a patient, and as unethical as that was, the world had lost order and judgement was never cast.

He adored his new bride, having never known such happiness, and her involvement in the mission united their focus. She granted him unlimited freedom to attend the unwell, until she wanted a child. Children had become rarities. The notion of welcoming a child into a dying world was a reckless action for most, but the doctor and his wife were not like the rest. They would be saved, along with their offspring, but despite this, the doctor rejected the imposition. A child would become an impediment to the many people needing his care.

His wife understood his pragmatic demeanor, but continued to persuade him that he possessed parental aptitude. Eventually, the conversation grew silent. The absence of a child was destroying them, and Mrs. Nyrmac became sad and aloof, grieving for someone she'd never met, so to repair their union and save his wife, Dr. Nyrmac agreed to start a family. He prayed that he could find love for a child as he had found love for her.

Mrs. Nyrmac had an uncomplicated pregnancy, and reveled in the experience. She spent her spare time preparing for the fine baby boy they would have, and her enthusiasm infected the doctor. He found himself securing obscure infant items to ensure his son's optimal stimulation and development. There would be time to love them both and remain committed to his practice. They would have it all.

Mrs. Nyrmac progressed to term without incident; however, she struggled during delivery and died, leaving her newborn and husband alone. Unable to comprehend a life without her or reconcile his inability to save her, Dr. Nyrmac worked tirelessly to save others. He fulfilled his parental responsibilities by ensuring that their son, Felix, was well cared for, but it wasn't enough. His absence would crack his son's tiny soul, allowing the innate resilience of childhood to seep out. Manifesting a fear of abandonment and desperate need for affection, Felix became aggressive, often throwing tantrums or hurling unkind words, not that any of his unruly actions garnered the attention of the doctor.

• • •

Felix's shoulders shook as he cried into the sofa. He was a heart-broken boy in an unknown place.

I pointed at him.

"Where is his mother?"

Empyreal knelt beside me and quietly explained, "He doesn't have one anymore." Then she guided my arm downward so that I did not appear rude before adding, "His mother died when he was a baby."

I felt terribly sad for him.

"Everyone must have a mother. Should we tell him that he can have one of mine? I have two."

Empyreal froze. Her lips were parted, but there was a long pause before she spoke, "I don't think that will work, but we can invite him to spend a few days with us. We can make sure that he meets everyone so that he feels happy and safe."

I nodded in agreement. It was a great plan. I crossed the room and grabbed Felix's hand.

"Come. You can be with us," I said, dragging him back toward my new mother. "We're new here too."

Felix didn't argue and returned with us to our pod. He stayed with us for a week while we became embedded in station life and was returned to his father as the station paused to celebrate Aqueous' inauguration.

The inauguration was the official dog-earing of the Gregorian calendar, marking the embarkation of our aquatic existence. In the infinite absence of the sun, it was the first of many parties to commemorate the milestones of maritime life. A seasonless life without day. A delicate life in the dark.

# CHAPTER TEN

Wearing our fitness SIDs, we proceeded to Athletics Development to practice for our physical trial. The trial challenges would not be revealed until the actual day, but we had been encouraged to continue independently with the conditioning program that had been structured for Y10s. I hoped that my progress would benefit me on the day of the trials. Cuvier assignment, in particular, was dependent on exceptional physical prowess.

Trainees spent five hours a week running drills designed to strengthen the mind and body, as well as condition us for life under the sea. Nursery-aged children played nostalgic games of red rover, four square, hopscotch, tag, hide-and-seek, and monkey in the middle; Y1–Y5s progressed to games like dodge ball, jump rope, and capture the flag; Y6–Y9s learned traditional sports like badminton, volleyball, decathlon, and basketball; whereas, Y10 activities were unconventional. We were given maps of the station and sent off on timed orienteering drills. We had to climb, hang, freeze, hold our breath, drop, squeeze, and sometimes spin. Our challenges were about survival and were not entertaining. Everyone had to swim.

All residents on Aqueous were allocated time slots in Athletics Development, but physical training was mandatory for all cuviers, officers, and trainees. Mobility marshals created unique, weekly programs for the various groups enrolled in mandatory fitness and recreational programs for users who enjoyed being active. Most residents participated.

Clear your mind and exceed the limit. That was the Athletics Development motto. It was visibly written at center court, across our nets, lengthwise down the running track, and as the lane divider at the bottom of the pool. Our drills and challenges were meant to strengthen the mind and body. We were instructed to clear our minds to make room for achievement by pushing out thoughts of disbelief, exhaustion, and fear. Healthy human bodies were far more capable than our minds permitted, so removing personal doubt was the first step in obtaining our goals. In basic terms it meant don't think, achieve.

Athletics Development, a standalone department spanning three floors, connected to the station on the main level, and was a large, open-concept, circular space consisting of various sporting facilities. From check-in, visitors could climb the stairs to utilize a five hundred-meter circular running track, located directly above the swimming pool, and traverse an elaborate high ropes course. Descending the stairs, visitors could utilize the pitch, courts, ice and curling rinks, and pools. The central structure, a thirty-meter carbon climbing tower, provided structural support for the department and anchored it to the seafloor.

When we arrived at check-in I surveyed the monitor for the recommended Y10 fitness routine, hoping that it would give some clues as to what would be on the trial. The suggested workout included five wall climbs, five motionless suspensions, five sprints of four hundred meters, five rope climbs with net rappel, five static apnea submerges, and fifty underwater swims of ten meters each. It was the standard stuff.

As we finished memorizing the routine, Fly emerged from the storage area with a stack of newly laundered towels. As our senior mobility manager, she was inspirational to children and adults alike. A petite powerhouse, with agility to spare, Fly was skilled at anything physical and addicted to endorphins. She was one of the happiest residents I knew.

"Hi, ladies. Here to squeeze in some extra training before the trials, are we?"

"No, we like squeezing into these absurdly tight and unflattering training suits for kicks," Naviah whined. "Could there be anything more humiliating? How can I clear my mind when I'm oozing out of this ridic getup?" Naviah wasn't interested in fitness, and to make it worse, she hated the one-piece, multi-sport suits we were required to wear while exercising. "This pinches in all the wrong places, and hasn't anyone heard of color contouring?" she continued.

"They could be improved, but you're both so beautiful inside and out, in whatever you wear, and you'll feel great afterward," Fly responded. "Log your results after each activity, and I can show you your progress and ranking at the end of your workout. Here are some goggles for the swim."

"Thanks," I answered.

I planned to work extra hard today, even though I suspected that I had already overtaken Creighton for top ranking. I liked being active, and I couldn't wait for Naviah to see my name at the top of the leaderboard.

The upcoming trials would be difficult. Aqueous trials were a closely guarded secret and known to be dangerous. Not open to spectators to reduce parental hysteria, the horrors of past trials were never corroborated. Former participants and instructors were barred from discussing their experiences, and not everyone succeeded. In honesty, most failed, but it was understood that any disgrace died with the trials and Y10s finished victorious, united by the experience.

"Let's go through the suggested routine as outlined. I'd like to finish in the pool because our lungs will be open and we'll be hot. It'll be a rewarding way to cool down," I said.

"So rewarding," said Naviah, with far less enthusiasm.

Starting our session at the base of the climbing tower, Naviah was able to complete the suggested wall climbs, but at a much slower pace than myself. She fell off multiple times, but persevered. I was proud of her. It was particularly high, which for many was a challenge unto itself. By the time she completed the task I was done with the sprints and rope climbs, so she skipped those activities and met me near the apnea tank.

"I think I'll ballpark my results on the items I missed. Let's be honest, Marisol, after the trials I'm never stepping foot in this place again."

"What about the steam room and the spa?"

"Oh, fine then. Twist my arm."

A fancy term meaning to hold one's breath underwater, static apnea was not complicated, but it took discipline and practice to become proficient. A lack of air caused alarm bells for the body, thereby increasing its heartrate. This adversely caused the body to use more air, diminishing the time that an individual could hold their breath. To master static apnea, a trainee needed optimal cardiovascular fitness and the ability to stay calm, which reinforced the motto: Clear your mind and exceed the limit.

When submerged in cold water, remaining stationary and calm, the static apnea diving reflex slowed the body's metabolic rate to conserve oxygen, and, with practice, trainees could maximize the amount of time spent underwater. This could prove useful in the event of an emergency, assuming that the bone-crushing pressure didn't finish us off first.

The water in the apnea tank was akin to pressing naked skin against the crystalized ice in Reggie's large walk-in freezers. It was so cold that it burned, and the square tank was deep and dark. It was a dimly lit abyss with long vertical ladders on each side.

During regular training sessions, Y10s were grouped in fours, one trainee for each ladder, and on Fly's mark descended into the water while holding their breath. The goal was to spend as much time at the bottom as possible before slowly ascending to the surface, but the tank grew darker with each lower rung, increasing the fear factor on the descent. The last trainee to surface and breathe was deemed the winner.

I borrowed a timer from the basket near the edge of the tank, and we entered the frigid water.

"Holy mother of Proteus. I can't hold my breath if it's been stolen," gasped Naviah.

"It's bad, so bad. Let's get this done quick. One, two, three."

We took last breaths, I started the timer, and we submerged together. For all of the discomfort, it was a different world once under. It was less cold somehow. Maybe it was the muffled noise, or the weightlessness, but there was solace in it.

Naviah's hair floated outward all around her, making her a mermaid after all. I waved at her, she laughed, then choked, and surfaced.

*Typical.*

Alone, I closed my eyes and focused my thoughts.

*Clear your mind and exceed the limit.*

I let my limbs float upward, allowing the water's cool embrace to encircle and support me. I was meant to be here. This was my fate. I had become an amphibious earthling capable of thriving in multiple habitats. Once of land and now of sea, static apnea was my thing.

I opened my eyes, grabbed the ladder and began my descent slowly, deliberately. The pressure grew with each lower rung, but down, down, down I went until I reached the bottom. I needed to breathe, but I refused to concede.

*The surface . . . What would it be like above us now?*

My lungs screamed for oxygen, interrupting my thoughts, so I plugged my nose and swallowed, hoping to quell their fears.

*Would the sun forgive and cease-fire its poisonous breath? Would life reemerge, sprouting forth once again?*

I was uncomfortable.

*Clear your mind and . . .*

I couldn't last any longer. I pulled my arms down and dolphin kicked to the surface, grateful to be reunited with dry, breathable gas.

I was greeted by Naviah's cheers.

"Three minutes and forty one seconds. That's a personal best! So on that note, I think we should call it a day and leave."

"But we haven't completed the entire apnea set or started our swim yet."

"Apnea schmapnea, and after five hundred meters underwater we'll be drowned anyway."

"It's not an underwater-without-breathing-swim. We breathe every ten meters."

"Oh. Are you going to wear flippers? Because that would make it a lot easier."

"Did it say assisted swim?"

"I don't remember."

She was lying.

"I'm quite certain it didn't, so I won't wear them, but if you want to wear them that's fine. I'm just happy you came, and I'm hoping you'll stay."

"I love it that you understand me, Marisol Blaise."

She eagerly grabbed a set of fins from the supply chest nearby, slipping them on and walking backward toward the water. They would significantly aid her swim.

The pool was a two-lane, circular swimming area that ran the perimeter of the structure. The water in the pool met the exterior station glass, creating an allusion of swimming outside. There was an infinite lane in each direction so that swimmers could swim as far as they pleased with no flip turns required. The transparent bottom was clearly measured in ten meter increments so that we could gauge how far we had travelled, and the circumference of the pool was five hundred meters. We only had to do one lap today, making it a relatively light swim.

"I suggest we swim in opposite directions and wherever we meet we quit," suggested Naviah.

"Now you're really cheating."

"Not really. Even with these flippers you'll still be faster than me. If you hurry you'll complete the majority of the swim, so tally ho. Off you go."

She was insufferable, but amusing. My mother could not have paired me with a better companion. We complemented each other, Naviah and I, and our friendship would endure after we were assigned. She was the integral member of my Aqueous CADRE, and I loved her like a sister.

I dove sideways into the water, determined to push myself for her sake so that she'd have a shorter distance to go. The apnea drill had opened my lungs, making the underwater sprints untaxing, and I counted the lengths as I went. I'd assumed that I'd meet Naviah somewhere around four hundred meters, but we did not meet. As I finished the full swim I saw her fins dangling at the edge of the pool, right where I began. I pushed myself up out of the water, and she extended a towel to me.

"Girl, you were quick. I didn't even have time to start, and now it's time to leave."

"There's still one more stop before we can call it a night. I need to log the rest of my results and check how they affect my ranking. We have to return our goggles anyway."

"Sure. Put me down for whatever you did. That'll be totally believable."

We walked back up the stairs to check-out with Fly.

"All done, girls? Feel amazing?"

Naviah shrugged, but I felt rejuvenated.

"Absolutely. I never get enough time here. Any chance you can show me the rankings?"

"Sure thing, Marisol. Let me pull them up." She accessed the system with her passcode before searching for the trainee results. "Here they are, the current standings for the Y10s based on those who have completed the additional recommended drills. You're currently fifth."

Naviah's eyes bulged out of their sockets, but she managed to suppress a verbal reaction.

"Fifth?" I confirmed.

"Yes, Marisol. You are fifth. Naviah, would you like to know your ranking?"

"Definitely not."

It was no secret that Naviah would be holding down last place.

"How can I be fifth? I've been here every day?"

"It's that time of year, in *your* year. All the Y10s want good placements, Marisol. It's getting real."

She had affirmed my worst fear: I hadn't worked hard enough.

"Can I see the list? I'd like to know who's ahead of me."

"I'm sorry. I can only show you your progress and your ranking. I can't share the standings for anyone else."

"Why is that?"

"Because there have been instances when primary contenders have sabotaged each other. They've done nasty stuff. Disgusting things that were often dangerous too, so we removed the temptation by removing access. You're training to overtake four trainees who are outpacing you. That's all I can disclose."

Fly abruptly logged out of the system before depositing our dirty towels into a hamper and carrying it back to the storage area that housed the laundry. The conversation was over, but I had to know who was ahead of me.

"I want those names, Naviah."

"Bad idea, and you promised me we could call it a night after you got your ranking."

"I said rankings. Plural."

Joen strode through the hatch in his dinner attire.

"Hi, Marisol. Hi, Naviah. Squeezing in some last minute training?"

"Yes, and apparently we're not the only ones," I replied.

"Joen, you're overdressed. To be accepted here you'll need to stuff yourself into one of these ultra-unflattering suits," said Naviah, but Joen was hyper-focused on fitness, so the suits suited him.

"I'm not training at the moment. I'm here to volunteer. I often relieve Fly at this time so that she can grab some dinner."

He walked behind the counter and began tidying up. I had been unaware that Joen assisted Fly, but it made perfect sense. His love of sport greatly exceeded any interest he had in science, except for the science of high-performance sport.

"So what is it you do, exactly?" I asked.

"I check-in the residents, explain the suggested drills, and show them their progress when they're finished. Straightforward stuff."

I sensed an opportunity.

"You probably have to login to the system for that, right?"

"Of course, Marisol. Why do you ask?"

I was about to lower my voice to explain when Fly emerged from the storage area in her dinner SIDs.

"Nutrition is my mission," she declared as she walked passed us toward the hatch. "Later, peeps."

"Enjoy yourself, Fly," said Joen as she vanished beyond the glass.

Joen had always been helpful, but he was unaware that he would help me next.

"Joen, I need you to login to the system, and show me the current athletic rankings for the Y10s."

"Oh," he responded, repositioning his feet and clasping his hands together in an uncomfortable manner, making no movement toward the monitor. "You must have heard that you're fifth."

"Joen! Focus on the task," Naviah demanded.

"I know how hard you've trained, Marisol, but I'm not supposed to disclose the list."

"Joen!" Naviah yelled again, slamming her fist on the counter.

"Alright. I'll do it. Calm down."

He punched several numbers into the keypad, typed in a quick search, and the Y10 rankings appeared on the screen. He turned the monitor toward me, and I scanned the list, top down. Creighton was first, Felix was second, then Joen, Lilith, Marisol . . . My mind began to race.

*How did Felix fit into this? He rebuked anything requiring commitment, always. And Lilith was ahead of me? She was a capable athlete, having an annoyingly good figure to show for it, but wasn't she usually painting or singing or stealing would-be boyfriends? Why was she taking the time to complete extra weekly drills? Was she doing them with Creighton? Training and stealing would-be-boyfriends at the same time?*

I looked up from the screen to see that despite his physicality, Joen had started chewing nervously on his thumb, and Naviah, who was leaning on my back, peering over my shoulder, let out a long, heavy sigh. I turned toward her, expecting empathy, but instead she said, "I wonder if Creighton plans to share his lemon squares with her too."

CHAPTER ELEVEN

It was sharing day for the Y2 flecks. It was always on the first day of our school week, Sunday, and we were seated in a circle on the carpet preparing to share our stories of Assuage. Assuage, by definition, was to mitigate, ease, or relieve, and every resident of Aqueous was designated one day of the week to break from science and relax. Station-critical schematics prevented full participation on the exact same day, but adhering to family-first ideologies, Command ensured that the parents of trainees rested together on Saturdays. This became a unified time to commune with loved ones, and was a valued respite from a saturated, six-day work week.

Assuage was a practice that had not been possible when we lived on the surface, when every minute was utilized to secure the survival of our race. This week my parents had taken me to meet the sous-chefs in our mess kitchen, where I was given a behind-the-scenes tour of how breakfast was prepared for everyone onboard. I learned how to make octopus-shaped pancakes, and I was ready to share my story.

"Lilith, would you like to tell us how you spent Assuage this week?" asked Miss Newing, the Y2 teacher.

Lilith, an independent child, was seated across from me, displaying equal indifference to all. Seated with erect posture, in perfectly pressed SIDs, she was all business, all the time, even during childhood, and looking down her nose at the rest of us, she was chosen first, and spoke emotionlessly of her day with her mother.

"I woke at 8:00 a.m. and proceeded to breakfast because my mother says that sleeping in is for the weak. I had an egg, and after eating that egg I practiced the piano for two hours exactly. Then my mother played the piano while I practiced my singing for two hours exactly. Then we ate lunch. I had fruit and a salad. Then we practiced ballet for six hours exactly. Then we ate dinner. I had fish. Then I washed my hair and it was time for bed."

Her arms had remained folded in her lap the entire time she spoke, with only her lips moving. She was robotic, and there was no smiling, ever. Julip, who was seated next to her, looked frightened.

Lilith's stories never included her father. He was the physicist who had powered our pods and systems. He had boarded Aqueous several times during its construction, but expired from an occupational hazard prior to station launch. His work was unparalleled, and the gratitude for his contribution remained strong, thereby securing Lilith and her mother residence on Aqueous, despite his passing.

Lilith's mother, an accomplished ballerina and pianist, solidified her value by becoming an invaluable conduit for the arts. In an environment focused singularly on science, her unique contribution infused invaluable leisure and entertainment into a mostly sterile environment. Like her late husband, her rigid demeanor and intense focus created an emotional void in the childhood of young Lilith. In the absence of humor and emotion, Lilith's childhood was fueled exclusively by schedules and results.

"Well, it sounds like you have dedicated yourself to the performing arts," Miss Newing commented. "Etan, what did you do?"

"I had a dream about heaven, and there were clouds and airplanes and spaceships and aliens, and then I woke up because Kade was jumping on me, so I pushed him off my berth and I smashed him on the ground, and my mom got mad at me and told me to be nicer to my brother, but he's so annoying," Etan said with a huff and an eye roll. "Then my dad took me, not Kade, to Athletics to blow steam, and we went swimming and played ninjas and arm wrestled and did play fighting. It was so cool. My dad is so awesome."

Etan was a naughty boy, uncontrollable, and he wriggled on the carpet in front of us as he boastfully recounted the abuse of his younger brother. The rest of us were able to sit still.

"Physical activity is necessary for healthy development. I'm glad you were active, Etan," said Miss Newing.

Sharing day was not about judgement. It acclimated us with presenting while honing our listening skills.

"What did you do, Mason?" Miss Newing asked, making her way around the circle.

"I went with my mom to Quality Control & Predictive Maintenance to help her repair stuff around the station, and I got to use all of the tools by myself. My mom says that one day I can be an engineer like her, and we can fix stuff together so that the station can get bigger and bigger and even more people can live down here."

Mason idolized his mom. She was one of the maintenance engineers assigned to repair and improve Aqueous. It was an ambitious task considering the unforgiving climate and finite resources. She repurposed machinery to marginalize mishaps, but she was equally talented at conceptualizing new machines to maximize the potential of underwater life.

"A necessary plan for our growing population," reflected Miss Newing. "Creighton, what did you do during Assuage?"

Creighton shifted on the carpet, keeping his eyes fixated on the floor. A small, shy boy, he preferred the company of his mother over the rowdy antics of trainees his age. Soft spoken and timid, he rarely engaged with his classmates, preferring autonomy and quiet activities over team games or sport. He did not respond to Miss Newing.

"Did you do anything interesting with your parents?" she asked again, rephrasing her question to encourage him to participate, but

Creighton remained silent. "We'd love to hear all about it. We're all friends here."

As Miss Newing continued to coax Creighton into engaging with the class, Captain and Mrs. Kress walked through the hatchway and approached the common area where we were seated.

"Captain and Mrs. Kress, thank you for joining us today. You're just in time for Creighton's sharing," she indicated as they looked at their son sitting silently on the floor.

"Oh, wonderful," commented Mrs. Kress as she approached him. She was a tidy, petite woman, but her usual pleasant nature had been replaced by uneasiness. She was nervous. "Creighton had a wonderful time with his father yesterday. They went to Command to learn about the rules of the station," she explained as she sat down beside Creighton and pulled him onto her lap.

Captain Kress remained standing across from them, wearing a disapproving look.

"Creighton, can you tell the children what happens if there is a falling object heading toward the station?" Mrs. Kress encouraged, but Creighton shook his head and turned to bury his face into her chest.

Mrs. Kress looked at Miss Newing, awkwardly. There were no other parents present, and it was unusual that the captain would leave his post to attend sharing day. Arms firmly crossed over his chest, he shifted on his feet before announcing, "Miss Newing, I understand your concerns now. The situation will be rectified privately, I can assure you. Now if you don't mind, I have to get back to matters of Aqueous security. Please excuse me." He pivoted efficiently and strode toward the door without further acknowledgement of his wife or son.

After watching her husband leave, Mrs. Kress looked back at our teacher apologetically as she stroked Creighton's blond head. Creighton had refused to share, but her husband's bad manners were far more embarrassing.

"I will go next!" shouted Naviah as she stood up and began theatrically circling the group.

It was a welcomed distraction for Mrs. Kress.

"Yesterday, my mom took me to the glamatorium to have my hair and nails done," she announced, thrusting her hands before each of our faces. "See how my nails look shiny? They were filed and buffed, and it's called a manicure. My hairdo is a French fishtail, side braid," she continued, twirling in a circle while stroking her long, ornate coif. "It complements my rounded face, and it's not tight, so it doesn't hurt . . ."

"It's not called the glamatorium," interrupted Lilith.

"Yes it is. Because I renamed it," explained Naviah.

"It's called Trimming Services," Lilith stated flatly.

"Well, my mom says I can call it whatever I want!" Naviah shouted, stomping her foot at exactly the same time. Her freckled cheeks had inflamed with anger in response to Lilith's comment. "She says it's even more important to shine brightly now that we live down here in the dark."

"Okay, class, that concludes our sharing time this morning," broadcasted Miss Newing in an attempt to diffuse the situation.

"But I didn't get to tell my story about the infirmary, where I got to learn all about the human body," whined Anit.

"Ew," groaned Creedan. "No one wants to hear about that."

"If you were not given a turn this week, you may come and tell me all about your Assuage adventures at breaktime. I'm always happy to listen," said Miss Newing. "Now, what do we say to our special guest?"

As we did for all visitors we chimed in unison, "Thank you for visiting us, Mrs. Kress."

She rose to her feet, disentangling Creighton from her limbs as she stood, and silently exited through the hatch. Miss Newing simultaneously reached forward and grabbed Creighton by his hand, preventing him from following his mother.

I had not been asked to share that day, but regardless, my enthusiasm had been thwarted by the telling experiences of my peers. Like Miss Newing, we had collected far more family intel than we wanted. Being rigid, unruly, and overindulged were three characteristics highlighted in our Assuage discussion, but they were not as unsettling as the backstage pass to the dynamics of family Kress. A shy little Creighton would undoubtedly be molded into the young man his father expected, and by whatever means he deemed necessary.

# CHAPTER TWELVE

The last few days had been a blur. The completion of projects were followed by the submission of individual theses, which were followed by our examinations. Professor Eseer and company had grilled us on the culmination of science we had digested during a decade of merstation immersion. We had become fact-spewing sea zombies over whom they exerted complete mind control. Eat, evaluate, sleep, repeat. That pretty much summed it up.

It was surreal to think that I had spent ten years of my youth in training, and that tomorrow, following the completion of the trials, childhood, as my peers and I knew it, would end. It was an inevitable, yet unfathomable, conclusion. We would be deemed adults and then, at graduation, assigned station responsibilities.

The day before grad would be a day of respite to reflect upon our journey. It was a surprising reward, considering that idle time beyond weekly Assuage was discouraged, but our evaluators needed the day to calibrate our academic and trial scores for appropriate assignment.

My peers, the first Y10s to complete the Aqueous underwater syllabus in its entirety, would be expected to excel at station life. The expectations were enormous and the pressure pronounced, but ironically, our day of respite would fall on my birthday, and although I had been excluded from event details, I expected that we would be partying, not pondering. Especially if my mother had anything to do with it.

"ATTENTION. ATTENTION. Empyreal Blaise has identified at your airlock," alerted the AI Assistant.

*Speak of the devil.*

I was surprised that she had time to visit, given the banger of a bash she would be busying herself with, but without further question I tapped the release allowing her to ascend. She was unusually disheveled.

"Mom, what's wrong?"

"I have some bad news, honey. Buckingham has died."

I let the gravity of her announcement overtake me, and I slid down the curved glass onto the floor as she took a seat at my desk. There was a moment of silence between us. He was a pet, and this would be worse if a resident had died, but I felt overwhelming sadness nonetheless.

"What happened?"

"He was old, Marisol. Duanra found him lifeless in his cage when she went to wake Naviah for dinner. Apparently, she needed a nap after the last exam today. It's been quite a tiring week for all of you."

"I didn't make it to dinner either. I was planning on an early breakfast instead. How's she doing?"

"As you can imagine, she is devastated. Duanra sent me a message asking me to inform you. They're taking him to be incinerated now, and then Naviah will spend the night with them in the commander's pod. Why don't you send her a message so that she knows you are thinking of her."

"Yes, of course. Poor Naviah."

I imagined Buckingham's incineration. Without the ability to bury our loved ones, it was the final stop on the subterranean tour. Whatever was left was left of him, afterward, would be recycled. Nothing went to waste. Even ash was useful on Aqueous.

Buckingham had been the last pet onboard. As our official animal ambassador, and the fleck's cottontail-in-training, he had been awarded the key to the station by the admiral himself. His bounding little presence had spread smiles across faces, like blossoms across meadows, and his passing would be more than the loss of a single pet. Former beloved fur babies, all of them, would be mourned with him today.

"I was hoping you'd be able to get a good night's sleep tonight."

"I wouldn't have slept well anyway. There's too much at stake tomorrow. The best I can do is rest. I will lie awake in my bunk, strategizing, while I enjoy the last moments in this pod. Who knows where I'll be living next."

"It doesn't matter," she answered flatly. "Most propulsion-pods are the same."

"Of course it matters! I'll be issued a pod near the department in which I'm assigned. How can you say that it doesn't matter?"

"You and your friends are well-trained, and each of you will have a suitable assignment. You'll meet new residents and you'll continue to see the ones that you care about. It doesn't matter how you do tomorrow. You have proven yourself already. Besides, we can sneak out in AP1 whenever we want. Try and get some sleep."

Although annoyed, I stood to hug her as she started to leave. There was something off about her. It was an emptiness. A distance. She had never before encouraged complacency or accepted anything less than my best. Buckingham's death couldn't possibly be this upsetting to her.

I stood a moment longer, after her descent, to ponder her unusual demeanor. Empyreal Blaise, typically, was nothing less than inspirational. A champion for making dreams come true, she was motivational to youth and had been instrumental in spearheading Osmosis, the merstation exchange program that invited trainees, like Sugar Tao, to complete their Y10 studies on Aqueous. She also coordinated biannual excursions to notable ocean relics in a mandate she had coined The Ocean Beyond. By engaging trainees in the planning of educational field trips, she strengthened relationships and averted our attention from the humdrum repetition of station life. She approached every trip with enthusiasm, eager to indulge our curiosity about what existed beyond the glass.

Ironically, the execution of these trips fueled my passion for diving. I found pod performance and maneuverability much more fascinating than the lifeless antiquities we observed. The concrete footings of an abandoned Golden Gate Bridge, or the rusty trusses of a stiff Ferris wheel, soused in a drowned Pacific Park, were static and inconsequential objects that I could research on my own. It was the pods we travelled in that were phenomenal.

Each trip involved numerous, long-range shuttle-pods. They were the same pods most residents had boarded at station launch, on their first descent to Mass Landing, and they were likely piloted by the same divers, undoubtedly cuviers, but despite my inquisitive small talk during our trips, they were never forthcoming. They were polite, but barely spoke, optimizing their efficiency by solely focusing on navigation.

Cuviers, by nature of assignment, were the faceless souls onboard. Their missions kept them removed from the educational epicenters trainees occupied, making them unfamiliar to us. We were encouraged not to distract them and to engage with our educators or chaperones instead.

My mother assumed a leadership role in the execution of every outing, and she was an ever-present chaperone in my shuttle-pod. On these outings she was, for all intents and purposes, Command, and the cuviers followed her instructions without confirmation of the admiral. She made it clear to them, by repeating it frequently, that under no circumstances were we to surface. Our excursions were to be singularly focused on submarine life, and the last hospitable habitat it afforded. The terrestrial ruins we observed under her watchful eye evidenced this, and any additional information we required about our terrene past could be obtained from Li-Fi once we were back onboard.

Duanra never joined us for The Ocean Beyond. Pod confinement had not been easy for her, nor would the passing of Buckingham. I logged into the system to send her and Naviah a note of sympathy. Then I forwarded the news to the rest of our class, before attempting to get some sleep.

## CHAPTER THIRTEEN

"Ladies and gentlemen, it is my great pleasure to applaud the Y10 class on the completion of their studies. They have shown great discipline and talent during their tenure on Aqueous, and as the first class to complete the entire subterranean syllabus, they are a testament to the strength of scientific learning, and an example of the great contribution future youth will offer our merstation upon the completion of their educational endeavors."

Professor Eseer's announcement was complemented by a life-wall depiction of athletes competing in various sports and accepting medals of victory on podiums of staggering height. I knew it to be past Olympic footage by the numerous flags waving above the participants and the colored rings symbolically uniting the continents. It was a nice sentiment, but success in the Aqueous trials secured the survival of a united species, not the ludicrous bragging rights of a patriotic nation.

Eseer continued to speak.

"Trainees, today you will face five trials. Designed to challenge mental and physical aptitude, your results will enable the Assignment Committee to assign you to the most appropriate Aqueous endeavor that will ultimately become your life's work. You have been given the skills to succeed today and every day hereafter, so without further ado, I bid each of you good luck."

Eseer applauded us as he stepped back from the podium to allow Dr. Pryor to speak.

"Parents, it is time for the Y10s to get started. Please keep your words of encouragement concise before exiting so that we may begin as scheduled."

We had gathered in the grand pavilion with our families for a private commencement breakfast at 6:00 a.m. Reggie had prepared smoked salmon on bug toast, with a side of berry soy yoghurt, and orange juice. There were double portions for the Y10s, but I had little appetite. I force-fed myself as much as I could, knowing that it would be a long day, but I eventually conceded and gave the rest of my plate to Murphy.

My parents were mingling with the parents of the other Y10s, reminiscing about how it felt like only yesterday that they had dropped us off at Sea Turtle's Nursery. Each of them dripped with pride, and I had a feeling that it would be difficult to get them to leave. Shooting my parents a look, my father became aware that he should cut his conversation short if he wanted to have time to wish me well. He strode toward me with outstretched arms, placing his hands on my shoulders.

"Honey, this is it. It's your big day. You've got this, sweetie. Don't overthink it. You've prepared well, and we are so very proud of you," he said. Then, pulling me in for a huge, public hug, he whispered in my ear, "Be sure to beat the boys."

"Roger that. I'll do my best."

My mother was next.

"Marisol, my darling, this will not define you. You'll be fine. Stay calm and be safe. An Aqueous assignment does not change the fact that you are an influential part of this community. Do you understand that?"

She was overly dramatic, and her hug was too tight and too long. *Odd.*

"Yes, of course," I lied.

At the end of the day, regardless of what they told us, not everyone would be a winner, and I did not intend to lose. I backed away from my parents, signaling that it was time for them to leave, and then I watched as all of the parents exited the hatchway, allowing it to be secured by our assessors. It was time to begin.

"Trainees, you are about to initiate the first of five trials, known as The Socrates Trial. I will be giving each of you a tablet to work from. Find a quiet place to sit alone and login. You will see a start button. When you are ready, hit the button and begin the timed exercise. Be aware that your heartrate, eye movement, expressions, and indecision will be recorded by the tablet. Choose the answers that most define who you are before the time expires. There are no right or wrong answers, there are no right or wrong responses, and you may begin when you are ready."

Dr. Pryor began to pass out tablets, and trainees began spreading out throughout the pavilion, claiming comfortable chairs to nest in while they completed the trial. I noticed that Julip looked particularly stressed and was having trouble deciding where to sit.

When I got my tablet I headed toward the rain wall, near the observation pond, hoping the running water would absorb any whispers or commotion that could distract my thoughts. Once seated on the ledge of the pond, I touched the screen and logged in. A blue start button appeared in the center of the yellow screen. I took a deep breath and tapped it.

*Here we go.*

The yellow screen melted away, slipping off the edge of the tablet like butter sliding across a pan, to reveal a black screen underneath. The phrase "Describe Yourself" appeared momentarily in the center before being replaced by four words: fun-loving, disciplined, athletic, friendly. Arguably all of those, I decided to tap "disciplined" as it aligned most with my preferred assignment.

Four more words appeared: brave, sensible, squeamish, timid. I chose "sensible."

Four more: determined, motivated, accountable, hard-working. I was all of those too, but due to my previous answers I tapped "hard-working."

The next four: stubborn, anxious, over-zealous, controlling.

*Ouch.*

They were less admirable characteristics, assumedly derived from my previous answers. I tapped "over-zealous."

The words swirled away and the phrase "Pick Your Preference" appeared and then vanished. A moment later I was presented with four squares: red, green, blue, yellow.

*Was that a joke?*

Blue.

The blue square expanded to display four more squares: a lobster in a pot of boiling water, a scuba diver surrounded by sharks, a blue flower, and a scientist swirling a test tube of blue liquid. I chose the sharks.

The sharks expanded to reveal a human-operated submersible observing a shark, a pot of shark fin soup, a fishery with a large shark hanging upside down, and a zoologist recording shark data at an aquarium. I tapped the submersible.

The submersible expanded to a children's submarine ride, a tourist snorkeling on vacation, long wavy strands of sea kelp, and a scuba diver welding underwater pipes. Welding.

It seemed easy, like I was leading my evaluators by the hand to the exact assignment I wanted.

The underwater welding expanded to a mother reading a story to her children by a fireplace, a chef standing next to a pizza oven, a repairman cleaning a furnace, and an explosion in a populated underwater habitat. I surmised that I had to demonstrate that I knew the risks surrounding a cuvier assignment, so I tapped on the explosion in a populated underwater habitat, knowing everyone inside was doomed.

The images on the screen swirled and the phrase "Make A Choice" momentarily appeared, then vanished. The black screen gave way to a central image of a young family trapped behind a hatchway with water rising around them. The image then split into two smaller images, both denoting the trapped family behind hatchway panels. In the left image the panel was green, signifying that the hatch would open, in the right image the panel was red, signifying that the hatch would remain shut. Opening a hatch during any sort of flood could lead to critical station failure, so I tapped the image on the right, theoretically sacrificing the young family.

A new central image depicting a catastrophic station fire filled the screen, before splitting into two smaller images. The left showed the fire threatening Aqueous food crops, while the right showed a teacher and nursery-age students trapped by the blaze. Saving the students meant risking the food source of all residents; thereby killing everyone. I surveyed the little faces of the young students. They looked terrified, and death by fire would be horrific, but I clicked left and saved the crops.

An image of a large crowd gathered before an escape pod appeared. The word "Evacuation" was written at the top. It split left to an image of the entire group loaded into a pod, and right to an image of half the group being abandoned as a properly loaded pod departed from the station. Overloading a pod would result in pod failure and death for all, so I clicked right to abandon half of the group.

The screen filled with an image of an ill mother and child lying on separate gurneys in an infirmary, and a doctor holding a single syringe. The image split left, isolating the mother, and right, isolating the child. Saving the mother meant saving a contributing resident, while saving the child left a trainee who burdened the community until she was assigned. Saving the mother would ultimately render her disabled by grief, but there would be enduring psychological ramifications of being orphaned also. The mother was physically larger than the girl, so perhaps she'd survive without the medication . . .

The scenario was less obvious for me, and the clock was ticking, so I clicked right on the girl, allowing the images to swirl once again to reveal the instruction, "Place your hand flat on the screen." I placed my cold, shaky hand against the tablet, and then the phrase "Biometric Analysis Complete" appeared briefly before the screen went black. I was finished.

I glanced around at my peers. Many had shocked expressions or could be seen rubbing their foreheads in discomfort. Julip's eyes darted back and forth as her hand hovered above her screen. She would be unable to make decisive selections before the time expired, and unlike our tutoring sessions, I would not be able to assist her.

Naviah gasped and clasped her hands over her mouth before standing up and flinging her tablet into an observation pond. Water from the pond splashed onto Purity, who shot upward in disgust, but despite her shock, managed to cling to her tablet, preventing it from shattering on the ground. Naviah would be reprimanded for that, but clearly something on the screen had struck a nerve.

Lilith sat, in perfect posture, with raised brow and slight smile, taking pleasure in the exercise. She was unfazed by the obnoxious laughter coming from Felix, and for once, unaware of Creighton, who had remained expressionless.

Creighton placed his strong hand on the screen, completing the first portion of his trial, and then looked directly at me, giving me a thumbs up as Dr. Pryor approached from a nearby table.

"Congratulations, Marisol. You've completed your first trial. You may proceed to the arboretum for the next one."

She took the tablet from me before returning to the table where her colleagues were pouring over the data from the Y10 upload. I had completed the task in the allotted time, but I was unsure about my last choice.

*Was I that child? Was that the decision my mother had to make? She chose without hesitation to create an orphan, thereby giving me the best chance for survival while drastically reducing her own.*

Questions unanswered, I rose from the ledge where I was seated and exited through the hatch.

## CHAPTER FOURTEEN

Leaving the grand pavilion, I proceeded through shades of blue toward the next trial. It was the most basic description of human submergence—blue, like the way I was feeling. From icicle hues near the station's exterior floodlights, to shades so close to midnight that they rivalled the darkest black, the ocean's watery embrace cocooned us in a kaleidoscope of blue that permeated the station and saturated our existence. Beautiful, beguiling, melancholy, and deadly, the blue arms of the ocean cradled us, danced for us, and threatened us. She was an intoxicating nymph, captivating and seductive, yet dangerous and unrelenting at the same time. As refugees, her blue shelter had welcomed us and then restrained us, knowing that we were powerless to escape, and it would be easy to forget the beauty of blue, were it not for the arboretum.

The vast, multi-levelled garden had hundreds of resident botanists assigned to its care. They watered, misted, pruned, plucked, pollinated, and planned crops from seed stock stowed safely away. As caretakers of Mother Nature, their gentle attention to invaluable crops helped to recycle wastewater, generate oxygen, purify air, feed hunger, and put clothes on backs. Their clever crop rotation eliminated food fatigue—a term used by residents who had been forced to digest an abnormally large harvest of one specific perishable. For example, growing sweet potato hadn't been considered since a bumper crop three Thanksgivings ago.

Mundane, yet important work, an arboretum assignment was not what I wanted; however, I did enjoy visiting periodically to imagine an earthly world. A world where healthy landscapes grew under a clean, clear sky, suspending a friendly, sunny star; a place where farmers felt the cool breeze on the glistening sweat of their skin as the hum of their heavy equipment drifted across an open field. The arboretum was a wondrous reprieve from a world full of blue.

A cornucopia of color, it was as if the greenhouse had been sucked downward to the seabed. Alien amongst its aquatic counterparts, the prismatic botanicals of the arboretum provided terrestrial colors predating earthly flood and fire. Saved by the scientists who preordained our salvation, the culinary botanicals living here had become the lifeblood that crept, crawled, and wondrously wound up as sustenance for our sea-dwelling population.

Connected by hatchways on the main and sub levels, I entered the department and found myself alone. A typically bustling place, the botanists had temporarily vacated for our use, so I meandered amongst the towering grow-podiums, looking for my evaluators. I was near the asparagus, in one of four climate controlled enclosures.

Plantings in the arboretum were categorized as hardy, half-hardy, tender, and extremely tender with each categorization cultivated on its own level. Since heat rises, plantings requiring higher temperatures were housed on higher levels than those benefitting from cooler climates.

Beneath each plant hung its exposed root system. Uprooted, like us, and hanging by a thread, our aeroponic farming techniques required no soil and little water. Produce yield was increased forty to seventy percent through a misting technique that delivered needed nutrients directly to the exposed roots. Creating various formulas derived from kitchen waste, hatchery water, and biosolids, Aqueous botanists ensured that each crop received the ideal daily dose of recommended supplements, thereby eliminating the need for additional synthetic fertilizers.

On land, potatoes had been grown below the soil and dug up at harvest, but on Aqueous they were grown suspended in the air and plucked off the root at maturity, but aeroponics were not ideal for all crops. Fruit trees and vegetables requiring a lot of space performed better in hydroponics—water and rock—growing first upward and then extending outward over strong cording. They created an organic rainbow of apples, cherries, oranges, pumpkins, squash, lemons, limes, cucumbers, and blueberries.

Continuing onward, I stumbled upon the tomatoes.

The shiny, red orbs stirred my imagination. They were a Christmas lattice of green and red against snowy light that dappled through them to the floor beneath; they were red like the war we had waged with the sun; and red like the blood pumping life through our veins. There were hundreds of thousands of tomatoes harvested in a single year, but they were more than just food, they were red balls of art and inspiration arching overhead to create a whimsical trellis of romance. They were more than food to empty stomachs. They were a connection to an imagined surface.

"Marisol," whispered a voice behind me.

I jumped. Startled from my daydreams by the whisper of my name, I spun around too quickly and whacked my hand across the speaker's face.

"Ouch," whispered Creighton.

"I'm sorry," I whispered back, unsure if we were even allowed to speak to each other.

We appeared to be the first two to arrive at the arboretum, and being alone under the tomatoes could have been magical had I not struck him.

"How'd you do with Socrates, Marisol? It looked like you were doing great."

"You were watching me?"

"Of course. Why?"

"Because the tablets monitored eye movement. Looking away confirmed indecision, anxiety, and possible surreptitiousness which could lead the evaluators to conclude that you are unfit for leadership."

"Surreptitiousness?" he asked, throwing back his head to laugh.

"Yes, surreptitiousness."

His laughter was replaced by an intense look, and then he moved closer to me, so close that I could feel his breath on my forehead. A slow smile formed on his lips.

"What are you smiling about?"

"You've always had a thing for using really big words."

*Were big words attractive?*

I couldn't tell if he liked or disliked big words, but he reached up and swept the hair from my face while scrutinizing my features as though he'd never seen me before. I averted my eyes. I had never been that close to a boy, and the next words he spoke transcended sound. He was so close that they carried warmth and scent.

"I hate to tell you this, but despite your hyper-developed lexicon, you did not understand the instructions."

"Of course I understood the instructions," I answered, defensively.

*Were we still speaking about the trial?*

"The evaluators told us that there were no wrong answers or wrong responses, Marisol, so I completed my trial to the best of my ability, honestly, and being true to myself, and that required that I periodically look at you because that's what I do. I watch you. I do it all the time." Then, bending closer to my ear he whispered, "Because I want to be the one assigned to look out for Marisol Blaise, forever."

I was confused, so I tried to step back to read his expression, but as I did he lifted his hand to my chin, tilting it upward to his lips, and kissed me. It was a small kiss, but a kiss nonetheless. Creighton Kress had kissed me and my world flipped upside down.

It was an unexpected action, and I could no longer feel the ground. I was Marisol Blaise, with Creighton Kress, under the tomatoes and snowy white LEDs between the trials, but I was suspended in time and space. I was in neutral. I was omniscient, exalted, and floating in a garden as glorious as Eden while the world paused and waited.

*Was this science or enlightenment? Did this happen to everyone, every kiss, and did I like it?*

I could feel every cell in every organism, everywhere.

As I levitated, questioning life as I had known it one millisecond before the kiss, Creighton tried to kiss me again, but bigger, and our teeth clanked together. The jarring knock of our ivories collapsed my clairvoyance, bringing me back to my body where my feet were next to grow-podiums, planted firmly on the ground. His arms were wrapped around me, and I could feel his body pressed against mine which summoned an instinctual need for escape. I pulled away, but then we were holding hands. I had no idea how our hands had found each other, but there we were, attached, under the enchanting tomatoes.

Footsteps and familiar voices approached.

"We have to let go now," I said unromantically, yanking my hands from his before we were spotted by the others. I wasn't ready for this.

"It's our hearts, not our hands, holding us together," he replied, dreamily.

*Was he medicated?*

I was still processing how I felt as Naviah emerged from an archway of eggplants. Notes of curiosity, triumph, and legitimacy were sounding off in my head, along with uncertainty and possible regret.

"I've found them!" she shouted over her shoulder. "They're under the tomatoes!" she yelled again, before looking back at us and asking, "What, in the name of Demeter, is going on over here? Is something wrong? Why do you two seem sleepy when the rest of us are stressed? We have been looking all over the place for you. Do you know how rude it is to make us wait? Today, of all days. We were supposed to meet near the brussels sprouts in hardy, and here you are under the tomatoes in tender. Come on people, let's get a move on. You're on the wrong level!"

We followed her, trepidatiously. Our tender moment had been squashed like a blueberry underfoot, but it was for the best. I needed to refocus on the trials.

"Did your psych trial go okay?" I inquired. "You seem agitated."

"That stupid psych tablet asked me to choose between relaxing in a beautiful angora sweater or snuggling with a rabbit that looked remarkably like Buckingham. I mean, who comes up with this stuff, the Aqueous Agents for Perverse Enterprise?"

"Oh Naviah, how awful. I'm so sorry," I said.

"Sounds like the tablets presented each of us with individualized choices," commented Creighton. "I wonder if that will continue."

*We will soon find out.*

Naviah led us down to the group, who were now lingering between the podiums of kohlrabi and cabbage. Professor Eseer and Florin Argro, a senior botanical engineer, were off to the side, briefing a small group of junior botanists, who I assumed were their aides for trial two. They turned their heads to us as we approached, simultaneously raising their eyebrows in a look of disapproval and question. Creighton handled it.

"Apologies for our tardiness, Professor Eseer, Miss Argro. We were unclear as to the meeting point and the arboretum is massive."

I felt Lilith's stare before I looked over and saw it. A thin grin was perched on her perfect complexion. Perhaps I was paranoid, but she was acting as though she was aware that there had been more to our alone moment than getting lost in the greenhouse. I hoped it was just gratification. She would be amused that I made an error and held up the group.

The junior engineers departed as Professor Eseer replied to Creighton.

"Thank you for your explanation, Mr. Kress. Dr. Pryor indicated that she may have forgotten to tell you and Marisol which grow-podium to rendezvous at, and it appears that is the case."

The satisfied smirk on Lilith's face faded.

"Going forward, I would like to emphasize the importance of time management. We are on a tight schedule today, and completion of the trials is mandatory. You will become mentally and physically fatigued, so let's try not to prolong the misery, alright? Miss Argro, can you please explain the next exercise to the Y10s?"

"Of course, Professor. Now that we are reassembled, let's weave together the premise for trial two—The Leizu Trial. Botany plays a critical role in Aqueous life. Unquestionably, it feeds us, but as you have learned, its advantages go far beyond that. I want you to remember that as you complete this trial. Remember your studies and you will do well. All of you possess the knowledge to be successful."

She began passing out individual tablets.

"This is a timed exercise. You have one hour, and at no point are you permitted to pick, pluck, or pillage any crops in the enclosures. The usual rules apply—we treat these plants with the utmost respect. You may begin."

Shifting my attention to the task at hand, I pushed aside the respective emotional highs and lows of my interactions with Creighton and Naviah. Without question, this trial would be more challenging than the previous psych assessment, so without wasting time I scanned my tablet for activity instructions. To my dismay, there weren't any. There was a poem instead.

> Steal a home to shelter yourself,
> The carpenter pays with its life.
> Boiled and seasoned a protein feast,
> Cold brings disease and strife.

Scour a sucrose forest,
For the fuel of your success.
Combine with friendly fungus,
And you shall pass the test.

Beneath the bolls of growing snow,
Find the tool you need.
To knit yourself together,
A community in SID.

Water for your wishes,
Is best if pure and true.
Journey to its cleanest source,
And you can make a stew.

Make known your full intentions,
To the atelier of the house.
Present the perfect process,
And you can make a blouse.

I had no desire to make a blouse, that was Naviah's dream, but surely this involved much more than sewing. The poem was a riddle, and to land my dream assignment I needed to dismantle it, verse by verse.

Steal a home to shelter yourself,
The carpenter pays with its life.
Boiled and seasoned a protein feast,
Cold brings disease and strife.

It made no sense. Aqueous "carpenters" were assigned in Quality Control & Predictive Maintenance, not the arboretum, and they were valuable assets to the station. They were some of our most talented engineers. We certainly wouldn't harm them. I decided to move on and return to that part of the poem later.

> Scour a sucrose forest,
> For the fuel of your success.
> Combine with friendly fungus,
> And you shall pass the test.

Sucrose, a form of sugar, was derived from sugarcane. It was a crop that never rotated because like many things on Aqueous, spatial limitations meant that we couldn't produce enough of it. Sugar was valuable, and though I could not recall longing for sweets until arriving at the station, I knew that if we took away the sugar we'd have one sour society. Maybe that's why Mr. and Mrs. Tao had named their daughter after it.

Sugar was everything, but where was the cane it was grown on? Every time I had been in the arboretum I was led directly to the plants of interest. I had never paid particular attention to the location of individual species or navigated the department on my own. What a mistake. I should have used my spare time to wander the enclosures, familiarizing myself with podium layout. My unfamiliarity would cost me time.

I looked around. The majority of the trainees were deconstructing the poem, but Amley was already gone. She wanted an arboretum assignment and would be well-versed in the location of each and every plant. I resolved to monitor her actions as I progressed through the trial. She could lead the way in the event I struggled.

Since heat rises, arboretum enclosures were sectioned by level, with cooler climates toward the bottom and warmer climates toward the top. I needed to return to the central staircase within the department and climb. Sugarcane was native to the temperate and tropical climates simulated on the highest level of the arboretum. Conceivably, Amley was already there, and I would arrive in time to discreetly follow her to the next enclosure.

Several Y10s started running at the same time, but in different directions, and I hoped I wasn't the only trainee who didn't understand the first verse. It was possible that we were attacking the stanzas in varied order, or that we had different poems altogether. Naviah was motionless, but Murphy was subtly trying to signal her to follow him. I was thankful for his assistance. I could not wait for her. I did not want to be caught working with someone else. I needed to act on my own interpretation, without distraction from others.

Making my way to the highest enclosure I passed through the hatchway to search for sugarcane. The humidity level was notably different when I entered, and a warm mist osculated on my skin. The tropical environment contained many species of plant life, including citrus fruit, mangoes, pineapple, a variety of nuts, tamarind, and bananas to name a few, but sugarcane, a tall perennial grass species, would be the easiest to spot. Stretching upwards to six meters in height, its cane-like stalks erupted into a tangle of fronds, creating a thatched canopy over those who walked beside it.

Locating the sugarcane grow-podiums, I began to search the rows of jointed spires until I found several identical buckets aligned beside a junior botanical aide named Ollan.

"Do I take one of these?"

The bucket contained a single piece of unprocessed sugarcane.

"Just one."

"And what do I do with it?"

"That's up to you."

His grin indicated that he was not permitted to assist me, but merely there to ensure that the trial progressed smoothly. Without supervision it was plausible that Felix or Creedan would encourage Etan to take every bucket, undermining the rest of us so that we'd timeout before solving the riddle.

I grabbed a bucket and quickly counted the rest. Eighteen of twenty-one were left. I was certain that Amley had arrived and departed before me, but I hadn't see her on the staircase. I pondered where she would go next, and who had the other bucket as I surveyed the poem again.

> Scour a sucrose forest,
> For the fuel of your success.
> Combine with friendly fungus,
> And you shall pass the test.

Sugarcane juice fermented with yeast yielded fuel known as ethanol. I looked in the bucket. There was no yeast, but I knew that yeast was classified as fungus and could be made from flour and water. Flour, for the purpose of ethanol, was made of wheat, and wheat was grown in hardy, located on the lowest level.

I was getting somewhere. Perhaps Amley had made a different summation because we should have passed on the stairs, but regardless, I headed back toward the arboretum staircase to make an abrupt descent.

*Who had the other bucket?*

A chorus of confusion echoed off the steps as I passed back through the hatch and into the stairwell. The Y10s were scavenging the department on the hunt for poetic comprehension. Lilith ran past me with cherry blossoms in her hair.

"Out of my way. All of you," she asserted, trotting effortlessly past others heading upward along the stairs.

I continued downward, as fast as my feet would allow.

"Slow down there, Aerosol," said Etan.

It was another failed attempt at humor as he walked slowly upward, following the others in a blatant display of disinterest intended to mask his botanical ignorance. His ridicule would not deflate my efforts. It became the catalyst by which I was able to move faster.

Passing through the hatch at the bottom of the stairwell, I scanned the area for podiums of wheat. I spotted them off to the right, beside an aide who was stationed near the crop. There were nineteen jars of yeast starter on a small table next to him, so I took one, noting that two trainees had beaten me to it.

I had not seen Creighton since we started. He and Amley were likely the first to decode "friendly fungus." I needed to work faster if I was going to win this, so I went back to my tablet to work the riddle once again.

> Beneath the bolls of growing snow,
> Find the tool you need.
> To knit yourself together,
> A community in SID.

There were four crops harvested for textile production on Aqueous: hemp, jute, flax, and cotton. The various outfits manufactured for SIDs were made from these crops, but only one of them was in rotation—cotton.

Back up the stairs I sprinted while dodging fellow Y10s as they descended toward me. The majority of them had found the bucket with the sugarcane and were running toward the wheat. I reentered at the highest hatch to search for the fluffy podiums of cotton, but after circling the entire enclosure I did not find it. I was in the correct climate, and cotton had distinct round and white tufts. It should have been easy to spot, but I could not see the crop. I began to scan for Argro's aide. Nothing. I could see no one. It was perplexing.

*Think.*

Cotton bolls were only present at maturity. Prior to that the plants displayed yellow and pink blooms, so I circled the enclosure again, and sure enough, I was able to spot a developing cotton crop in bloom.

Miss Argro's aide was seated nearby, and as I approached I realized that it was Kade, Etan's little brother.

"Hooray, a friendly face," I lied. "What have you got for me, Kade?"

"Shhhhhh," he chided. "You're way too loud, and if I mess this up I'll be in even more trouble."

"Why are you here? You're only a Y8. You haven't been assigned yet."

"I'm in detention because my music was deemed inappropriate and clamorous. As if I know what clamorous means, but apparently it's no good. So much for freedom of expression."

"Bummer," I said, but Kade serving detention didn't surprise me. "I'm in a bit of a rush. Do you mind telling me what I'm supposed to do?"

"All I've been told is that you can take one of those and then move on, quietly. Do not tell anyone where I am. I want to stump everybody, especially Etan," he said, confirming the longevity of their rivalry.

"Oh yeah, for sure. I won't be telling anyone, don't worry. I'm in it to win it today."

I grabbed one of the items below the podium while trying not to annoy him further. It was a spindle. A simple tool used to twist plant fibers into usable thread, it did relate to cotton, but I was not given any bolls.

"Is this it?"

"Yes, that's it. Now get lost before you get me into more trouble."

I had nothing to spin.

"Is there a mature cotton crop hiding nearby?"

"How would I know?" he snarked. "Now beat it."

"Fine, I'm going."

The Biggott boys had sharp edges.

I put the spindle into my bucket with the sugarcane and yeast, but I was stumped, so I returned to the first stanza.

Steal a home to shelter yourself,

The carpenter pays with its life.
Boiled and seasoned a protein feast,
Cold brings disease and strife.

I had missed it before, but now I understood. In addition to hemp, jute, flax, and cotton, Aqueous botanists harvested silk from silkworms. Our history lessons had taught us that silkworms had been consumed by other cultures due to their high protein content, and I knew that they were susceptible to disease if exposed to cold temperatures. I had fixated on plant material and forgotten about the worms, but it was so obvious now. The trial was named Leizu, after the empress who invented the silk loom. Silkworms spun themselves into cocoons of silk threads before emerging as moths, and the cocoons were harvested and boiled to unravel individual threads before they were spun together into stronger, usable thread. Unfortunately, the worms perished in the process.

I needed to visit the silkworm receptacle, near the mulberry podium, on the level below. As I turned to leave, I heard Naviah's voice on the other side of the cotton plants.

"Murphy, no one else will know this, but the cotton crop isn't mature. The snowy white bolls won't be visible yet, so this will confuse a lot of trainees. We can make up some time and get ahead!"

I didn't want to disrupt her, so I slipped away unnoticed, but I was relieved to learn that she was doing well. I should not have been surprised. If there was one trial she would excel at, it would be the one pertaining to textiles.

Naviah had a point about getting ahead. It was evident that many trainees were simply following the leader. If I returned to the staircase it was probable that others would follow me to the silkworms, and I didn't want that. I needed a different route. Perhaps the supply lift was viable. The others would likely not think of it, as it was built to haul heavy comestibles, and with every resident of Aqueous fully mobile there was an unspoken expectation to take the stairs.

I rounded green bunches of coconuts and proceeded toward the adjacent department of Comestible Silos & Refrigeration. Located within the arboretum, and fitted with temperature-controlled storage, the facility preserved harvested items until they were needed by neighboring departments, like the kitchen, which was located above and connected by the supply lift. If I could access the lift, I could move undetected to complete the trial.

I pressed the button and waited for the aluminum doors to slide open, and when they did I was saluted by a surprising silhouette—Felix.

"I wondered when you'd get here," he said with a smirk. "The rest of them are far too daft to figure this out. What have you got in your bucket?"

"Mind your own business," I replied, swinging my bucket behind my back as I entered the lift. "We're not supposed to work together."

"Oh beans. This challenge is as much about alliances as it is about individual sleuthing. I specifically listened for Florin to discourage teamwork, but she did not. Trust me, Marisol, they are monitoring who is working together and who isn't. It's a big indicator of how we should be assigned."

Maybe he was right. Some assignments were more suited toward group work.

"Well, I can't work with you or anyone else. My preferred assignment requires independent problem solving."

"And that's what I like about you. You've always been a feisty one. A fighter. A survivor," he added as the doors opened. "Fine, you get out and I will ride around in this thing a little longer. It's fun in here, and besides, if anyone deserves to have their dreams come true it's you, Marisol."

He vanished behind the closing doors, leaving me to contemplate his comments.

*Did Felix Nyrmac just act like a complete gentleman? How bizarre.*

The silkworm receptacle was located near the mulberry podium, adjacent to the offices of the botanists. I walked to the entrance of it, opened the door, and found Marglo, an aide, perched on a stool inside. Next to her, on a table, were twenty-one bowls. I was ahead of Amley. I was first! For someone who detested botany, I was blossoming.

I surveyed the bowls and found that each of them contained an empty silk cocoon. Sugar had told us that on Sihai Longwang they consumed boiled silkworm larvae. Hopefully the former inhabitant of this cocoon had emerged as a moth, and not as broth, but who knew.

I selected a bowl and put it in my bucket.

"Congratulations, Marisol! You're the first to decipher this part of the riddle," exclaimed Marglo. She was an enthusiastic botanist with a cheerful disposition. "Perhaps an assignment in our department is in your future."

*Not happening.*

"Oh, well, Marglo, I hadn't considered that, but just look at those worms. Aren't they fun."

I managed my way out of the receptacle without being rude, but internally I refused to dedicate my life to worms.

It was time to review the final stanzas of the poem.

Water for your wishes,
Is best if pure and true.
Journey to its cleanest source,
And you can make a stew.


Make known your full intentions,
To the atelier of the house.
Present the perfect process,
And you can make a blouse.

The ultimate goal was to demonstrate the process by which materials from the arboretum could be used to make a blouse. A silk blouse. I was not making a stew. The transformation of a silk cocoon into silk thread required 'stewing' the cocoon in clean, boiling water, and the cleanest water on Aqueous was found in our kitchen.

After filling the bowl with the clean water, I would need to locate Alfrid Shru, Atelier Director, and explain that by fermenting the sugarcane and yeast to produce ethanol, I could ignite the ethanol, boil the water, and stew the cocoon in the water to release individual silk threads. Then I could use the spindle to wind the threads together, making stronger, usable threads for blouse construction.

I could use the supply lift to pass directly into the kitchen and save an enormous amount of time, so I returned to it, pressed the button, and bumped directly into Felix as the doors opened.

"Boom. We meet again, Marisol Blaise. Just as you are about to win this one. See you in the kitchen?"

I watched him walk toward the silkworm receptacle. Aqueous was covered in surveillance cameras, and our evaluators would be watching our every move. They would already know that he had let me win.

"I'll wait for you."

He stopped and turned toward me.

"What?"

"I will wait for you, and we can finish together."

"Are you serious?"

"Yes, Felix, but only if you hurry up. I haven't got all day."

He smiled and quickened his step.

"Awesome! I'll be right back."

He was in and out of the receptacle in a flash, shouting, "Yeah, whatever, cool," to Marglo on his way out.

"Not interested in an arboretum assignment either?"

"Not a chance."

We ascended in the lift together, into the kitchen, and as the doors opened we could see Reggie feigning wiping down the countertops nearby. His face lit up as we stepped out, evidencing the satisfaction he took from being involved in the trials.

"Do either of you need any water?"

"You're not supposed to help us, Reg."

"That isn't helping you, young lady. You may be tired or thirsty from doing whatever it is you're doing today, so I'm offering you some of the finest, cleanest water we have on this station. Alright? And you too, Felix. You look like you need some extra clean water. Get over here."

Reggie filled our bowls with enough water to submerge the cocoons, and then he pointed toward the hatchway.

"Did you know that Mr. Shru is sitting in my office reviewing menus for the anniversary? He wants to make sure that the décor matches the food. Can you imagine? Salmon on the plate, and salmon on the drapes! Ha, ha, ha! Go and check it out for yourselves, and congratulations you two. You did a good job today."

*He was so easy to love.*

Felix and I walked to the back of the kitchen where Reggie's office was located. Alfrid was seated at Reggie's desk, with his back to us, but upon hearing our steps he turned to peer at us through the wire-framed glasses atop his long, pointy nose. He was a small, thin man with impeccable manners. His SIDs were custom-made, exclusively for him. He wore a unique uniform accrediting his creative license and flare for all things fantastic. He stood as we approached and extended a manicured hand, first to me and then to Felix, and I felt as though I should kiss his ring, but settled on a handshake.

"Welcome to you both. I offer congratulations on a fine achievement. Being the first to complete the exercise, and in record time, is truly outstanding."

"Thank you, Mr. Shru. Would you like us to explain the processes we formulated to satisfy the clues in the poem?"

"No, no, that's quite alright, Miss Blaise. I don't need that. I can see that you've got it. I've been watching your progress on Reggie's monitor. Quite an interesting finish, don't you think? You did not work together, and yet you've taken pleasure in standing shoulder-to-shoulder now, as partners. Why is that?"

"We didn't think it was against the rules to finish together," I admitted, worrying that we had made a mistake. My heartrate increased as I struggled to find a satisfactory excuse.

"Well, I prefer to be with friends," said Felix. "You know, my crusaders of adventure, daydreams, and rainbows evermore."

I looked at him, dumbfounded.

"Oh yes, Mr. Nyrmac, what a delightful way to live. It's preferable indeed to be with those you care for. So very well said, and on that note, I will ask you both to proceed across the dining hall and wait for Professor Eseer in the bethel. Once all are amassed, he will lead your group to the next trial. Bravo to you both!"

## CHAPTER FIFTEEN

Contemplation is a reflective state of deliberation. It's an opportunity to examine oneself, and that is what most of the Y10s did as they waited for the remaining trainees to arrive in the bethel.

After Felix and I completed the trial, the rest of the trainees had been given clues, in ten-minute intervals, to aid their progress, but even with the assistance, several trainees, like Julip and Mason, failed to solve the riddle in the allotted time. Their disappointment was visibly weighing down their shoulders. They would need to excel in the last three trials to avoid undesirable assignments.

Satisfied with my efforts thus far, my contemplation was significantly different. I was replaying Felix's words in my head: "I prefer to be with friends. You know, my crusaders of adventure, daydreams, and rainbows evermore." He had recited the family acronym of my past—CADRE.

As children, in the absence of his father, Felix and I had spent considerable time playing together. It was plausible that I had recited the acronym many times, ages ago, when we were much younger. When girls and boys still played together, uninhibited, before the influence of hormones, crushes, and the universal teenage syndrome known as awkwardness took hold of us. We had been close friends, Felix and I. Childhood confidants united by the loss of our parents.

"Ah, you're all here," said Professor Eseer as he arrived, but his ardor faded as his eyes evaluated our despondency. We were droplets of saline in a sea of sadness.

"It's time to move on," he instructed. "There's no point in dwelling on it further. What's passed is in the past. Follow me."

Our uneasy cohort shuffled behind him, passing numerous residents along the way.

"Come on, you guys! You got this!" shouted Hurley Jett.

Duffel Cowl gave a whistle and hollered, "Enjoy the experience. You're doing great!"

Neither of them had had to participate in trials. They had stepped aboard with an education and an understanding of their significance, but our futures were undetermined and our anxiety was pronounced.

"I see a brand-new batch of seaworthy scientists," exclaimed Catalina Phool. "What a smart looking group."

Mason, who was walking next to me, muttered, "I guess she didn't see me then."

Our procession marched forward on a wave of ignorant encouragement. There were few who could relate to this day, and how it felt like a funeral. It was not a friendly competition, so I quashed the memories of my childhood in consideration of the challenges ahead. The degree of difficulty would increase. The pressure would rise.

• • •

Pressure was abundant on Aqueous. The weight of the water was in perpetual conflict with our existence. Swaddling us from the dangers above, it was the savior and the captor that separated us from the elemental necessities of land life. We lived in an infinite war, battling to soothe an inhospitable host, and the Y10s were the next fleet to answer the call of duty, assuming that we could complete the third trial.

We were positioned at tables throughout the labs, waiting to begin. The rooms were spotless. Devoid of all materials related to scientific study, they appeared larger and cold. All ingenuity had been removed and replaced with space.

"Your task is simple. Identify a threatening characteristic of station life, and create a solution," directed Professor Eseer. "You have one hour. Please begin."

"One hour?" Crimson questioned. "We can't accomplish anything in an hour!"

Leop was unnerved and scanning the room wildly.

"This place is empty. What are we supposed to use?"

He had failed, as expected, to finish his thesis before the deadline; thus, running out of time to prepare for anything else.

"Anything at all," grinned the professor as he tapped the tablet in front of him.

"ATTENTION. ATTENTION," alerted the AI Assistant. "The Elucidation Trial has commenced. Please make all available resources available for the next sixty minutes. Repeat. All station resources and personnel are to be available to Y10 trainees for the next hour."

"You will be informed when your precious hour is up," said Eseer. Then he stretched out his arms, positioned his hands behind his head, rocked back in his chair, and closed his eyes.

*Everybody panic!*

I needed an idea and subsequent plan immediately. The two biggest concerns at the bottom of the ocean were pressure and oxygen. Pressurization to avoid being crushed, and breathable air because we didn't have gills.

*Boring. Think.*

Empty chairs rolled backward across the room as trainees dashed out the hatch to scavenge for needed materials while I remained motionless.

"Push me again, Kyro, and you'll be sorry!" yelled Naviah as she dashed to get through.

"What? You slammed into me!"

Kyro would never push anyone. In fact, he avoided crowded spaces, but pandemonium had erupted as the Y10s raced from the room.

I couldn't think of a threatening characteristic of station life that I wanted to solve, but Naviah would solve some sort of imagined catwalk crisis, Felton would tackle tech, and Lilith, being super annoying like always, would probably carve a working violin with matching bow from a one of the trees in the grand pavilion and then play it flawlessly for the remaining forty-five minutes.

*Ugh. What was I going to do?*

I looked at my desk, and it looked back at me with a blank expression.

Aqueous needed recycling.

*Boring.*

Residents needed food.

*Boring.*

We needed light, powered by electricity, and our electrical needs were met partially by the energy capture of the turbines and ocean currents.

*Boring.*

We needed energy to fuel our . . .

*Hello!*

I had found my idea. If my focus was to become a cuvier I should demonstrate how hydrogen could be captured and used as a sustainable pod fuel source.

Hydrogen technology, a highly combustible and clean alternative to petroleum, had been conceptualized decades prior to the collapse of terrestrial life, but the cost to develop it greatly exceeded existing oil refinement infrastructure, so a ban on fossil fuels was never issued. Our carbon footprint stamped out any chance of reversing the effects of earthly environmental damage long before we utilized known alternatives. Our predecessors continued to burn pollutants, knowing that naturally emitted hydrogen bubbled up from the vents at the bottom of the sea.

There were two types of hydrothermal vents in the nodule fields throughout Monterey Canyon: white smokers and black smokers. White smokers ran cooler, generating temperatures of only three hundred degrees Celsius while the black smokers were hotter, generating temperatures above four hundred degrees Celsius. The intense heat of black smokers caused the thermochemical water splitting of hydrogen and oxygen, and thanks to the ingenuity of Aqueous engineers, these elements were captured and used within the station.

As an alternative to electrically charged fuel cells, the hydrogen from black smokers had been deemed an ideal, zero-emissions fuel that we used to produce hydrogen fuel cells, and these, in turn, were used to power our pods. That's what I needed to demonstrate, but venturing outside the station to bottle up some hydrogen wasn't feasible, so I would have to simulate water electrolysis at my desk instead. It would be a simplistic demonstration, but given the time constraints I did not have much of a choice.

I needed a plastic tube, some test tubes, a battery, battery cables, two sharpened graphite lead pencils, water, a rubber tub, and sodium bicarbonate, also known as baking soda. I leapt from my chair, sending it rolling backward to join the others. I needed to go back to the kitchen.

There was so little time to gather supplies that I decided to run, rather than walk. On regular days I preferred a brisk stride, running was childish and unsafe, but today was remarkable and failure was not an option.

After passing through the hatch I ran along the MP corridor to the grand staircase and took the stairs two by two. I entered the dining hall and then ran to the kitchen.

"Where's Reggie?" I yelled, forgetting all formality.

Ajdan looked up from where she was working and silently threw her chin in the direction of his office. Her hands were busy loading ingredients into a commercial sized mixer that was slowly churning a vat of cream colored batter. I hoped it was coating for fish. Battered fish and chips was an infrequent treat.

"Reggie, quick! I need a small rubber tub!" I demanded as I rushed into his office.

He looked up from the storage log as he fumbled to get out of his seat.

"They weren't kidding when they said make all resources available. Look at you, all bossy and shouting," he chuckled. "One small rubber tub coming right up, Miss Marisol."

He clambered past me toward a supply cabinet. There were stacks of them on a stainless steel shelf where Ajdan was working, and as he passed me one I said, "Oh shoot, I could have asked Ajdan."

Ajdan nodded and shrugged in agreement. She had mastered non-verbal communication.

"No worries," said Reggie. "I'm happy to help. Anything else?"

"Baking soda."

"You bet."

Reggie moved quickly to the industrial spice cannisters along the back wall. He was a large nimble man, and I followed him and said, "Just dump some into the tub, Reg. I'm going to mix it with water when I get back to Malice."

"You got it."

He ladled in a heaping portion, and I turned to sprint away. There was no time for formal goodbyes, so I yelled over my shoulder, "Sorry to bother you both, and thanks!"

I ran back across the dining room and down the grand staircase. My next stop was Robotics & Automation for a rechargeable nine-volt battery. It didn't have to be particularly powerful. I only needed a slight charge for the purpose of my demonstration.

Running through the hatch I was surprised to see Captain Kress seated near the glass, looking outward at the canyon. I stopped immediately and tried to slow my breathing, to gather myself before speaking.

"Sir, excuse me. We are in the process of our . . ."

Without looking up he said, "I am aware of the Elucidation Trial, Marisol. What do you need?"

His omniscience was impressive.

"Sir, I was wondering if I could borrow a nine-volt battery. I will return it later today."

"I believe Professor Eseer is responsible for the redistribution of borrowed supplies, but I appreciate the offer. Due to fire hazard, all batteries, big or small, are housed in storage locker number six. Take what you need and leave the items on your table when you are finished."

"Thank you, sir."

"You're welcome, Marisol," he said, without averting his gaze from the sea.

After quietly retrieving a battery from the locker and silently backing out of Robotics, safely away from the intimidating aura of Captain Kress, I sprinted back toward the grand staircase, but as I neared the hatch Murphy sprinted through and slammed into me, sending my sodium bicarbonate flying into the air. It shot upwards like a geyser, before falling like mist onto the polished, white floor.

"Murphy!" I shouted. "Look what you've done!"

"I'm sorry. I didn't see you," he said, dropping to his knees. "Here, let me help you scoop it up."

I joined him on the floor in a desperate attempt to salvage as much of the squandered electrolyte as possible.

"Where's the battery?"

"What battery?"

"I've lost a nine-volt, Murphy. Look around. It's got to be nearby."

As Murphy crawled around at the base of the stairs, I surveyed the corridor until I spotted it near the hatchway of the mechanical room, and as I bent down to collect it I overheard voices nearby.

"You're kidding," said an unknown voice.

"No, I swear. I saw them kissing under the tomatoes," answered someone else.

I recognized the voices. It was Joen and Creedan.

"No way. Felix is going to be crushed," replied Creedan.

"He doesn't stand a chance now, poor guy. Let's keep this between us until after the trials," suggested Joen.

"All hail the prince and princess of the Aqueous," Creedan stated, sarcastically.

"It's coronation day, for sure," said Joen as they shared a laugh.

*O.M.G.*

Joen had seen Creighton and I in the arboretum, Creedan couldn't keep a secret, and I dreaded being the topic of discussion, but I didn't need the stress right now, so battery in hand, I hurried back to Murphy to collect the rest of the items he was holding for me before returning to the labs.

• • •

Professor Eseer helped me to gather the rest of my supplies, which allowed me to assemble a rudimentary apparatus exhibiting the principles of water splitting. It was in no way indicative of the sophisticated, energy-efficient electrolysis units operating on Aqueous, or as awe-inspiring as the towering chimney of a black smoker, but it worked. Each test tube successfully captured oxygen near the anode and hydrogen near the cathode, based on the respective negative and positive charge of the nine-volt battery. For display, I placed a hydrogen fuel cell and a tablet picturing a pod next to my experiment to highlight the application of hydrogen in station life, and with five minutes to spare, I was done. I tidied up my table to join the some of the others who had finished near Mason's desk.

"Did you just touch poop?" asked a smirking Crimson as he sprinkled a handful of dark, composted material into a fish tank. He had demonstrated how recycled waste could be used as a food source in our hatcheries.

"I got it from Biosolids & Compost, and it's called aquarium meal," he shot back.

"And everybody knows I want the fish assignment, so why didn't you convert the fatty acids from poop into paraffin instead?"

"What for?"

"Because you can power tools with it."

Mason's face fell as he started to understand what Crimson was saying. He had failed to consider the Elucidation Trial as a reflection of his preferred assignment.

"Well, I think you're brilliant, Mason," said Leop.

"Thank you," said Mason, his cheeks flushing scarlet.

"Because now the rest of us don't have to worry about a crappy assignment," Leop added with a smirk.

Creedan, who was doubled over with laughter, shouted, "Epic fail, man!"

"It's the only experiment I could remember," whined Mason.

"And soon the only thing you'll be remembered for is flushing the bowl," Creedan continued.

We knew that Mason wanted to be placed in Quality Control & Predictive Maintenance, and I too was concerned that he had given our evaluators the wrong impression, but mocking him was cruel and unnecessary.

Mason looked toward Creedan's table.

"What did you come up with, Creedan?"

There was a monitor on Creedan's desk with a dot rebounding back and forth across the screen.

"Oh, nothing. I just coded a new game."

It was a simple game, possibly not new, but it was enough to Titanic Mason's pride.

I surveyed Lilith's workspace. She'd painted a mountainous landscape with jewel-toned sunset on a large banana leaf, and was justifying it as art therapy.

*Useless.*

"ATTENTION. ATTENTION. The allotted time for the Elucidation Trial has expired," alerted the AI Assistant.

Anyone still working set down their instruments, took a step back, and then subtly scanned their neighbor's workspaces to see how the competition had fared. Murphy's attempt at meat growing was smoldering and smelled more like barbeque than cloning, but the majority of our group had made significant progress toward demonstrating an environmental solution for a specific challenge of station life.

Felton's desk was covered in speakers, and when he tapped the keypad in front of his monitor the AI Assistant sang a reworded rendition of Yankee Doodle Dandy.

> Felton Bytes has won this trial
> All without a pony
> Reprogrammed my dull broadcast
> To prove he's not a phony

The evaluators looked impressed. Digital communications were an integral part of Aqueous life and tethered us to our sister stations. His simple song demonstrated his superior programming skills. He slayed it.

Tackling our clothing needs, Naviah had created a braided belt from corn husks. She had attempted to dye it pink in a bath of drowned raspberries that, unabsorbed, oozed from the belt onto her desk in a wasteful pool of belt juice.

Felix had a satisfied look on his face. His ambitious attempt to create a miniature, aquatic rover had succeeded, and I watched as he controlled its movement through a water tank on his desk.

*When had he become intelligent?*

I had grossly underestimated him. His robot highlighted the simplicity of my demonstration, which was akin to a Y6 experiment. My demonstration was basic and boring.

Creighton had constructed a catalyst for splitting toxic carbon dioxide into oxygen and carbon monoxide. He then demonstrated how the residual carbon monoxide could be combined with hydrogen to create methanol, a biofuel. Its application was necessary in many departments, so theoretically he could be assigned anywhere, but someone as capable as him would surely receive a top assignment. He was the full package: intelligent, well-mannered, tall, handsome. He was a leader without being aggressive or loud.

Sensing my stare, he turned to me and smiled, which set my cheeks aflame. I looked away, awkwardly, toward the other tables.

Sugar had also split carbon dioxide, but had done so to make liquid glycerol, a colorless, odorless sweetener like her name.

*Punny.*

Ironically, Yarrow demonstrated how the same product could be produced from biodiesel plants like soy, hemp, and flax.

"Can I borrow a cup of sugar?" quipped Julip.

"You're gonna need a huge cup," said Etan, looking directly at Sugar.

"No, Etan. Sugar, not Sugar. That's what they used to do. Neighbors. Rather than run to the store in the middle of a recipe, when the oven was hot and the family was hungry, they'd run next door and borrow a cup of sugar."

Her explanation was lost on Etan, who continued to look at Sugar, nodding absently.

"Julip, when was the last time you saw any of our parents operate an oven?" asked Creedan.

"Never, but I want to operate one."

Julip was comforted by the precise measurements and detailed instructions offered in recipes. She had churned out formic acid, also known as methanoic acid, an effective food preservative, and was feeling confident once more.

"ATTENTION. ATTENTION. The Elucidation Trial is now complete," alerted the AI Assistant. "All departments are to take inventory of supplied resources and ensure their return while adhering to best practices."

"Ladies and gentlemen, this concludes the lab portion of the trials," announced Professor Eseer. "Assessors from Robotics & Automation are waiting for you. Please proceed there now."

## CHAPTER SIXTEEN

Conditions at the bottom of the sea were less than hospitable. To start with, it was always cold. Beyond the station walls, away from the vents, the body would quickly succumb to hypothermia, but only after suffocating. Without air, the body could not sustain life for more than five minutes. Not usually, anyway. There were old news articles of young people surviving submergence in frigid water for up to thirty minutes, but that was without extreme water pressure. The weight of the water in Monterey Canyon would crush someone before they suffocated. It just wasn't an easy place to live.

Protection from the elements was a vital part of seabed life. Unlike space, where a relatively thin suit shielded astronauts from harm, sophisticated pressure-stabilizing pods provided the only safe opportunity for human survival on the exterior of Aqueous, and although routine diving activities would only be assigned to a select few, diving training, as a necessity for emergency situations, was mandatory for all. Hence, a diving trial was paramount in the completion of the subterranean syllabus.

Walking at the back of the group, deflated by the elementary and dull nature of my Elucidation demonstration, I could see my peers stiffen as they passed through the hatchway into Robotics & Automation.

"Welcome, trainees," said Captain Kress as they entered the department.

*That explains why he was here during the Elucidation Trial.*

"Line up in front of the viewing panel," he instructed.

"Today, as your captain, I am charged with the oversight of The League Trial. Each of you have completed the mandatory one hundred hours of pod management, which I am told was sufficient time to familiarize you with the basic mechanics and maneuverability of the various types of submersibles we operate here. It is my opinion that these one hundred hours are grossly inadequate; however, in consideration of the limited number of trainees who will actually qualify to hold the elite assignment of cuvier, it is understandable that the majority of you should focus your efforts on more manageable tasks."

*RIP.*

"It is my intention to challenge you in order to identify the trainees who possess the desirable attributes needed to conduct life-threatening work. The individuals who regard the safety of those onboard before the safety of themselves. Divers can face unforgiving scenarios that push the boundary of ethics and expectation. Those who understand this trial will undoubtedly be considered for the most coveted station assignments, and those who don't, well . . . Let's just say that unlike terrestrial life, down here, half a league beneath the sea, there is some sort of an assignment for everyone."

A small squeak escaped from Purity as he critically scanned the youth before him. This was a make-it-or-break-it moment. No one spoke. There would be no questions directed to the captain.

We had expected that each trainee would operate a pod at some point during the day, but likely from Mass Landing. Some of us enjoyed operating the submersibles, while others found it arduous. We stood before the viewing panel as instructed, attempting to ascertain what we were observing.

"Lieutenant Commander Lowry Keel will be providing you with more specific details of the task you are to complete, but let me remind you that nothing on Aqueous is accomplished in solitude. Albeit subtle at times, teamwork is a key component of station life. Checks and balances are the key to our success. No single resident should play hero for the rest. Check on each other during this trial, and it will balance itself," said the captain, and then, hesitating, he awkwardly added, "And best of luck," before abruptly turning on his heels and exiting the department.

"He is so scary," whispered Yarrow, who was standing next to me. "He's like a tyrannical android pretending to be human."

It was a more personalized statement than usual from a man who did not concern himself with things beyond regimented textbook protocol. Perhaps it was the participation of his son, Creighton, that was thawing his icy demeanor.

Our attention shifted to Lieutenant Commander Keel. There were few residents on Aqueous that I was unfamiliar with, and he was one of them. Undoubtedly a cuvier, his work would have taken him beyond the station, ferrying delegates, repairing damaged items, and collecting resources. The details surrounding his missions would often be classified, so it made sense that I did not know him.

Cuviers, preferably single and childless, carried out the most dangerous Aqueous activities. Collision and corrosion were their primary concerns, but they also monitored surface volatility, which was rumored to be exceedingly toxic. Any potential risks were reported to Command and then relayed between merstations. Information sharing was essential for our survival.

"Good afternoon, trainees. As Captain Kress indicated, my name's Keel, and I'm excited to tell you that today, some of you will get to pilot a cozen—the Lamborghini of all pods!"

His enthusiasm was met with blank stares.

*Lamborghini?*

"What I'm trying to say is that the machine is the fastest, most maneuverable submersible in our fleet. Defying previous limitations, it combines intense speed with compact, robotic capabilities that allow a single occupant to venture farther, faster, for interaction with the outside environment. These pods are reserved entirely for cuviers, so today, for those of you who get to operate one, it will most likely be the only time you will be permitted to do so."

*Wait a second. Did he say "some" of us will get to pilot the cozen?*

I had never heard of a cozen before, but I didn't intend to watch. Our pod management instruction had utilized simulated trainers and remote robotics to allow us to develop our diving skills. I had excelled in the training, and although I had been unaware that cozens existed, I was not going to miss this opportunity.

"Are they clean inside?" asked Purity.

"Ah, yes, of course," said Keel, looking bemused. "They are extremely clean, and you will be working in pairs. Each pair will be assigned a cozen that you will maneuver in a game similar to capture the flag."

"Excuse me, Lieutenant Commander," Anit interjected. "If the cozen only holds one person, why are we working in pairs?"

"Good question, Anit."

His exuberance made us relax and smile.

"Each pair will consist of a diver, who will pilot the pod, and remote roboticist providing tactical support. This will optimize the potential of each team."

"I'd like to request the role of roboticist, sir," said Kyro.

"Unfortunately, the roles for this task are selected randomly. Like many things in life, Kyro, you do not get to choose."

"How small is the cockpit?" Kyro asked.

"Cozens are cozy. That's for sure. There's no wasted space. They were built for efficiency, not luxury."

Kyro gulped. He would not do well within the confined cockpit of a cozen, whereas I would not do well without one. Working in pairs was a relief to many, but my heart sank. There was a fifty percent chance that I would not be selected to dive, and my aptitude for diving could not be showcased from a dashboard in Robotics.

"Please join your partner as I call out your names," instructed Keel. "Mason, you will be working with Lilith."

Lilith theatrically rolled her eyes, making no effort to disguise the displeasure in her match.

"Yarrow, you're with Creedan; Naviah, please join Kyro; Amley, find Sugar . . ."

The lieutenant commander continued to call names as they were generically generated by a matching application on the tablet that he held. As the number of available partners reduced, I realized that my two strongest competitors had not been called, making them potential allies.

"Felix, you are teamed with Creighton. Please join him," Keel instructed.

*Seriously?*

A tsunami-like groan rolled through the room. Our task had become twice as hard, and a smirking Felix crossed in front of the group and bro-hugged a rigid, refusing to gloat, Creighton. They were the dream team, and I would make it my personal mission to rejig the matching app before additional trials took place next year.

*So unfair.*

"That leaves three," summated Keel. "Elsby, Marisol, and Purity, we have an odd number of trainees, so you'll become an augmented team with two divers and a sole roboticist," he concluded.

A silver lining. My chances of being selected as a diver increased by thirteen percent.

"But Lieutenant Commander, sir, will you impose a penalty on the three-trainee team?" asked Leop. "They have an advantage."

Keel looked at our group.

"No, I don't think it's necessary, Leop. The design of this trial does not benefit from additional pods."

Choking, stifled laughter could be heard as Etan shouted out, "Especially when you're as useless as Purity."

Keel frowned and shook his head.

"Trial success is achieved with a clear mind, Etan, and I believe that you need additional time to gather yourself. When it is time for you and your partner to choose pods and remote dashboards, take a moment to calm your thoughts while the other teams select theirs first. You and your partner may utilize whatever is left over, and commence your trial after their departure."

"Damn it," seethed Felton, who had been paired with Etan, but Etan nodded, unaware that they had been penalized.

"Before we select our divers and roboticists, let's discuss the object of the game. We have hidden a target beyond the walls of the station. This unknown object requires rescue. As a team you will work together to identify and retrieve said object with efficiency and safety. The team to achieve this will be awarded top marks; however, the scoring rubric is robust. It values the attributes and abilities of teamwork in addition to individual skill, as such, this trial can produce many winners," encouraged Keel.

Lilith, standing slightly ahead of me, shot a sideways glance toward Mason and let out an unconvinced, definitive huff.

"What are we looking for?" asked Amley.

"You already possess the information to complete this task, Amley," answered Keel.

He had impressive recall. I didn't think he had met any of us before, but he knew who each of us were.

"Are we supposed to be observing something through the viewing panel?" asked Crimson.

"Not specifically, that I am aware of," said Keel.

Crimson raised her eyebrows, dramatically.

"Then why did the captain make us line up here?"

"To organize you into a line, and to grab your attention. You're going out there, well, some of you are going out there, into the abyss. Look at it and respect it," said Keel.

It was a tad alarming. There was no room for error out there.

"Now, let's draw numbers. The ones will become our divers and the twos will become our roboticists," he explained.

Purity's hand shot up.

"Where do the roboticists sit?"

"The roboticists will be providing support from here, at observation dashboards."

"Are the dashboards clean?"

"Yes, Purity. They are clean."

Keel passed before each of us, extending the tablet each time.

Lilith tapped the screen and became a one, making Mason a two by default. She would dive and he would assist. Naviah became a two and Kyro a one. She tilted her head to one side and shrugged. The League Trial didn't interest her, so she would have no advantage as a roboticist or a diver. She would rely heavily on Kyro to see them through. Etan and Felton became one and two respectively, and so on and so on until the lieutenant commander was in front of me. I touched the screen: two.

"What if we don't like our number? Can we switch?" shouted Etan, oblivious that Keel had already told Kyro that that was not possible.

Keel looked over to him, blankly, with no intention of answering the question for a second time, and as he did I grabbed Elsby by the arm and pulled her in front of me. I had not worked this hard to become a two.

"What is certain in life is uncertainty, Etan," Keel replied, and then looking forward again stated, "Elsby, you are a two, which by default makes Marisol and Purity ones."

As Keel moved onward Elsby quietly asked, "Why did you do that? That hurt."

"A positive result is more likely with this configuration," I whispered. "Trust me, this is better for all of us."

Purity, who had already placed her hand on her forehead, had a shocked look on her face, accentuated by her mouth, which hung open. There was a very high probability that she would be completely useless at this activity, but as the additional diver she could follow my lead.

Down the line, as the last trainees were sorted, Felix threw his arm up in the air and choked back his displeasure after generating a two. Creighton remained dignified.

# CHAPTER SEVENTEEN

With the roboticists stationed at their observation dashboards, the divers were led to a hidden hatch. It opened to reveal a staircase that we descended to discover that tucked away, beneath Robotics, there was a discreet cozen dock. It was a windowless room with a ring of circular markings on the floor. The circles on the floor were either red or green, and they surrounded a central table. The contents on the table had been covered by a large sheet.

This restricted area, which appeared to be for cuvier use, was probably their strategy room. Risk aversion missions would be formulated here and not shared with Aqueous residents. Panic, stress, and fear were not ideal at the bottom of the sea, so the cuviers would ensure our safety and ignorance when it pertained to anything deemed frightening. If any bad things were occurring, we probably wouldn't know.

"I'd like to welcome you to Sub-Command. You may position yourselves at your desired airlock, but not you, Etan. You will not move until I give you the signal," warned Keel.

Etan, not understanding why he was told to stay put, nodded proudly in agreement.

"The League Trial has begun," Keel announced.

There were no visible airlocks. The room was empty. It would be difficult to choose an ideal pod if I couldn't find its access point. I looked at the ceiling. It was opaque. I approached the table, but I didn't have the audacity to uncover the shielded objects. Maybe that was the test. We would fail by uncovering or not uncovering the hidden items. No one touched the sheet.

"Oh man!" shouted Kyro, nearly falling to the floor. The ground beneath him had shifted, creating a hole, a tunnel, to what must have been the interior of a cozen. "They're beneath us! Under the rings!" he shouted.

We started running, everyone but Etan, to the nearest rings, unaware of the consequences of choosing one color over another. I jumped inside the boundary of a red ring and began to descend. Purity gingerly stepped inside a green ring and nearly lost her balance as it started moving downward.

As I sank lower I surveyed the room. Several of the trainees were sinking like myself, while others, like Kyro, stepped off their rings altogether. Creighton quickly moved from a red ring to a green one.

Descending airlocks were used for propulsion pods. They were different from the mini-pods we inhabited which were engineered and balanced to float unobstructed to the surface, during an evacuation. With propulsion, cozens dangled beneath Sub-Command, ready for deployment, and could be propelled in any direction a diver chose.

Once descended from view, my airlock stopped.

"ATTENTION. ATTENTION. Prepare for cockpit entry," alerted the AI Assistant as the floor of the airlock gave way and I slid downward into the seat. "ATTENTION. ATTENTION. Fasten your safety restraint," it continued as I fumbled for the harness. "ATTENTION. ATTENTION. Launching will commence in three, two, one."

My cozen disengaged, and like a fledgling falling from its nest, began tumbling, powerless, to the bottom of the sea. The interior was dimly lit, and although I had managed to get my arms through the harness, I struggled to see how to buckle it together, but the cockpit was so tight that I was not tossed about as it rolled out of control.

*Click.* I was secure.

Ignoring the whirling landscape and the dizziness it inspired, I scanned the cockpit interior for clues as to how to power the pod. There were two sets of controls located beyond the arm rests, on each side of the craft—power and maneuverability on the right, and communications and accessories on the left. Normally backlit and color-coded, the controls were dead. I frantically tried to power the pod before I . . .

*Crack!* I hit the bottom.

The nose of the cozen collided with the seafloor and rolled onto its roof. I hung, suspended by my harness, like a World War II paratrooper hanging from a tree. I was winded and gasping for air as the pod rolled onto its side, allowing me to observe several trainees zipping through the water above. Their cozens were alive with light and propulsion, but there were others, like mine, that were already aground, or plummeting toward me, incapacitated, on a collision course with the Earth's crust. I estimated that half of the trainees had crashed their pods as I did, revealing the important difference between the red and green circles.

From across the seafloor, a functional cozen approached. It was Purity. Her jubilation was evident in her huge smile and happily waving arms. She had chosen correctly, a green circle, and was coming to my rescue.

*Bang!* Purity slammed her pod into mine, sending white pain slicing through the right side of my neck and clavicle. The friction from my restraint had torn my skin, and I yelled in agony as Purity's hands shot upward to hide the 'oopsies' expression on her face. Her intent to liberate had lacerated me instead.

Above us, the roboticists were visibly suspended in individual dashboards. Sunken into the floor of Robotics & Automation, Elsby appeared to be floating in an air bubble trapped under the station. Swiveling in her chair to locate Purity and myself, she had a three hundred and sixty degree view of the dimly lit seafloor, and a panel of useful instruments before her. If utilized properly, her assistance could be pivotal to our success.

I assumed we could do better than Etan, who had caught up, but was upended in a pod beside mine, unharnessed and throwing himself against the glass in an attempt to flip his cozen over.

*Idiot.*

Bright search lights approached from above, making it appear that the trial had ended. What a complete disaster. I tried the start controls again, but there was nothing. The light became much brighter and then dimmed as it pulled along beside me. It was Creighton. Of course it was Creighton. He'd followed his gut, selected the green ring, and was now fully operational.

Creighton was holding something. He pointed at it and then pointed downward, and sure enough there was an acoustic wave communication device in a storage compartment beneath my seat. I turned it on—static. I looked back at Creighton and he held up three fingers, so I adjusted the dial to channel three.

"Marisol, are you alright? You hit pretty hard."

My burn was throbbing, and it was difficult to lift my right arm, but I replied, "I'm fine. Bruised ego is all. I need to get this thing going."

"Look up. Some of the roboticist's dashboards are dark. I think the trial administrators sabotaged half of the pods and half of the dashboards so that each team would have a dilemma to solve. We'll have to troubleshoot on these devices until we can restore pod-to-station communications. Try to find the channel Elsby is broadcasting from."

I nodded my thanks and looked upward. He was right, some of the twos were seated before dark dashboards, but Elsby's appeared to be functional. I was regretting my intervention to become a one.

I began changing the channels on my device.

Channel 4: "Mason, it's Lilith. I don't need your help, so sit in the dark and wait. Over."

Channel 5: "Kyro, I've pushed every button on this stupid board and I'm giving up. Naviah out."

Channel 6: "Anit, stop brushing your teeth and answer me."

Channel 7: "Marisol, can you hear me? It's Elsby."

*Bingo!*

"Elsby, it's Marisol. I'm so glad I've found you. I need to get this thing running."

"Are you alright down there? Those pods hit hard."

"We're good. Purity has a functional pod. Should she start the search?"

Elsby ignored my question, politely confirming that she had no faith in Purity's ability to complete the trial on her own.

I held up seven fingers so that Purity, who had located her communication device, could talk to us, and when she connected she said, "Marisol! My cozen is spotless."

*Stop with the damn cleanliness!*

"Is yours?"

I wanted to scream at her, reprimand her for her carelessness, but summoning the strength of the ocean, mustering every ounce of self-control I possessed, I calmly answered, "Aside from the blood pooling beneath my safety harness, it's very tidy, Purity."

"We need to get you operational, Marisol. After that I can use a mapping app to pinpoint specific areas not yet searched by the other trainees," said Elsby.

"Roger that," I said.

"I wish I could figure out why your pod is malfunctioning. My systems all check out. From where I'm sitting it looks like you've got a healthy machine."

"There's got to be a remote override, Elsby, and it's probably controlled by someone with high security clearance. Maybe someone in Command? An officer? We need to contact them. Let's try all of the channels on our devices," I suggested.

> Channel 8: "Amley, stop crying. I will get you back to the station even if I have to swim out there and drag that cozen in. I promise."
> Channel 9: "Creedan, it's Yarrow. If you can hear me, I want you to know that I have no idea what I'm doing. Sorry, buddy."
> Channel 10: "Murphy . . . ? Murphy . . . ? Murphy . . . ?"
> Channel 11: "Etan, it's your pod-master calling. If you're unable to read my mind, try answering the phone."
> Channel 1: "It's Crimson, reporting live from all the cool stuff that's swimming around down here."
> Channel 2: Static.

"Channel two isn't being used. Should I say something?" asked Purity.

"Request a cancellation of the system override on Marisol's cozen," Elsby instructed.

"Okay." Purity cleared her throat about four times before saying, "Sir Command, we'd like to request a cancellation of the override system."

> Channel 2: Static.

"Try being more specific and less awkward," I suggested. "Address the question to Lieutenant Commander Keel."

"Okay." There was more throat clearing and some deep breaths taken before she said, "Excuse me, Lieutenant Commander Keel, we'd like to request the removal of the override system."

> Channel 2: Static

"We're going to keep trying," I stated. "Address Captain Kress. He was there earlier. Perhaps his involvement is greater than we expect."

There was no throat clearing or breathing exercises this time. "Captain Kress, requesting cancellation of the system override on Marisol Blaise's cozen," she said.

> Channel 2: "Copy that. Cozen system override cancellation granted for Marisol Blaise."

The lights came up in my pod and it started to vibrate.

"I have power!"

"OMG! I actually did something right!" shouted Purity.

"You sure did. That's amazing work, team. Now let's try to determine what we're looking for," Elsby encouraged.

We were elated, but possibly lagging behind the rest of the group. It was time to get to work.

Despite the pain near my right shoulder, maneuvering the cozen was effortless. Once mobile, the pod righted itself and hovered just above the ocean floor. Using my right hand I was able to ascend and descend, turn left and right, and increase and decrease my speed as needed. My left hand was able to access the onboard communications system, which was now activated. There would be no further need for the devices; the three of us were hands-free.

The cozen had various functional capabilities that had not been apparent while the interior was dark. It could dig, saw, retrieve, and weld.

"This thing is unbelievable. I hope we get to try the welding option," I confessed.

"Let's be satisfied with finding the flag, Marisol," Elsby replied.

*Note to self: schedule cozen playtime for another day.*

Purity and I began to fan out, making a wide swath under the station as Elsby gave indication regarding areas that hadn't been searched. An hour went by to no avail.

"We've searched the seafloor over and over. It's not plausible that we missed it. It's time to try something new," I suggested.

"There's no one else here," said Purity.

"You're right, and that's odd. Where are they?" I asked.

"I have a grouping of cozens under Command," noted Elsby.

"Maybe they've found something. Let's proceed to Command for visual confirmation." I said, pivoting my pod and accelerating upward with Purity following behind.

Command was the highest section of Aqueous, located on the observation deck at the pinnacle of the grand and officers' staircases. For safety and security purposes, Command had exceptional visuals on the entire station, and as we approached, I spotted the pods of Lilith, Creighton, Crimson, Murphy, and Leop surrounding an out-of-place object. It was a mini-pod, and what an odd place to find one. With the MP corridor far away, it could not have detached and become stuck under Command randomly. It had been positioned here.

As Purity and I circled closer, Creighton indicated that the group was communicating on channel four.

*Always so helpful.*

I switched channels and joined an ongoing debate.

". . . leave him here. We found him, so now we're done. Let one of the cuviers retrieve him. That's their job," stated Crimson.

"It's capture the flag, not find the flag. We can't leave him here. We have to take him back," explained Leop.

"If my cozen pushes, and the rest of you maneuver slowly above him, it's possible that we could direct his MP into the decompression chamber, and voila, everybody's happy. No barotrauma," drawled Lilith in her seductive, I'll-get-what-I-want voice.

"You can't push him, Lilith. He'll float to the surface. How would we explain that? Had a great time at the League Trial today, Admiral Blaise. Oh, and by the way, we lost Captain Kress," said Murphy.

It was odd that they were still utilizing the communication devices we had found in the pods, instead of switching to hands-free.

"Risking the safety of the captain, my father, or anyone else for that matter, is completely unacceptable. There must be another way," said Creighton, diplomatically.

"Since the game is called capture the flag, I would expect you would use the winch," said Elsby.

It was a good point, so I attempted to engage the winch.

"The winch doesn't work," I announced.

"You're late to the game, Blaise. We already tried that," said Leop.

"That doesn't make any sense," Elsby replied. "We need it."

"Wait, I'm getting a winch indicator warning. It says remote access only," I said.

"Remote access . . . That's you, Elsby. You're our remote roboticist today, so you have to activate the winch," said Purity.

*Way to go, Purity.*

"Marisol, does your team have control of both pods and the dashboard?" asked Felix, who sounded as though he was still sitting in the dark.

"Yes, of course. Don't you?"

The rest of the divers hadn't successfully cancelled their system overrides to engage their roboticists. We were the only fully functional team. I positioned my cozen next to the mini-pod Captain Kress was relaxing in and noted a smile on his face.

"Elsby, please activate my winch and proceed to remotely attach it to MP78," I instructed.

"Roger that, Marisol. Winch deployed and attaching."

"Purity, please position your pod on the other side of MP78 in preparation for winch activation." I instructed.

"Yes ma'am. Repositioning now," replied Purity.

Once in position, Elsby remotely deployed and connected Purity's winch. Then we commenced a slow tow of Captain Kress' MP toward Decompression and victory, proving that our underestimated girl squad was in a league of its own.

• • •

My success in the League Trial was due to the combined actions of a group of people, also known as teamwork—something that I dreaded. Autonomous tasks, where I could prove my knowledge and assign value to my individual skills, interested me far more, but the League Trial had been designed to identify and sabotage those who could not collaborate. I, in particular, was thankful for the assistance of Elsby and Purity. Had I chosen a green ring, like many other divers, I would have attempted to reach Captain Kress on my own, unknowingly sabotaging our team.

After depositing Captain Kress in Decompression and returning our cozens, Purity and I had been instructed to proceed to the Habitat Hatchery locker rooms in preparation for our physical trial. It would be the last, but most exhausting activity of the day.

Elsby had waited for us and was walking with Purity ahead of me. They giggled as they recounted the events of the trial, energized by our win, and did not notice the sound of footsteps behind us.

"Marisol!" called Lieutenant Commander Keel. "I'm glad I caught up to you. I wanted to say congratulations on a successful trial. Who would have thought that the little girl I piloted to the station ten years ago would become such a fierce competitor."

I froze. This man had met me on the most vulnerable day of my life. Something few residents had witnessed.

"I knew you looked familiar, but I couldn't place you."

"Cuviers . . ." he said, breaking into a smile. "We're an elusive breed."

They were an elusive breed, one that I rarely got to interact with, so it seemed like an ideal moment to blurt out, "I'd like to be a cuvier. It's what I want more than anything. Girls are as worthy of the assignment as boys."

He looked shocked.

"The first female cuvier? It's a prodigious idea."

*Prodigious as in impressive, or prodigious as in unnatural?*

"Do you actually get to detonate explosives to dislodge sediment near the start of the canyon?"

"To generate the turbidity currents? Yes, we do that, but only because it's advantageous to manage sediment before it slumps and buries the vents, or worse, the station."

"Wow."

"It's all very routine. We keep odd hours and leave the station often. I spend the majority of my time ferrying experts between Morskaia Derevnia and Sihai Longwang. It's less exciting than you imagine."

*Was he being modest or discouraging?*

"Whatever you've heard about cuviers, Marisol, it pales in comparison to the wonderful things I've heard about you."

"From who?"

"Your mom. She really misses you."

I shot him a confused look and stated, "But I see her every day."

"What? Oh! Right. It's because you're growing up. Becoming independent. It's a normal thing moms go through. Forget it."

He was surprisingly flustered.

"What I was trying to say is that your parents are exceptionally proud of you, and they're right to be. I monitored your activity in the cozen, and I was impressed."

*He was impressed with me? Best. Moment. Ever.*

"I hope the Assignment Committee decides in your favor, Marisol. Now if you'll excuse me, I need to get back up to the infirmary."

He pivoted and strode quickly away, like I needed to do also. I was sure to be the last to the locker room.

## CHAPTER EIGHTEEN

"Your athletic suits are waiting for you inside. Please put them on and return for further instruction," said Professor Eseer.

"Awesome! I love fish," said Crimson, but no one rejoiced with her.

This would not be a fun-filled fishing trip. There would be some sort of unexpected twist that would likely be unpleasant, and my fellow trainees appeared uneasy, for all had gone quiet as their heads filled with dread. The idle chatter about the previous trial had died—buried beneath the gravity of the unknown task at hand.

I followed the girls into the locker room. Commotion ensued once we were behind closed doors.

"Fish cannot be as bad as being upside down on the outside of the station. It took them so long to drag us back," said Amley.

"Well, I did not sign up for this. How does fish farming have anything to do with fashion?" Naviah complained.

"I'd rather catch a fish than wear a skirt," said Crimson.

"It'll be much worse than catching fish," said Lilith, smiling as she spoke.

She enjoyed watching trainees suffer, but she was correct. The physical trial would be designed to test fitness under duress, and our evaluators would have taken creative license when deciding which fears they would subject us to.

"Let's not worry about the unknown. They wouldn't give us a challenge we couldn't complete. Try your best and remember your training. If you clear your mind you will exceed the limit."

It was the best unplanned pep talk I could manage, and Naviah took a deep breath and nodded in unison with the other girls while Lilith scowled at me with an intensity that could etch borosilicate glass.

I turned and moved away from the group to change. I wanted privacy. My shoulder was sore, and I hadn't yet inspected the wound near my neck. Finding a secluded spot toward the back, I whimpered as I pulled my arm from my sleeve.

"Marisol, what happened to you?"

"Julip, I didn't see you there. It's nothing."

"Your skin is raw."

"It's a small burn from the cozen harness. It's fine."

"It doesn't look fine. I think we should tell Professor Eseer."

"No! No. I don't know what he'll say, and I want to finish the last trial. Help me put this on."

"Okay, but . . ." She looked uncertain, as usual. "I've got a little sister, and I know what can and cannot be healed with butterfly kisses. They wouldn't work on this."

"I promise to go to the infirmary when we're done. Okay?"

"Okay."

I stepped into my suit and pulled it up to my waist, but had Julip help me guide my hand through the opening for my arm. Then I let her fasten it while I told myself to block out the pain of the tight material rubbing against my clavicle. I would clear my mind and exceed the limit.

We exited the locker room to rejoin the boys on the metal platform above the tanks. The department, officially known as Habitat Hatchery, held many slang names. It was most commonly referred to as the pond, but was also known as the fish bank, the fish nursery, the fishing hole, bait & lure, or wiggle & stink. Likewise, Aqueous aquatic species technicians had various nicknames including fish nannies, sole seekers, shell fishers, bred herrings, stinkmongers, and flippers. It was an infinite world of piscary humor, but today was no joke.

I had anticipated a return to Athletics Development, where I was familiar with the equipment and drills Fly regularly prepared for us, but instead found myself standing before multiple large aquariums. I was apprehensive, but aside from a minor wound, I was in excellent physical condition and trainee safety would be paramount, so whatever this task was, I could do it.

Unlike meat and poultry grown in the labs of Proteins & Cloning, the pond farmed many live varieties of aquatic species for future consumption by residents. It was a two-story space. The main hatch was located on the sub level of Aqueous, but was elevated above the tanks located below. For safety and observation, a labyrinth of metal ladders and walkways extended across the department, connecting each tank and creating an escape route for the technicians should they fall in.

The rows of tanks housed various animals, including shellfish and crustaceans. It was trippy to witness the production of fish when there were many wild species swimming beyond the glass, but alas, the ones outside were trickier to catch.

Each fish species in the habitat had their own series of life-cycle tanks, with pumps circulating water of appropriate temperature and salinity throughout their habitat. For each species, the first tank consisted of brood stock for the creation of fertilized eggs. The eggs were then moved to a small hatching tank, where they would emerge as minnows. With growth, the minnows swam to the next larger tank, via a lock system, as more fertilized eggs were deposited into the tank they vacated. The fish continued to move into larger tanks as they grew, ultimately reaching maturity in the last tank. When the last tank was full, appearing to have more fish than water, Aqueous dietary analysts would determine how many were needed for portion preparation in the kitchen. The rest would be designated for storage in Comestible Silos & Refrigeration.

I became aware of a floating course set up on some of the bigger tanks toward the back of the department. We certainly wouldn't be fishing; traversing seemed more likely.

In the first tank, large clear inflatable balls bobbled on the surface of the water. They were the training pods used by the flecks to practice mini-pod evacuations, and their movement appeared to be caused by the multitude of adult fish slashing beneath the surface.

The tank beyond that had half a dozen flimsy and transparent tubes strung across it. The tubes did not look sturdy enough to support much weight, making it unclear what the activity would be, but the tank itself was teeming with fish.

The last tank, aside from the water it contained, appeared to be empty.

We were greeted by Fly and Nesme, our senior aquatic species technician, otherwise known as the fish nanny, as I pondered what we would be doing in the last tank.

"Trainees, welcome to the pond! Nesme and I are so excited to test your physical and psychological agility in the Glaucus Trial. This looks like everyone," Fly confirmed by counting heads. "Please follow me to our starting point."

We traversed the suspended platform above tanks of various fish: salmon, eel, tilapia, black tiger prawns, cod, carp, and trout. Nesme gave commentary on each species we passed. She was a proud fish momma.

"Our task today is comprised of three challenges requiring physical prowess and emotional control. In addition to being physically fit, you must learn to eliminate the most detrimental feeling of all, fear. Fear impedes our thoughts and actions, causing a performance paralysis powerful enough to prevent happiness, achievement, and in the most dangerous situations, life. Fear can be different for everyone.

Something that scares one trainee, may not frighten another. Will you be able to conquer today's fears?" asked Fly.

Felix and Etan began to snort in a fit of stifled giggles.

"He's unlikely to be a conqueror," said Etan.

Fly paused to address them. "Mr. Nyrmac, will you please explain the joke."

"No ma'am. There's no joke. The only thing here is fear."

His response generated even greater snorting from Etan, who, as it turned out, was watching a large red salmon flop about on the floor below.

"It's not a he, it's a she!" shrieked Nesme. "And we need to save her eggs!"

Crimson, who was close to the ladder, had already started descending to aid the stranded fish.

"I've got her, Nesme. Don't worry," she said, after easily scooping up the salmon. She cradled it in one arm as she ascended the ladder with the other, gently easing the creature back into its tank.

Crimson would be a contender in this trial.

"Very observant, Felix. By now you should understand the valuable resource these animals are to our viability. How about a fifteen second delayed start time?" Fly offered. "Would that be funny?"

"No ma'am, please. I will try harder to be more serious."

"You *will* try harder. Let's make it a thirty second delay instead."

"What? That's unfair!"

"Would you like forty-five?"

"No ma'am. Definitely not."

His face was red like the salmon. He was displeased with himself.

"Wonderful. We are agreed on thirty seconds then," she said, turning again to lead us toward the starting point.

"And what about me?" asked Etan. "How long is my penalty?"

She ignored his question. Etan could not afford a penalty.

"Please pay attention. I will say this once, and there will be no questions," she explained.

*Focus on her words, Marisol. This is your future.*

"Our task begins at the catfish tank, where each of you will be placed in a floating training pod. You will find a cap and goggles inside. Put them on. The pod will be sealed with you in it. When the trial begins, you must unseal your pod and escape, making your way across the pool and up the ladder to the platform between the catfish and the tilapia tank. On the platform you will find many metal hoops, vertically fastened to the ceiling above. Each hoop is the entrance to a long, narrow, perforated tube. Enter the tube and traverse the tank. The tube may be torn if you need to exit and cannot complete the task, but be aware that purposely tearing the tube is an immediate disqualification and failure of the Glaucus Trial."

I looked for Kyro, but could not see him. The tube would not be easy for him.

"Assuming you successfully traverse the tilapia tank, you will emerge from an identical hoop on the other side, on the next platform. From this point you will be able to start the third task, a diving exercise. Dive to the bottom of the third tank and recover four, five-pound kettlebells without surfacing in between. Climb the ladder to deposit all four kettlebells on the platform at far end of the third tank and your trial is complete. If you surface to breathe before placing all four kettlebells on the platform, you will need to return to the platform between tanks two and three and start again.

"This is a timed exercise. Efficiency counts. If at any time you feel overwhelmed by danger, or if you are unable to complete the task, call out for assistance and our emergency personnel will remove you from the trial. The trial begins at zero."

We arrived on the platform next to the catfish tank. There were thousands of them thrashing about at the surface of the water. Peering out from behind whiskered faces, they appeared to be jostling for a look at us. I tried to convince myself that they weren't that bad. I could manage a few fish.

Anit raised his hand and asked, "Where's zero?"

But having given the full instructions, Fly simply pressed her palms together under her chin and silently nodded her encouragement. There would be no more words. She turned and walked away in the direction from which we came, pausing momentarily for Nesme to follow her.

It didn't sound as bad as I thought it would. I would open the pod, swim to the end of the tank, crawl up the ladder, go through the tube, and then dive down to retrieve some weights.

*Simple.*

I needed to locate the zero.

The sound of a sliding hatchway vibrated through the hatchery as Fly and Nesme exited, and a line of official looking men entered the department. They were dressed in tight, rubber suits. Their faces were covered by masks, making it impossible to identify them, but I knew immediately that they were cuviers. They were the motivators I needed to sail through this exercise, proving to everyone that I was worthy of joining their ranks.

They walked toward the training pods that had been loosely tethered at one end of the tank. There were twenty-one of them. One for each of us. They opened the circular seals and motioned for us to join them. Following the others, I climbed into one and watched as my assigned cuvier sealed the opening above me.

With the cuviers holding our training pods in place, it was not difficult to enter, but I could feel the fish thrashing below me as my weight sunk the pod slightly into the water. I had never experienced anything like it, and to be honest, it was kind of fun. I watched as other pods were sealed with trainees inside before searching again for the zero, until my cuvier began banging on the side of my pod. He pointed to the cap and goggles that I was supposed to wear, so I quickly tucked my hair into the cap and pulled the goggles over my head, leaving them to dangle around my neck. I probably wouldn't need them until the third tank.

I looked around again. Our group appeared to be set.

*Let's do this.*

One by one the cuviers detached our tethers, allowing the pods to bump into each other. Then they each stepped back from the edge of the tank and held up their left arm with a closed fist. It was the start signal. When the last arm went up we were startled by an AI announcement.

"ATTENTION. ATTENTION. All residents are to prepare for a mandatory thirty-minute lighting failure drill. Repeat. All residents are to prepare for a mandatory thirty-minute lighting failure drill. The drill will commence in one minute. Initiating countdown: 59, 58, 57, 56, 55 . . ."

*Wait. We have to do this in the dark?*

The cuviers stepped forward and pushed each of our training pods toward the center of the tank. The untethered pods danced across the water to the rhythm of the frenzied fish, unseating their uneasy occupants. Some pods moved advantageously closer to the ladder while others drifted away, but one remained relatively motionless. It was empty.

*Who's missing?*

"42, 41, 40, 39, 38 . . ."

Muffled cries of alarm, insulated by the closed seals, could be faintly heard. I could see Naviah on all fours, looking downward at the rolling school of fish beneath her hands and knees. I doubted that she would be able to make it out of her pod.

"29, 28, 27, 26, 25 . . ."

The countdown continued as I thought about what I needed to ascertain before the lights went out. I examined the seal, paying attention to how it worked, and then I rotated the opening to the top.

*Where am I now? Where am I trying to go?*

The ladder leading to the next platform was ahead of me.

*The lights will go out, I will climb out, and then I will swim straight ahead to the ladder. Control the fear. Control the fear.*

"15, 14, 13, 12, 11 . . ."

The cuviers' masks were obviously night vision, and thankfully so. They'd need to monitor our progress, and rescue some of us, like Purity, who was already sobbing. She wouldn't withstand the filthy water, and my heart broke for her.

Felix was calm, sitting in his tethered pod with his arms and legs crossed. Lilith was also relaxed, laughing loudly to garner the attention of the boys. Creighton, as usual, was looking right at me in a show of encouragement.

"3, 2, 1 . . ."

Darkness. We were at zero, at the bottom of the sea, and it was terrifyingly black. I reached upward with my good arm and fumbled for the seal until I found it. My hand was shaking, making it difficult to open, but after yanking hard, it yielded. Then I heard a scream and someone choking.

Trainees were already out and making contact with the catfish, signaling that I needed to move faster. From kneeling I took a small step forward with one leg, lowering the opening slightly before attempting to dive through, but I didn't make it all the way out before hitting the water. The pod rotated on top of me as the upper half of my body submerged with my legs still inside, and there were catfish everywhere. They were in my face, behind my neck, around my torso, and as I pushed my arms upwards, through them, to free my legs from the pod, I sank deeper. The tentacles of the hairy fish entered my nose and ears.

*Should have worn the goggles.*

I no longer knew which way was forward, but it became imperative to breathe first and determine my location second, so I kicked off the pod, let my legs submerge, and then kicked again, harder, hoping to surface. I hit my head on a stationary pod as I tried to breach and swallowed the foul water.

*Felix.*

He was still tethered at the side of the tank, motionless, waiting out his penalty.

Coughing, gasping, I had managed to get my head out of the water to register the activity in the tank. It was manic. Arms and legs thrashed wildly against the disequilibrium of the churning fish. Trainees abandoning the trial screamed in fear, calling for rescue, while those seeking victory were silent.

*Game on.*

The dirty water stung as it saturated my wound, but abandonment was not an option for me. Without sight, the position of Felix's tethered pod, which had not moved since we lost the lights, became my primary directional guide. Then I used the sounds of my panicked classmates, whose voices collided with the end of the tank and ricocheted in the opposite direction, to gauge distance. I could not see, but I could hear, and the hysterical sounds of my peers would lead me to the ladder.

I quietly made my way to the side of the tank closest to Felix's pod, avoiding collision and further injury. I was calm, and it was working. The splashing of my cohort altered the motion of the water, sending waves forward and up the end of the tank, to crash loudly on the platform. I was getting closer.

I could hear Naviah's rescue as she was pulled from the tank by a cuvier. I was relieved for her, but more happy that she provided another clue. Her whimpers and footsteps, plus the footsteps of the cuvier who assisted her, confirmed that I was heading in the right direction.

*Bump.*

"Ouch! Watch it! Wait. Who is that? Do you know where the ladder is?" It was a sharp voice that softened to purr like a catfish.

*Lilith.*

She was traversing along the same side of the tank, attempting to find the ladder. I let go and swam past her, hopefully taking the lead, but she was doing well.

*Irritating.*

When I got to the end, I could hear the suction and subsequent drippings of water falling off others exiting the tank ahead of me.

*Dammit.*

I wasn't the leader, but it was impossible to see who was ahead. It was so dark, but I located the ladder and began to climb. One, two, three, four rungs and I was up. It was good to be free of the fish, unlike many of my friends.

I needed to locate a hoop. I got down on my hands and knees and proceeded to crawl until I could feel the edge of the next tank. I was careful not to get too close. Being tossed into a kettle of fish once was plenty enough for me.

Making my way along the edge of the platform, I waved a hand ahead of me until it collided with a hoop. I found the tubing and entered headfirst.

*Mistake.*

I slid down the slippery tube until I collided, yet again, with thousands of thrashing fish, but that was not the worst part. I started to sink. The flimsy tubing collapsed around me and simultaneously began filling with water. It was perforated. Unlike the pod, which had structure and ample oxygen, the collapsing tube was closing in, and I felt certain I would drown.

There was no width to turn around without tearing the delicate material, so I started to back up as the water seeped in and I continued to sink. Soon there were fish above me, and the steep, slippery incline to return to the platform where I had entered was preventing me from exiting.

*Oh no. Oh no.*

I was hyperventilating. I couldn't tear the tube and fail, but if I didn't I would die.

*Breathe, Marisol. Breathe.*

*Bang.*

"Ugh, I'm sorry. Who did I bump?" said a familiar voice.

"Cr-Creighton?"

"Marisol? You're ahead of me? You're doing awesome!"

"Creighton, be still. Don't move. The water is coming in, and the tube folds in around us making it difficult to breathe. Back up. I need out. I need out right now!"

"Whoa. I agree with you. Let's get out, but forward. Backing up won't work. It's wet. We'll just end up sliding back in, and I think we're halfway across already."

"No. We'll drown. I'm drowning!"

"I can feel the water, and it's barely trickling in. You're not drowning. I promise. The tubing doesn't hold its shape, so it compacts around us as we move and the fish move. We feel like we're drowning, but we're not. It's an illusion. We have enough air, and we're completely safe."

"You're sure?"

"One hundred percent, and you know what else I'm sure about?"

"What?"

"That you want to win this, and that I want to beat you, so get moving."

He began pushing on my feet with his hands, and I started to breathe again. He was right. There was only one way out, and it was me moving forward toward victory. I had lost a few minutes to fear, but Creighton was the motivator I needed to get myself back in the game.

"ATTENTION. ATTENTION. Fifteen minutes of the mandatory

lighting failure drill remain. Repeat. Fifteen minutes of the mandatory lighting failure drill remain," alerted the AI Assistant.

No further encouragement was necessary. We wriggled and squirmed like furious tadpoles toward the end of the tube where a rope dangled, making it possible for us to pull ourselves out. I emerged from the tube, shaken.

Crawling along the deck to locate the third tank, my limbs were unsteady beneath my torso, but the finish line was close. Now was not the time to falter.

*Clear your mind and exceed the limit.*

There was movement behind me.

"Let's go," whispered Creighton, brushing my sore shoulder as he dove directly into the third tank, but I would not follow. I would prepare for a longer dive by taking a deep breath and holding it to expand my lungs.

I tried to block out the pleading whimpers of desperate trainees behind me, sinking in the tubes, and a rescue as someone attempted to tear themselves free. Creighton and I appeared to be leading the race, but it would not be a victory if we were beaten by the clock.

I put on my goggles and crawled to the edge of the tank. I stood up, took a last deep breath, and not knowing how deep it was jumped in feet first. It was a mistake. I could not get low enough. I would have to surface and try again. Pulling myself back onto the platform I heard Creighton surface and gasp for air.

*Good.*

I dove in headfirst and pulled myself down to the bottom to discover things that felt like rocks. It was an oyster bed, and the kettlebells would be hidden beneath them. Kicking with my feet so that I could remain at the bottom, I started to dig between them, searching for a weight, when something big brushed against my leg. My heart-rate elevated.

*Was that a massive fish?*

I tried to stay calm and kept searching, reminding myself that this portion of the challenge would not be testing our resilience to fear. We had already completed that. This was purely physical. This task demonstrated how long we could stay under and if we could surface with the additional weight. That was the measurement of success.

I had not yet dug to the bottom of the tank, and there was more movement. I was not alone. Others had caught up, and I was running out of air. I would have to resurface soon.

*A weight!*

I grabbed the handle of the kettlebell, but I needed to breathe, so I surfaced with it. It was heavy, and climbing out with all of them would be challenging.

I swam back toward the distressing sounds from tank two and climbed back onto the platform. Trainees were emerging from the tubes to begin the task in tank three. Lilith had arrived, and I could hear her talking to a cuvier.

"Just tell me where the bells are. I won't tell anyone that you did."

*Ridiculous.*

I dove back down and buried the kettlebell I had found next to the wall, hopeful that it would not be discovered and taken by someone else as I searched for three more. I began running my hands over the mounds of oysters along the bottom of the tank. Their dormant, bumpy shells were a welcomed relief to the slimy bodies of the catfish. I was calm and enjoying the cool silence of the tank.

*Another bell!*

I started swimming it over to my first one when a hand clamped down over mine and tried to pull it away from me.

*No way. You are not taking this from me.*

I turned my body and kicked as hard as I could with both feet in their direction. It was a direct hit, and I didn't care if it hurt. They would not take my bell.

*Get lost.*

I headed back to the wall and found a third one near the first that I hadn't noticed before.

*Lucky.*

It was time to surface again. I climbed onto the platform and took a small breath to recover. There was more activity in the final tank now. I had to finish this before someone stole my bells, and before the time expired. I dove down to the first three and took them with me as I searched for the fourth. They would be beneficial in weighing me down as I surveyed the bottom.

Crossing the bottom of the tank was daunting. This was not like static apnea, where we held our breath without moving. This was a workout, and I was running out of breath.

*Clear your mind and exceed the limit; clear your mind and exceed the limit; clear your mind and exceed the limit; . . .*

I repeated the phrase over and over again until I accidently dropped one of the bells, but found a fourth while rummaging for it. I had them all. I continued forward until I hit a wall, and hopeful that I would surface on the far side of the tank and climb out to victory, I kicked upward with the additional twenty pounds immobilizing my arms. I had used all of my strength, all of my breath, and almost all of the time. I could not start again.

To my surprise I surfaced, reached upward, and found the ladder. I grabbed a rung and pulled myself onto the platform, hurling the kettlebells ahead of me. I was exhausted, but I had done it. I completed the Glaucus Trial first, and I would become a cuvier after all.

"Hey there, Marisol. What took you so long?"

"Felix? Is that you?" He was the large fish I had felt in the tank. "Are you finished?"

"Yeah, for a while now. It was less challenging than I expected."

"But you had the penalty, and I didn't hear you as I worked through the tanks."

"Stealth mode, but I'm not surprised to see you. Once again we're the first male and female to finish. We make a good team, Blaise. We should celebrate."

*Celebrate second place?*

"I think I'll go to bed early instead. It was a big day, Felix."

"Ah. Okay. As you wish."

His tone was unusual, but it was dark, so I couldn't see his expression to determine if it was disappointment or indifference.

"Well done, Miss Blaise," said a nearby voice. "Would you like a warm towel?"

It was the cuvier assigned to me.

"Yes, please."

I would have enjoyed discussing his awesome assignment, but I was tired, sore, and second.

We sat in our warm towels and waited quietly, Felix and I, as the other trainees dove and resurfaced to restart and dive again. Creighton was next to finish, followed by Joen, Lilith, and Leop. Then the lights came on, signaling the end of the activity.

"ATTENTION. ATTENTION. The mandatory lighting failure drill has now concluded. Repeat. The mandatory lighting failure drill has now concluded. You may resume your usual activities," alerted the AI Assistant.

Then the jubilant voice of Professor Eseer wafted toward us across the tanks. "Trainees, we would like to congratulate you on the completion of your trials!"

All of the evaluators were with him, clapping as they approached.

"This is no small feat, and the activities of the day will remain in your memory and hearts for years to come, uniting you through this shared experience. There are no losers here. Only winners moving forward on their suited path. We are so proud of you. Your integrity and courage will serve you well," he said.

Only six trainees had completed the fifth trial. The rest of our entourage were humbly seated in various groups between the first and third tank. Many had not made it to the first ladder.

Naviah, wrapped in a towel next to Murphy, was still visibly shaken, and Murphy had put his arm around her in comfort. All-talk-no-action Etan sat next to them, along with Yarrow and Purity, whose ichthyophobia had prevented her from participating.

Anit, Crimson, Amley, and Creedan had been beaten by the tubes. Large openings were visible in two of them where trainees had made the decision to evacuate, disqualifying anyone else inside. Crimson was visibly angry, but it was unclear which of them had torn their way out.

Sugar, Felton, Elsby, Mason, and Julip had made it past the second tank only to run out of time in the third.

The trainees on the platform beside me were the victors, but it didn't matter. Collectively we had accomplished something far greater—we had completed a journey we commenced together, in Y1. Felix was right, we should celebrate. Celebrate the past we shared and the future we would forge together.

I turned to him to tell him that I had changed my mind, but was arrested by his alarmed expression. Gone was his usual indifference, and for the first time, he appeared worried. Creedan was the first to inquire.

"You okay, buddy?"

Felix's eyes jumped from face to face, tallying the trainees on the platforms before he shook his head and asked, "Where's Kyro?"

## CHAPTER NINETEEN

To make known publicly through proclamation, to commemorate an important event, was to celebrate, and celebrate we would. The anxiety that occupied each of us the day before had dissipated, creating a vacancy where joy could, once again, reside. It was the morning after the trials, and it was my birthday.

*Was I sweet at sixteen?*

I would attend a coming of age party to celebrate the loss of my childhood, the completion of the trainee syllabus, and my readiness for my assignment. I was sweeter yesterday, when I was still a kid.

My mother had ensured that the details of my party had remained a guarded secret. It was easily kept during the stress of final assignments and the trials, since none of my friends had had time to think of anything else. I knew that Naviah had created an outfit that I was going to wear. A gift, I suspected, that was more for her than me, and although conspicuous, I would do my utmost to showcase it properly. I was honored to be the one to make her happy.

In fact, that would become the intrinsic theme of the evening—making others happy. My sixteenth birthday was also the tenth anniversary of my separation from my mother. It was a day rooted in sadness, and even though I was to be adorned like a princess, I did not wish to be paraded around like one. I was done with stories. My adventures died long ago, with the last inhabitants above. Today, I was more comforted by math and science and the happiness of others.

Fulfilling the hopes and dreams of my Aqueous parents and my best friend would be my altruistic gift.

And my gift would be given soon. It was getting late. Pre-party jitters had ruined my sleep and completely abolished my appetite, so I had remained in my pod, MP124, all day, enjoying laziness in the familiar surroundings of the corridor I had enjoyed for the last five years. I would be moved immediately after graduation, which created a desperate need to drink in the space by memorizing the smells, sounds, the feeling of each surface, and the view before surrendering it to the next, equally deserving, Y10.

A lazy day was now as unfamiliar as heavy slumber under a sunburnt sky. Even Assuage was spent learning, exercising, or interacting with others. We needed to be lazy more often, excusing ourselves to build mental armor as a necessary guard against the nonstop grind. That had to classify, loosely, as science; therefore, not wasteful at all. Because there was no waste on Aqueous, we all knew that.

Mental fortification aside, if I was to be the perfect model for Naviah, it was time to leave the comfort of my berth, walk around the corner to the lav, brush my teeth, trim my nails, and drag myself into the shower, immediately, before putting on some clean, casual SIDs. I wanted to be neat and tidy when my friend arrived. I would surrender and become a willing victim, ready to be beautified.

"ATTENTION. ATTENTION. Naviah Hark has identified at your airlock," alerted the AI Assistant.

*Uh-oh.*

She was early. I got up and hit the release, allowing her to ascend, but I couldn't see her. She had been consumed by a giant ball of midnight blue fabric.

"Is that you in there?"

"It is! Are you excited to see your new dress?" she shouted through the layers of material blocking her face.

"I'm more excited by the fact that you were able to navigate here with complete visual impairment. Maybe this is the breakthrough we've needed to eliminate our need for light."

She deposited the dress on my chair.

"Occupational adaption, or at least I hope it will become one. Let's dress to impress and we'll see where it leads."

"Your wish is my command, all-powerful leader. Suit me up."

"Hmm. I was expecting difficult Marisol. Agreeable, smiling, happy Marisol is a refreshing change. This will be less painful than I expected, with the exception of your bedhead and bad breath. What a pleasant surprise."

"What do they call it . . . Turning over a new leaf? This is my new and improved, adult self you're looking at. I mean, I'm just giving my fans what they want."

I held straight face for as long as I could before we both burst out laughing. There was no fooling her. She knew that being presented to my peers in an elaborate garment would be challenging for me.

"Well, despite your newfound brazenness, you'll be relieved to learn that I did not envision a slinky, sexy little number for your birthday celebration. You will not be expected to strut half-naked, soul-exposed, before your peeps tonight. This dress is fun and flirty, but fully covers you. There's a ton of fabric here, constructed in a way that will make you look fashionable and feel fantastic. This dress is your friend."

She moved it onto my desk and began smoothing it out so that I was able to examine it further. There were folds of crisscrossing fabric forming a fitted bodice that created a chevron pattern in the front and back. The skirt was full. Constructed of hundreds of fabric petals resembling the layered head of a peony, it was approximately knee length, and the color was exquisite. The majority of the blue and purple petals were matte, but were highlighted by random, shiny petals that reflected light like the translucent wings of a dragonfly.

"Naviah, this is incredible!"

"Of course it is. I made it especially for you, and I knew you would love it. Happy birthday."

Forgetting about my bad breath and bedhead I reached out and gave her a massive hug.

"You're so talented."

She pulled away and proudly replied, "You're not the only amazing one, Miss Blaise."

That was true. With her abundant popularity I had never stopped to consider her aptitude, and thinking about it for the first time, it may not have been particularly easy to be my friend. My family name alone cast a long shadow, and I had outperformed Naviah both scholastically and athletically for as long as I could remember. I was glad that her artistry would be displayed tonight.

"Now that we've been introduced, I guess I should try it on. Pass it over."

I cast off my SIDs, throwing them onto the floor, as Naviah passed me the dress to step into it. Zippers were limited, so the back consisted of hidden hook and eye closures that I never would have been able to manage on my own. I turned around and let her do it up.

"Don't think I haven't noticed that this is strapless and knee-length. Those are both characteristics that make it fall into the half-naked category."

"True, but I made sure the neckline was high, and it goes down to your knee. Anything longer would have swamped you."

"It feels like it fits perfectly."

"It should. I went to Atelier and got your most recent measurements from Alfrid before I started cutting. I didn't want to measure you myself because I knew it would stress you out. Sabotage was a much better strategy. Now turn around and let me see you."

I spun toward her as instructed, worried that the injury I had sustained in the League Trial might detract from her creation. Julip and

I had visited the infirmary for numbing, antiseptic ointment, but the mark was still unsightly.

"Does it look alright? Am I wearing it right?"

"Better than right. I've been working on this for a while, and it wasn't the most straight forward design, you know. I'm actually so impressed with myself right now."

"Me too. And totally relieved that I don't look like a complete freak with a big burn across my neck. "

"The burn is badass, and the cut of the neckline won't rub against it."

*Only a true friend would call my injury badass.*

"You're amazing, Naviah Hark. I scored big ten years ago. I mean, just look at us now, two happy mermaids at the bottom of the sea."

"You know it. Now go and have your shower. We need to tame that hair. More Sedna, less Medusa, would be nice."

## CHAPTER TWENTY

Transformation complete, Naviah had returned to her pod. She left behind a large handheld mirror that she had indefinitely borrowed from Atelier so that I could come to terms with my polished appearance. The hair around my face had been twisted, pinned, and adorned with tiny petals of matching fabric. The back of it hung loose, and was easily tolerable. She had slathered my arms and legs in coconut oil to illuminate my skin. I had never noticed the definition in my shoulders, which were completely exposed above a Queen Anne neckline, and granting myself impunity for vanity, I admitted that I looked good, possibly great. The only problem now was that I would look notably different from everyone else, but that also meant looking different from Lilith. I hoped Creighton would like this new version of me.

Naviah would meet my parents and me at the undisclosed, secret location of my party. I didn't know who was going, but I assumed it would be intimate. Most probably my class and the adults I was close to. That was the usual protocol, but I would receive more attention as the daughter of the admiral. It was a burden that some, like Lilith, would relish, whereas I resisted, but looking down at the elaborate fabric consuming me alive I made a pledge: I would savor the moment. If Lilith could do it, so could I.

"ATTENTION. ATTENTION. Admiral Blaise has identified at your airlock," alerted the AI Assistant.

"Tell them I'll be right down," I instructed.

"Affirmative," it replied.

*There's no going back now.*

I looked nervously toward the shelf that housed the memories of my birth mother, seeking her strength, then put down the mirror and slipped on the black, rubber ballet slippers that Naviah had instructed me to wear. I hit the release, descending in my airlock, bracing for my parent's reaction. They would be the first to either marvel or malaise over my major metamorphosis.

The black shoes of my father came into sight as I sank. From his pant legs I could see he was dressed in formal SIDs, which meant that everyone else would be also. The gap between my ornate appearance and that of my guests had shrunk. I'd never been so thankful for formal wear.

My mother's feet were farther away. She would, undoubtedly, be planning to allow my father to escort me to whatever unknown setting awaited.

My heart began to race. Their expressions, which always gave them away, would communicate volumes before they managed any words. They had accepted a child in rags and had seen her every day since in SIDs. This would be a shock.

My father, who had been conversing with my mother, turned toward me as I completed my descent. His happy smile froze, then slipped from his face, audibly shattering into a million pieces as it collided with the floor. My mother gasped. Her hands involuntarily shot upward to her mouth, attempting to stifle the sound she had made as my father attempted to speak.

"Marisol, look at you," is what he managed.

He stopped speaking to process the scene before him, and I thought I saw tears in his eyes. He turned toward my mother, seeking her input and support. I had never seen him at a loss for words.

My mother looked from me to him, appearing more shocked

by his reaction than my physical appearance, and said, "Marisol, it seems your father isn't ready for you to grow up."

She approached and gave me a hug before she continued to speak.

"If the world were as it was we'd be accustomed to seeing you like this, but it's a good reminder why our new world cancelled the production of material goods—to reduce the strain on the planet through uniformity. I'm sorry it's your only dress, sweetheart, but it was worth the wait."

She hugged me again, but as she did I could not help think that this was not my only dress. I had another on my shelf in MP124, and if the world were as it was I'd still be with my family.

"Shall we go, ladies?"

My father extended a bent arm toward me, and I linked my arm through his, willing to be led toward whatever escapade had been planned. Milestone birthday antics were a tactical distraction meant to mitigate the mundane constraints of station life, and the admiral's daughter would have a sixteenth celebration like no other.

We began walking.

"Where are you taking me?"

"I've been sworn to secrecy," replied my father. "If I tell you, I'll have to kill you," he added with a wink. "At least, that's what your mother said."

My mother, frolicking beside us, asked, "You still don't know? I was so worried that someone would let it slip, and I was close to telling you myself because I was so excited," she confessed. Joy radiated from her like the glow from a lantern.

"I can't tell which of you is more affected by all of this," my father interjected.

"I have no idea what is about to happen, but I assume that there'll be a meal, embarrassing speeches, and cricket cake."

From my first mouthful, when I turned six, I knew that I loved cake, but grains were difficult to grow on Aqueous. With longer grow-cycles, and the utilization of numerous grow-podiums, crickets became a favorable substitute. Ground into flour, they created a nutty-tasting baking alternative that was high in protein and easy to obtain, and with a thirteen-day incubation period they outpaced every grain. I could already taste it. The cake, not the crickets. As you can imagine, crickets on their own were disgusting, and I had eaten way too many bugs as a child.

"With your mother in charge, I'm sure your party will exceed anything we could have imagined."

We walked to the grand staircase, and I stiffened with the realization that I would soon be visible to residents proceeding to dinner. I should have completed my thesis on invisibility.

"Keep breathing, you'll be fine," assured my father, pulling his elbow closer to his side to keep me in forward motion. He placed his free hand over my linked arm in a calming gesture that helped. I kept walking and breathing and, remarkably, did not pass out.

To my relief, we descended at the grand staircase, avoiding the dinner rush at the dining hall, but we couldn't avoid everyone. Several friendly faces were quick to offer congratulations, birthday wishes, and positive comments on my appearance, making me feel especially loved. Any inhibitions I had experienced earlier subsided. My birthday was becoming fun.

We entered the arboretum and descended to the lowest climate zone.

"We're partying at the farm?"

I looked around to see where everyone was hiding.

"No, silly, you were just here for the trials. I couldn't plan a party in a space associated with that. We're just making a quick stop for some souvenirs," my mother explained.

True. I'd been here yesterday, but my strong dislike of botany did not negate the importance or natural beauty of the arboretum, and Creighton kissed me here. For the rest of my life this would be the place where I had had my first kiss with Creighton Kress. My face began to flush. I would be reunited with him shortly.

Creedan and Joen knew about the kiss, but I hadn't told anyone else, and I certainly didn't want my parents figuring it out. I refocused my attention on the angular shoulders of my mother as she swept past podiums of parsnips. We followed her to the back of the enclosure where, tucked away against the rear wall was an incubator housing a single, flowering plant. My mother switched off the contraption, allowing us to see the true color of each blossom.

"We won't be needing that anymore," she stated proudly. "These little beauties are at their peak."

"Beauties indeed," said my father. "What are they?"

"I give you boronia heather," replied my mother. "I infiltrated the clandestine plan of a certain young seamstress to become privy to the shade of your dress, allowing me to select seeds that would yield a complementary corsage. I think this shade of magenta will strike the right tone for the evening. There is a sprig for each of us to pin over our hearts."

The blossoms my mother trimmed were tiny but impactful, with each pink bloom bursting riotously from the bright green foliage it clung to. Pinned to my dress, the tiny adornment was well-suited against the dark fabric. A cultivar from the past, produced from precious seed stock, the flowers were fanciful embellishments underpinning our commitment to each other.

"This is very thoughtful, Mom. Thank you."

"And I have never felt so handsome," added my father as my mom positioned the flowers on his uniform.

"Let me help you, Mom. I can pin yours."

My mother stood still, bashfully smiling as I attached her corsage.

"You're going to love this party, Marisol. Now, let's go!"

Flowers in place, we blazed ahead, weaving our way through the vertical gardens to exit the arboretum and climb toward a destination still unknown. There was nowhere to hide from the tidal wave of diners, but with growing confidence I welcomed cheerful birthday wishes from those happy to share, even for a moment, in my rite of passage. Aqueous residents rejoiced as the adopted first daughter reached adulthood, thanks to the graciousness of her humanitarian parents. It was a fairytale story, and I was starting to feel like an actual princess.

We continued upward, toward Command, which was far too secure to host a party.

"There's no way you were able to fit everyone inside AP1."

"It's the biggest pod on the station," said my father.

"Come inside and you'll see," said my mother.

We descended the airlock together, but there was nothing to see. AP1 was empty.

"What the heck? Where is everybody?"

"Hold your horses, Pony Express," said my father. "We're about to get to the good part. Empyreal, please explain."

"Marisol, we know how much you love diving, and how well you did in the trials, so we were wondering if you'd like to dive us to your party tonight."

"What?" I screeched. "Are you serious?" I screeched again. "This is sick!"

"What was that? You're sick?" jested my father. "Okay fine, I'll dive then."

But I was already behind the controls, thumbing the instrument panel and dreaming that a midnight-blue party gown could become the official SIDs of the first female cuvier.

"I should probably know where we are going."

"We are going, young lady, off the grid, to a place rarely seen and hardly spoken of. A never-before inhabited land we like to call Auxiliary," announced my father.

"Seriously?"

I had expected them to pull out all the stops, but this scenario hadn't occurred to me. I spun my chair toward my mother to witness the uncontrollable delight that had infected her. She was jumping up and down like a small gleeful child in what onlookers would have described as a mega mom-moment.

"Seriously, kiddo, but we haven't got all night," said my father.

"Right," I said.

Confident from the Glaucus Trial, I spun back to the controls and powered up AP1 to initiate our launch. Then, detaching the pod from its dual airlocks, I maneuvered away from the station.

The Aqueous Auxiliary, also known as Aux, was an expansion site developed for future generations. Unlikely to be utilized during my lifetime, the uninhabited station sat like an estranged cousin, dormant and dark, waiting to be reunited with its family. Its earnest motionlessness masked its desire to be called to action and welcome occupants to its lonely corridors. I had only ever seen its silhouette, through clear water, when the ocean's sifting silt had been minimized by continuous days of idle currents.

Aux had been submerged in pieces prior to the Aqueous launch, and assembled by resident engineers after Aqueous occupancy. Robotics teams worked for years erecting the marine megastructure that moonlighted as a restless, watery ghost.

Positioned on the opposite side of the closest turbines, the unlit structure was largely invisible and forgotten by Aqueous inhabitants. It was difficult to see through the walls of rotating blades. Monitored remotely via cameras and wireless operating systems, custodians were deployed infrequently to clean it, and with minimal energy requirements, Aqueous Auxiliary sat in perpetual standby, steadfast and willing if ever conscripted.

"Be cautious as you crest the turbines," my father instructed. "The surrounding water is unstable, and we don't want any mishaps."

Heeding his words, I delayed my descent until we were adjacent to Aux.

"I'm not sure where to go from here. Is there an Aux Mass Landing?"

"Starboard. Just there," my father pointed, "Approximately one hundred meters ahead, at the bottom."

A faint glow was visible at the base of the station, marking the location of the entrance to my party. I approached with minimal sink rate, not wanting our diving adventure to end, and a slow descent optimized our viewing enjoyment as we idled in parallel to the exterior glass. As we neared our destination, it became obvious that the glow was emitted from exterior floodlights illuminating available airlocks for docking. I pivoted AP1 into alignment beside the shuttle-pods already there. There was no visible light emitted from the station interior, and the lights of AP1 bounced back, off of unlit departments. It reminded me of the boarded, seaside storefronts I had seen while studying typhoons in meteorology class.

"Are we certain there's a party in there?"

"You'll find out soon enough," said my mother. "Cold feet?"

"Of course not."

"Don't worry," said my father. "The pod will align itself automatically once you are within distance."

*Did he think I was getting cold feet about docking?*

I glanced at my mother who was seated behind us, and she shot me an eye roll that confirmed that the admiral had completely misunderstood our conversation, but I decided not to correct him and remained agreeably silent as I docked and powered off AP1.

"Well done, Marisol. Now, if you and your father will follow me up the airlock, to the little soiree I have planned, I'll be forever grateful."

*Aw, she was so cute.*

Ascending together into the unfamiliar station, the first thing I noticed was the sound. It was hollow with the exception of the bewitching notes of Bach's Cello Suite No.1 wafting along the dimly lit passageway. The dramatic melody beckoned us onward with promises of magic and delight, and was the perfect complement to the mysterious setting—a candle lit corridor leading to a destination unknown.

The candles cradled flames easily ignited and extinguished, but the wax sustaining them was less common. The Aqueous apiary housed the last known honeybee colony and fraught with challenges in a synthetic habitat, beekeeping, for the purposes of pollination and a possible return to the surface, was a delicate business. Honeybee commodities were almost obsolete, yet the pathway to my party was alight with hundreds of bees wax candles blazing a golden runway toward a hanger of hospitality. It was unacceptable opulence, and made me uneasy.

"It's okay to enjoy them, Marisol. I promise they'll be extinguished when we arrive at our destination," my mother said.

I relaxed, and we started forward, hand-in-hand, toward the music, the mystery, and my moment. On our way we passed labelled hatchways with mundane names like Aux Mech, Aux Systems, Aux Robotics . . . Then, arriving at a nondescript staircase we ascended two levels to enter what should have been a grand pavilion, but it was far from grand. Lit with emergency lighting, most probably powered by back-up generators, the walls were lifeless. There were simple seating areas and the opaque ceiling was low, making it feel cramped by Aqueous standards. Life in Auxiliary would be stale by comparison.

It was a disappointing end to such a grand entrance. The music had stopped, and the magic was fading fast.

*Where was everyone?*

"Marisol, in order to appreciate how fortunate we are, sometimes we need to see things from another perspective. Aqueous Auxiliary was built purposefully, not extravagantly, but it has one single feature that is out of this world. Would you like to see it?" my father asked.

"Of course."

"Lights please!" he hollered, and in an instant everything went dark. The emergency lighting was switched off which allowed me to notice that the candles behind us had been extinguished too. Black stillness surrounded us with the exception of the end of the room, which was marginally illuminated, although I could not see the source.

We moved toward it.

"I've got your arm. Try not to bump into the chesterfields," my father said.

*Chesterfields? What decade was he in?*

We shuffled together, toward the end of the room, where there was a large window showcasing our station, Aqueous, from tip to toe in all its splendor. Rising from the ocean floor to tower above the turbines, like a castle behind moated walls, it commanded our attention.

"Wow," I said. "It's so beautiful. We are always so close to it, even when we're diving, that it's hard to see the entire thing. Magnificent. We are so fortunate."

"And that's exactly how we feel about our life with you. You are beautiful, magnificent, and we are so fortunate to have you. The best ten years we've had have been our years with you, Marisol, and we love you much more than we can explain," said my father.

"For many years we lived on the surface with everything at our disposal, but none of it was as fulfilling as becoming a family with you. There are times when station life is repetitive, but I wouldn't trade one second of it for a life above without you," said my mother.

"In fact, everybody loves you. Isn't that right, guys?" my father asked loudly, spinning around to address the empty room, or what had been an empty room.

The ceiling had come alive. It was a digital life-wall depicting a night sky, and the long arms of the Milky Way swirled above us, creating an infinite canopy of comets and constellations. And there was music again, but not a somber cello. There was loud, festive, dance music being piped in from a DJ booth on the other side of the room.

"Happy Birthday, Marisol Blaise!" he shouted into the air. "It's time to get this party started!"

My father's cries were answered by my friends, who emerged from the seating areas they had been hiding behind. I was surrounded by my favorite faces. There were the Y10s, some of their siblings, former trainees, and the adults I was the closest to. There would be no evaluations or trials this evening. This was a party.

Reggie and his crew entered with floral centerpieces and repositioned and reignited the candles on tables. Trays of food were carried in from the kitchen and placed near a large cake that had been rolled in on a stand. The entire party appeared, instantaneously, from the darkness of the abyss, and all we had to do was dance beneath the stars.

## CHAPTER TWENTY-ONE

The night whirled by as we twirled and sang, tipsy on the jubilation of stresses gone by. My sixteenth birthday marked the culmination of an Aqueous childhood and scientifically structured learning, celebrated collectively by myself and my peers. It was the prom we'd seen in many movies, but knew we'd never have. It was a teenage landmark of significance, that few our age had lived to experience. We had survived to make this milestone, and we would make it a night to remember.

What it wasn't was a night for small talk or polite formality. The party was a rager like we'd never seen before and probably wouldn't see again. We danced in a large group, barely stopping to enjoy the hors d'oeuvres prepared for the occasion.

Sugar, who had become hilarious since settling in to Aqueous life, taught us how to dance like a robot, and Sergeant Reginald Eirome, who dominated the center of the circle, showed us the floss, grapevine, running man, and shoot. He threw down serious moves onto DJ Kade's fist pumping beats. For such a big man, he was Neil Armstrong—weightless.

My mother had intuitively made the right decision to primarily limit the guest list to teenagers, but the few adults invited let their hair down and cut loose. My father, who could barely side-step, delighted my mom with his gyrating theatrics, Commander Hark spun Duanra around the room countless times, and Captain Kress, who was usually so stiff, seized the opportunity to dip his wife backward and plant a small kiss on her lips. It was a softer side I hadn't seen from him before.

Professor Eseer had the men carry me above their shoulders in a chair as his wife, Eeman, let out a trilling ululation. I was up there for a while, giving me no opportunity to talk to Creighton, but I had felt his eyes on me several times. The night was still young, and there would be plenty of time to talk. We hadn't discussed the trials, or other things, but we would do that later.

When my chair returned to the floor I realized that my feet hurt, so I decided to remove my shoes. I was dizzy and could not take them off while standing, so I grabbed a seat at a nearby sofa.

"You look incredible, you know," cooed a familiar voice.

*Lilith. Ugh.*

The room was dimly lit and I had sat down on the same sofa as her. She moved in even closer.

"I don't know why you insist on not standing out, when you are clearly so outstanding. Every girl wants to be you, and every boy wants to be with you, but you are completely oblivious, Marisol. Why?"

"Well, um, I-I don't think that's true, but if you think it's true then it can be true, I guess."

I started to laugh. The room was warm and I was sweating. It was difficult to focus on Lilith's face. She was blurry, but nice.

"Are you feeling okay?"

I couldn't be sure, but I thought I could see that little smile of hers, the one I used to think was evil, spreading across her face, but now it was funny.

"Because my mother steals potatoes to make vodka, and I poured some into the punch," she said.

"What did you pour into the punch?"

My breaths were broken, like I was panting, and I could feel my face and chest heating up from the inside out. Something was not right.

"Vodka. It's an alcohol made from potatoes. I expected this party to be painfully dull, so I spiked the punch. Look at how much fun everyone is having now."

I looked up, but the room was spinning in sync with the galaxy on the ceiling, so I closed my eyes to make it stop. I braced my arms on the seat of the sofa and waited a few seconds before reopening them to refocus on Lilith.

"I drank a lot of that. It was so spicy, but I was thirsty from . . ."

*Whoa.*

The floor was tilting dangerously to one side.

"They should shore up the foundation in this place. I think we're being sucked into the turbines."

"You're drunk," she said, standing from her seat. "Stay right there. I will get you some water."

"Okay, I'll stay right here," I repeated far too loudly.

I stared openly as she sauntered away. She was so beautiful and perfect, and it was nice of her to bring everyone vodka. I'd never even heard of it before. Her mom was talented.

The centerpieces caught my attention. Spiny plumes of purple aeroponic sage, complemented by edible honeysuckle and hibiscus, were potted in the large bowls that Yarrow had crafted. They dotted each table with ornamentation that would become dinner, tomorrow. The dancing flicker of candlelight animated the blooms, creating a mesmerizing show of color and light, unless the flowers were actually dancing. I couldn't tell, but Empyreal had said the candles would be extinguished.

*What a trickster.*

Lilith returned with the water.

"Here, drink this, the entire glass, and then we're going to get some food into your stomach. You're such a lightweight, Blaise."

"You would make a great doctor. Have you considered working with Dr. Nyrmac?"

"As if. The only thing I'd consider is becoming his daughter-in-law, but alas, there's another boy who's head-over-heels in love with you."

"What? Felix? He only loves himself."

"All the boys have confessed their feelings for you to me. Creighton, Felix . . . You are so smart and so stupid."

"Hey, I started to like you today," I blurted out, accidently spitting on her at the same time.

"Charming. I'm going to get you something to eat. Don't move until I get back."

I watched her sashay away. It was an incredible night. I was in Aux, and it was tilted to one side, possibly sinking, and I had a new friend named Lilith.

*Best. Night. Ever.*

I heard my name being called from behind me.

"Marisol! Marisol, what a sea-freaking great party! I've had so many compliments on your dress. It's a dream come true," said Naviah. Then, looking at me more closely she asked, "Are you alright? How much of that punch did you drink?"

"Vokda. There's vokda in that punch. Watch out," I informed her, hitting her in the face as I pointed my finger at her. "You don't even see it coming."

Lilith returned with ice water and a big slice of cake.

"Look what you've done to Marisol, Brizo."

"What did she do to Marisol?" asked Felix, approaching from the dancefloor looking genuinely concerned.

"She got her drunk!" snapped Naviah.

"I didn't pour it down her throat, Hark. Geez, I had no idea how inexperienced she was."

"Not true!" I declared. "I am experienced. Creighton kissed me."

"What!" shrieked Naviah.

"Really?" drawled Lilith, casting her eyes to Felix to catch the disappointment on his face.

"Creighton kissed you?" he groaned, slumping into a nearby chair.

"That's right, people. Kissed. I was kissed by a tomato, not a potato."

As I made my shocking declaration a piece of cake fell out of my mouth and landed squarely on my lap, causing me to laugh uncontrollably.

"Does everyone know about this?" asked Naviah, annoyed.

Felix simply shook his head and then buried it in his hands.

"She's a train wreck," Lilith stated.

"Huh?" queried Naviah.

"Train wreck. Like when they come off the rails."

Lilith's attempt to clarify only confused Naviah more.

"Forget it. We need to make tracks and get her out of here, now. Who's got the keys to the pod?"

• • •

Life is a journey filled with learning, and I had learned that headache and stomach disorder were two of the many unpleasant physical side effects following the overindulgence of alcohol. Unfortunately, they paled in comparison to the mortification and ignominy of one's pride, following the realization of the events that occurred during the alcohol consumption. My innocent summation that the unusual taste of Reggie's potent punch had been created by the addition of one of his seaworthy delicacies was my first mistake. Continuing to speak after I had consumed way too much of it was my second.

It was late morning, and Naviah had left after spending the night with me in MP124. After the initial shock of learning that I had not shared the details of my kiss with her, she eventually found my state of disorientation and discomfort humorous and spent most of the night laughing at my expense. She'd taken good care of me: getting me into my sleeping SIDs, hanging up my dress, and making sure that I had plenty of water.

I would be fine, and I was grateful that I had been removed from the situation before I had embarrassed myself further, but it was not the ending I had anticipated. I didn't get to speak with half of my guests, reminisce about the trials with my peers, or have some one-on-one time with Creighton. Naviah indicated that once she informed my parents that I needed a rescue, they met Felix and me at AP1 for the short ride home. Lilith had stayed behind to run defense, making excuses for my hasty departure, and enjoy an amazing party that continued long after my absence.

I wasn't sure how the others had fared with the vodka, but it was likely that many residents were feeling less than the best this morning. Unfortunately, there would be no empathy for our delicate conditions, for today was graduation day. I needed to recuperate in time to receive my life sentence—also known as my assignment.

"ATTENTION. ATTENTION. Felix Nyrmac has identified at your airlock," alerted the AI Assistant.

I was still unable to move anything more than my eyes, and I could only imagine how badly I looked. Summoning all of the energy I had left, I tapped the intercom.

"Felix, I am not well."

"I expected that, so I brought you some breakfast. Open up."

"I don't look that great. It's better if we visit at grad."

"It's not better, and we all have the same sleeping SIDs, so I know exactly how you look. Besides, I didn't get a chance to give you your gift last night, so open up. Please."

*My gift?*

Gift giving was not customary on Aqueous. Kindness, togetherness, and helpfulness were the daily gifts we were encouraged to give. This was unexpected, and my instincts told me to let him in, so I tapped the release.

Felix ascended, balancing a kitchen tray in one hand and his gift, hidden behind his back, in the other.

"I asked Reggie, who asked Ajdan, to make you a greasy breakfast sandwich with egg and sausage, and they suggested tomato juice instead of orange juice because it's supposed to be the best thing for a hangover."

"A hangover?"

*New word alert.*

I had never heard of a hangover.

"Your self-induced condition."

He clarified his statement by pointing his finger up and down at me.

"It's what you're suffering from," he added.

"Oh, that," I said, nodding, even though it hurt to nod, and climbed down from my berth to accept the tray at my desk.

"You were right, Marisol. You do look terrible."

His joke was funny and made me laugh, even though it hurt to laugh.

"What a disaster. It was a good party until I took it too far."

"Such a good party! By far the best ever until wild-child Marisol Blaise had to act irresponsibly again. When will she learn to be serious like the rest of us?"

"Exactly."

I took a bite of the sandwich, and it was good.

*When did Felix become caring?*

"I'm glad you're okay. Over the past few years we didn't hang out as much as we did when we were kids, and I started to miss it. Finishing the Leizu Trial with you reminded me of the time I spent with you and your family when we were young. It was nice. Anyway, I don't know if you noticed, but during the Elucidation Trial I attempted to finish a miniature rover that I designed for Creedan to use in Gaming & Amusement," he stated, revealing the rover that he had been concealing behind him. "We plan to make lots of them and host game nights. Felton ironed out the last coding kinks yesterday, and Kyro helped with the original design . . ."

*Where's Kyro?*

"Wait. What happened to Kyro?"

I was ashamed of myself for not asking sooner.

"He got hurt, Marisol."

"How hurt?"

"Really hurt."

Felix inhaled and then paused. He put his free hand on his hip, as he considered how to deliver the bad news.

"It's been difficult to get information, but he was obviously terrified of the cozen. He couldn't manage a small space like that, and everybody knew it."

"Even Keel?"

"Probably, but Keel refused his request for a dashboard, so Kyro attempted to descend into the cozen rather than disqualify Naviah and himself."

"Did he have an operable pod?"

"No, and I've learned that he had a severe panic attack. He wasn't able to fasten his harness before slamming into the ground."

"Oh, Felix."

"He's still in the infirmary, but the nurses won't let me in. They did let it slip that he was recovered by the cuviers, unconscious."

"Unconscious!"

"I got the impression that he had a brain bleed and several fractures."

"Surely your father, or my father, can give us more information?"

"Trial details are guarded, Marisol. Nobody's talking."

I felt terrible. I had spent my time partying while a friend was fighting for his life.

"Don't feel guilty, Marisol. There was nothing any of us could do.

Pray that he wakes up. We need him to see that I had the courage to give this to you," he said, handing the rover to me then thrusting his hands in his pockets, looking bashfully proud. "It's the prototype, and I know how much you want to be a cuvier, so I thought you'd enjoy it. The range is unbelievable. You can go completely around Aqueous."

I was dumbfounded by his generosity and thoughtfulness.

"Felix, this is incredible. You should keep it."

"No, I want you to have the first one. I never thanked you and your mom properly for looking out for me when I was younger. It's important to me that you have this."

The rover had lights, a tiny winch, and a camera. It would dive like a pod, but unoccupied. I could explore Monterey Canyon without ever leaving the station.

"It's amazing, Felix. Thank you for giving me this, and for helping me get home last night."

The depth of his relationships and his physical and academic prowess were becoming more pronounced.

"You did well in the trials. I was surprised you made up for the time penalty and finished first. How did you manage that?"

"Oh, instead of exiting the training pod immediately, I crawled inside of it, allowing it to roll until it collided with the far edge of the tank. Then I opened the seal right beside the ladder. I didn't even come into contact with the water or the fish. It saved a ton of time."

"Smart. I wish I had thought of that. I panicked a bit in the tubes. If I had kept my head together I may have beaten you."

"I don't know about that. I had a lot of extra time in the oyster tank. I tried to pass you a kettlebell, but you kicked me, so I left it at the bottom of the ladder where you were reentering instead."

"What?"

"The kettlebell you found by the wall. I was already done and thought that it'd be nice to finish together again, so I placed it there for you."

An uneasy feeling took hold of me.

"You helped me?"

"Only a little. You're not mad at me, are you?"

The floor dropped from beneath me, and the room started to spin again, but this time it wasn't because of alcohol.

"I didn't need your help, Felix. What if the cuviers, with their night vision, or heat seeking vision, or whatever those goggles were, saw you? I won't get credit for my efforts. And how am I even to know if I would have finished second? I know you think you were being nice, but this could have the opposite effect."

I sounded hysterical.

"I'm sorry. I wanted to be a good friend, and I can hold my breath for a ridiculously long time. That's why it's so easy for me to be ob-noxious—big lungs."

He was pleading for forgiveness. It was the first time I had ever seen him look distressed.

"Everybody knows that you've worked hard. Harder than anyone, actually, and you're deserving of the role of cuvier. My help won't impact the result. You're the admiral's daughter, so . . ."

"What? Are you saying that I can get whatever assignment I want based on nepotism?"

My voice, high pitched and loud, caused Felix to become increas-ingly flustered.

"No. I didn't mean it like that. Can we start over? I'm sorry. I won't ever help you again. Well, I will, but never in an oyster tank. I promise."

"Felix, I think you should go. I'm not feeling well, granted it's be-cause of my own naivety, but it's an important day, and I want to rest before the ceremony. You need to leave now."

I stood up and motioned him toward the airlock.

"I understand. I'm so sorry, Marisol, and if it's any consolation, I want you to know that I truly believe you would make an exceptional cuvier."

He looked gutted as he descended the airlock, leaving me all alone with my half-eaten breakfast and the rover he had given me. Not only had I humiliated myself last night, I had forgotten Kyro and was rude to someone who had shown me tremendous kindness. Feeling guilty and ashamed, I climbed back into my berth and cried.

# CHAPTER TWENTY-TWO

Graduation can be described as the receiving of an academic diploma, and the division into degrees on a graduated scale. Today would be both. Cresting the watery summit of our scholarly development, we had arrived at a day of achievement and conclusion. It was a transition into the world of responsibility and adulthood, determined by the degree of our educational success. At graduation, the Aqueous Assignment Committee would divulge where we had landed on the assignment scale.

I had had a good, therapeutic cry. The kind that washes away sadness, remorse, and anxiety, and as the last tear fell I was ready to surrender. I would surrender to adulthood with the knowledge that I was imperfect; I didn't have all of the answers, and I would accept my place on the scale of life with dignity and grace, regardless of where I landed.

I showered and changed into the specialty SIDs created for the occasion. A light blue jumpsuit, paired with short, rubber booties, was to be worn by all Y10s, and we would don our jumpsuits for subsequent graduations in remembrance of our year. There had been nine graduating classes prior that had each received a similar jumpsuit in a color selected for their class, and they would be proudly worn tonight.

I had intended to get ready early, dedicating any remaining minutes to spatial awareness, but the unexpected visit from Felix had exhausted my extra time, hindering my intent to indelibly commit every inch of my mini-pod to memory. Last night was the last time I would sleep here. It was the end of many years that I had inhabited this corridor. My assignment would determine the new location of my housing, adjacent to my department. New relationships would be forged, aligned through common goals, but never as it was with a set of peers of the same age and development. In the whirlwind of activity leading up to this day, I had not anticipated how much I would miss this place, but as I stood on the ledge of adolescence, overlooking maturity, my will to retreat to the sanctity of pupilage was outpowering my desire to leap toward my assigned future.

"ATTENTION. ATTENTION. Naviah Hark has identified at your airlock," alerted the AI Assistant.

"Tell her I will be right there," I instructed.

"Affirmative," it replied.

Naviah and I had agreed that she would pick me up on her way to the labs, where we would gather with the rest of the Y10s before proceeding to the ceremony in the dining hall, but I needed one more second in front of the view.

"Naviah Hark says, 'Hurry up,'" chirped the AI Assistant.

She knew I was being nostalgic.

"Naviah Hark says, 'Your new pod will be nice also,'" it chirped again.

"Affirmative," I barked at them both.

I was tired and grouchy, but it was time to get going. My scant possessions would be moved to my new pod during the ceremony.

"Goodbye, MP124. You were great."

I ran my hand along my desk and surveyed the view for the last time before descending the airlock. Naviah stood in the corridor with arms crossed and shoulders back.

"Are you seriously delaying graduation to mourn the loss of your pod?"

"This corridor has been my home for the last five years. Weren't you a little sad to leave yours?"

"Absolutely not. The next one is going to be way bigger and farther away from Malice. Win, win."

We walked away, forever, heading toward the labs, and I noticed that she looked pretty. She had pulled her hair back into a low, messy bun, adorning it on one side with a large orange fabric flower that she had constructed from a cloth napkin. I had uncaringly tied my hair back with an elastic.

"The flower's a nice touch. How'd you make it orange?"

"I wasn't feeling great after the physical trial, so my mom dragged me to the infirmary to be examined by Dr. Nyrmac. He boiled some eucalyptus for me to inhale, and I noticed that the roots turned the water orange, so I begged him to let me have it. Then I forced my mom to go to the dining hall and steal a table napkin. It has made me, my hair, and my outfit feel way better."

"Well, as long as your hair and outfit feel alright, that's what really matters."

"Apologies that I didn't make one for you, but do you know what I had to threaten Duanra with to steal one lousy table napkin for me? That woman is impossible."

"That woman, your mom, loves you, and you're lucky to have her."

"It took her five years to be able to look out the window, Marisol."

"And she only did it to try and see your pod."

We laughed at that. It was true that Duanra was delicate. She was not the typical adventurous type Aqueous summoned, but she was kind and she loved her family above anything else. Beyond that she was happy to read a book or knit.

We arrived at the labs to find an excited group of graduates. Joen, Etan, and Creedan had hoisted Professor Eseer over their heads and were crowd surfing him around the room. Felton had instructed the AI Assistant to sing Queen's, "We Are the Champions," which sounded odd as a computer generated rendition. Amley was polishing Yarrow's oversized eyeglasses, and Mason and Murphy were adding some zing to their latest secret handshake. Felix sat alone, watching.

"Nyrmac, I always expect to see you in the center of the chaos. It's a tad late to start behaving," said Creighton, sarcastically.

I was surprised by the tone in which he addressed Felix. Neither of them had noticed Naviah or myself.

"I've got a bad case of nostalgia. This is the end, man. Nothing will be the same after today."

"It's not the end. It's only the beginning, and based on how your trial went you should have a spectacular assignment, provided you aren't penalized for a decade of disorderly conduct. The station is your oyster, or maybe that last tank was your oyster. I guess we'll find out soon enough, but you can finally make your father proud."

Naviah raised her eyebrows. We had never witnessed cruel behavior from Creighton, but his words were undeniably demeaning. Felix didn't retaliate.

"Yeah, I'm not sure he can make it. Last I heard there was a possibility of someone developing an allergic reaction."

"But surely a possibility could wait. Unless he prefers his practice over parenting."

Creighton's unnecessary comment must have stung, but Felix kept his cool.

"It's odd that after the eradication of disease, a doctor could be so busy," Creighton continued.

"My father likes to be in the infirmary. He is a workaholic, a micromanager. I didn't see him much after I moved to my mini-pod in Y6. That's no secret."

"But everyone thought it was weird."

"I didn't. I had my classmates," Felix said, looking around the room. "Did you know that Leop is an excellent operatic singer, and

Anit has a passion for cultivating succulents? Elsby's a poet, and Sugar can burp the alphabet in several different languages?"

"I did not," said Creighton, indifferently.

"Etan's dyslexia was so bad that we had to do special puzzles to help him keep up."

"He didn't keep up," slammed Creighton.

"Whoa, dude. Is this how you're going to act today? Like a sore loser? Better luck in the next trials, Kress."

The conversation was interrupted by a flying boot that stuck Felix in the back of the head.

"Ouch!"

"Nyrmac, come on. We're supposed to be celebrating. Stop being all feelings," Creedan called out.

"You're dead, Wylde!" Felix yelled, jumping up to chase him around the room.

And with that, the atmosphere went back to normal, but the conversation between Felix and Creighton had been telling. Roughhousing camouflaged Felix's true self. He had long worn a mask of indifference to hide his delicate heart, but underneath it all he was a good person. Creighton was jealous.

Turning to watch Felix sprint away, Creighton noticed that Naviah and I had arrived, and his demeanor returned to normal.

"Marisol, you made it. How's the head?"

Way to run defense, Lilith. Apparently, everyone knew what a hangover was and that I was suffering from one.

"It's her pride and her head," said Naviah, answering for me. "Fill him in, Marisol, while I spot clean Murphy. He's wearing his breakfast again. What a mess."

She left. Leaving the two of us to talk.

"I waited hours for Kade to play "Time After Time," you know, by Cindi Lauper, only to realize that you'd already left. I didn't even have a chance to wish you a happy birthday."

He had planned to ask me to slow dance in front of everyone, including the parents. I would have died. As much as I liked Creighton, he should have known how uncomfortable it would have made me feel, dancing intimately in front of everyone at the party.

*Thank you, Vodka.*

Professor Eseer interrupted before I could formulate a response.

"Okay everyone, I know we are excited about today, and you deserve to be, but before we destroy a perfectly good laboratory, let's settle down. There is someone here who would like to talk to you, so please take your seats."

The hatchway slid open to reveal, much to our surprise, Mrs. Hark.

"Mom, what are you doing here? I told you and Dad that I would meet you in the dining hall," chided Naviah.

"I know you did, and I'm sorry, but I needed to stop by to give each of you a small gift."

Naviah looked perplexed.

"Gifts?"

Duanra addressed the class.

"We live in a tiny community, in the least forgiving climate imaginable, and it was not easy for me to move here. The thought of our existence below the weight of sea was paralyzing. It prevented me from being assigned, so instead, I volunteered my time chaperoning all of you. When I was on playground duty, or sitting with you at lunchtime, I could hear your laughter, your stories, and it helped me to relax. You may not have realized it, but I found my way through my anxiety with your help, and listening to you interact with each other, I got to know you. By Y6 you no longer needed a chaperone, and my interaction with most of you concluded. It was a big loss for me, so I decided to continue volunteering with the flecks, making childcare my self-assignment."

We had never heard this story before. Even Naviah stared in silent amazement as Duanra continued.

"Because you are so significant to me, I have crafted each of you an individualized item to remember this day. These gifts might be silly, but with limited resources down here, we do not have possessions, and although you may not remember our past lives above, it was nice to be individual and have things that were ours alone. So, if you will allow me, as a sincere token of my appreciation to each of you, I will pass these out."

"Oh yes, Mom!" cried Naviah, leaping toward her mother and almost knocking her over in a massive embrace.

"And I should also add that you helped me deal with an overly active and dramatic child."

There was agreeable laughter as Duanra proceeded to call us up to receive our special mementos. Naviah remained by her side, proudly passing the items to her, one-by-one.

I received a long wrap bracelet with seven metal beads that looked to have been made from a fork. It was braided with two colors of yarn. There were four beads on the tawny yarn, two beads on the cyan yarn, and a single, dragon-shaped bead uniting them in the middle. It was my family, past and present. I hid my tears as I hugged her extra tight. There was more to Duanra than any of us knew.

She continued passing out her gifts.

Leop got a sweater that said *If Rocks Could Talk*, Felton got a necktie with repeating ones and zeros, Sugar got a jacket with *VIP Visitor* stitched across the back, Anit got a face mask with the word *SMILE* on the front, Lilith got some leg warmers, Purity got a pair of germ-proof gloves, and Yarrow was presented with a pretty floral pin.

"Perfect for a guy with a girl's name," said Etan.

Yarrow surveyed Etan up and down, slowly.

"I will have you know, Etan, that yarrow, the plant, also known as achillea millefolium, is named after Achilles, the son of a fearless soldier and cunning sea nymph. He was the hero in the Trojan War, and because of that, and other reasons, I will accept my pin with pride."

Etan tried unsuccessfully to process what Yarrow had said while Duanra continued to call the Y10s. Each presentation had a personalized meaning, demonstrating that her quiet attentiveness had been overlooked, until now. With every gift, crafted from appreciation and admiration, she needled herself into our hearts.

I admired my bracelet as the rest of the items were given. My mother had told me to find my dragon, and here it was, braided into the yarn of my new trinket. Assumably unpredictable beasts, possessing fearsome strength and above-average intelligence, folklore dragons were known for their courage and honor.

My thoughts were interrupted by Professor Eseer.

"What a handsome bunch! And I'm delighted to tell you that you are welcome to wear your new decorations with gratitude. Never have I seen a more accessorized ensemble, and I certainly hope there will be more of this to come," he said, nodding toward Duanra. "Now follow me, graduates. Your futures await!"

# CHAPTER TWENTY-THREE

Aligned alphabetically, we proceeded up the grand staircase toward the dining hall so that our families, who would be seated by now, could admire us as we entered. On Professor Eseer's cue, we would proceed to the stage where we would sit, facing the audience, as my father summoned each of us for the big revelation—our assignment. The first day of forever had arrived.

Our line-up was organized alphabetically by first-name, so I had the diminishing pleasure of plodding along in Lilith's far-reaching shadow. I should have tried harder with my hair. A low, lifeless pony-tail was insufficient now that I was here, in the moment.

Mason was directly behind me, tromping on my heels. He was wearing his new gift.

"Are you nervous, Marisol? You've lost your smile today."

"I'm fine, Mason. It's a wonderful day."

I responded while scouting for nearby waste bins. There was a possibility that I would hurl, and I needed to know where to aim.

"I like your tool belt. You'll be perfectly placed in Quality Control & Predictive Maintenance."

"I hope so, but I really screwed up in the trials. I only completed the first one. I guess I can only go uphill from here."

It was true that he and Naviah had had abysmal trials, but his abundant confidence and enthusiasm was admirable.

"Marisol!"

It was Creighton again. He had left his position in the line for one last chat. He was wearing an olive-colored beanie with the word COMMAND stenciled on the side. It was his gift from Duanra, and it certainly commanded my attention. I'd have to remember to thank her for that.

"We got interrupted, but I had planned to tell you that it's going to be fine. Take a deep breath," he said.

Why was it that absolutely everyone knew I was a neurological mess today?

"Do not pass out while we're on that stage, Marisol. Do you hear me? Do not embarrass me again," said Lilith.

She issued her warning without turning back or slowing down, so I ignored her.

"I'm fine, Creighton. Honestly."

Sometimes dishonesty was the best policy. In addition to a sub-optimal headache, my anxiety was at an all-time high.

"Your bracelet looks pretty on your wrist," he said softly.

"Oh, gag me," snapped Lilith. "Get back in line, Creighton, so that the rest of us can graduate."

"I'll go back to the front, but remember, Marisol, I'm always right beside you."

His monotone voice and even-keeled manner was making me seasick, and I forgot to compliment his hat.

Pausing before the entrance of the dining hall I could hear our families and friends greeting each other over excited voices. There would be a large turnout today. Any resident without station-critical responsibilities was welcome to attend, and former graduates and school-aged children were expected to be present. The dining hall was at capacity.

There was a tap on my shoulder. It was Naviah.

"Good luck!" she squealed, wrapping her arms completely around me to squeeze the nervousness out. "You'll be the first female cuvier.

You're making sea haven history here. Fist bump, jellyfish," she said, raising her knuckles to impact mine while mine stayed motionless at my side.

"If this is history, why do I feel so uncertain?"

"Because the rest of us played it safe. We know what we're getting. You're the only real gamble here, Marisol, but you'll get it. Don't sweat it."

She was holding the knitted bunny that her mother had made for her.

"Can I see your bunny?"

She passed it to me.

"Isn't it amazing? Duanra, my mother, is amazing! I didn't even know that she could make such nice things. Most probably because I have never taken the time to get to know her. I mean, it's mainly about me, right? That's how the mother/daughter dynamic was intended, for sure, but there are probably so many talents she had above that she hasn't been able to utilize here, below. I can hardly remember that life. I need to talk to her more, and I want to help her with future grad gifts, if she'll allow me to."

With each subsequent year our graduates would have less recollection of what it had been like above, until there was no firsthand knowledge beyond the curated life-walls, but there *was* a life before Aqueous, and my age group vaguely remembered it. For them it was a comfortable memory. A notion of survival, but a not unpleasant experience. The children of Nebulous had not struggled like I had. My limited time on the surface had been singularly focused on staying alive, and it remained vivid, raw.

I too had an amazing mother, like Duanra. She had smiling eyes and a melodic voice that still danced in my ears. It was a sound that continued to surround me when I needed solace, as did the scent of her hair and the softness of her skin. She lifted my spirits in her arms of recollection, like a ghost unable to cross over, reminding me that I was a lucky one. She had given me away for a chance to survive, and today, once again, I would bravely move forward without her, making her memory proud. I was happy and sad, lost and found, ignorant and wise. My tragic years on the surface left deep scars that even the most powerful ocean could not wash away. I had lost everything—my family, my identity, my name. This was something my cohort could not comprehend. Their families were here, present and participating in the celebration of their success, while mine had been abandoned beyond the darkness.

I passed the bunny back to Naviah so that she could assume her position in the line as we waited to begin our slow procession behind Amley.

"Graduates, the time to shine has arrived. I have cued the choir, so please follow Amley to your seats when the music begins, but take your time to greet residents along the way. If they try to hug you, shake your hand, or give you a jovial high five, reciprocate. Don't be stiff. Enjoy the attention. You've earned it. Now, big smiles everyone!"

I was half expecting him to insist on jazz hands as the choir launched into the Aqueous graduation song, with customized lyrics for our class. A station tradition, it was an a cappella rap/roast poking fun at the graduates on the verge of adulting.

Our feet fell in step with the humorous verses as we passed through the hatch to witness the magnificent transformation of the dining hall. The colors of the ocean, beyond the glass ceiling, had been enhanced by billowing strips of fabric in pastel hues of purple and blue to complement our newly fashioned jumpsuits. The tables had been removed and replaced with many rows of chairs to accommodate the hundreds of residents who had gathered to witness our rite of passage. My anxiety washed away as my eyes met many familiar faces, fondly expressing their admiration for me and my friends. It was a good feeling, and it would be a good day.

We had been instructed to proceed to the stage through a center aisle that had been created between the many rows of chairs. Energetically lining the aisle were Aqueous' littlest wonders—the stinkers and the flecks. They jumped and cheered and gave us high fives as we filed past. Starren was front and center to cheer on her big sister, Julip, but threw her arms around my waist instead, refusing to let go. I had to peel her off before I could proceed, but it felt great. We were treated like heroes as we worked our way to the front, proving that Eseer was right, this was our moment to enjoy. There was no need to rush.

As Amley continued to lead us, we met another graduation tradition. The remainder of the aisle was lined with former graduates, each of whom had worn their graduation jumpsuit. Standing in full salute, they proudly paved our pathway with ten years of station wisdom. It was an Aqueous rainbow of scholastic success.

The runway of handshakes and good wishes concluded with our families as we got to the front. The unofficial theme of the evening appeared to be tears and handkerchiefs, which best described the decor in the first few rows. Our parents were emotional, to say the least.

Making it onto the stage as the rapping ended, we did not sit. We had been instructed to remain standing so that we could be admired while the choir transitioned for the anthem. The dining hall lights were dimmed as the members of the choir were spotlit in white light. They silently raised their arms and eyes to the glass ceiling above, looking upward toward the water that embraced us, and beyond it to the land that had cast us away. Unified by humility, they began to sway from side to side, marking a somber tempo with their steps to lead us into song.

> *Scorched earth blooms beneath the sea*
> *For those we lost new seeds we'll be*
> *A call to save humanity*
> *An Aqueous for you and me*
>
> *Peril shames our past unjust*

*So now we live to work and trust*
*Together standing as we must*
*United below death and dust*

*Aqueous, united you'll save us*
*Aqueous, together forgave us*
*Aqueous, remembered the bravest*
*Aqueous, a heaven you've made us*

*Deep frontiers a wild new world*
*Where time and sound doth it absorb*
*No poisoned wealth to us unfurl*
*Sins washed away by thy tide's swirl*

*Raise up our eyes to pasts above*
*In hopes one day return to love*
*But 'til the day we fly the dove*
*Our hearts will beat for Aqueous*

It was a hymn for the future and a pledge to never forget. We took our seats as Professor Eseer walked onto the stage. He was followed by Dr. Pryor, Admiral Bojing, Admiral Afanasy, my mother, and my father.

"Good day, residents! Thank you for joining us to celebrate the tenth graduating class of Aqueous."

His words were met with deafening applause.

"For many of us, this day is filled with individual reflection on the days of yesteryear, when we attended a traditional school system based on a syllabus unrelated to our futures. It was difficult to understand why we needed to learn the things we studied, or what we would do once we graduated, and employment decisions were often based on geographical proximity or salary. On Aqueous, students are free from the constraints of class and wealth. We've created an ideal learning environment where teachers can identify and nurture the interests of each student to match them to rewarding life work. We have a tremendous team of talented educators who, year after year, construct amazing tutorials and lectures for our students, thereby engaging the powerful minds of our youth in preparation for today, the day of assignment. The graduates before you now are well-equipped for day-to-day station problem solving and improvement. Look at them shine before you. Our future is bright."

There was more applause as Lilith leaned toward me and whispered, "We're in the darkest depths of the ocean. Our future is dark."

"And without further ado," continued Eseer, "I will pass the mic to our esteemed Admiral Blaise, who will introduce each graduate and announce the exciting assignment that they have received."

Whispers could be heard above the crowd. This was it—the moment of truth. I spotted my mother in the sea of anticipation, but she did not appear joyful. Her expression was distressed, and she was wringing a handkerchief in her hands.

*Was she ill?*

My father rose from his perch on the stage and approached Eseer. The two men shook hands before my father accepted the mic.

"Thank you, Professor," he said. "This station, this new life, would not be possible without your hard work."

Applause.

"In fact, it takes a station to raise a child, so I would like to thank each of you. You were directly involved in the development of these fine youth. You helped to feed them, clothe them, and ensure that they had lighting, heating, clean water . . . The list is long, and as your admiral I am humbled daily by the self-sacrifice all of you make for the benefit of the greater good. We are saving the race, and we will eventually save this planet."

More applause.

"How exactly are we saving the planet by hiding down here?" Lilith whispered to me.

"I've always dreamed of surfacing," replied Mason, who had leaned across me to whisper back to her.

I shot each of them a discouraging look.

"Oh sorry, we forgot that that's your dad," Lilith said, unapologetically.

"Now, I appreciate your enthusiasm, but I implore you to please hold further applause until we've assigned the last graduate. I am told that we are proceeding alphabetically, by first name, so I will begin with Miss Amley Birch."

Amley rose from her seat to join my father near the podium.

"Hello, Amley."

"Hello, Admiral," she greeted, letting out an uncertain giggle that spurred laughter from the audience.

"You look nervous."

"Yes, very," she admitted, wringing the monogrammed gardening gloves she'd received a few minutes earlier.

"Well, there's no need for that. For those of you who know Amley, she has a keen interest in plants, mutagenesis to be exact. Her Y10 thesis involved the improved utilization of gamma rays to increase crop yield, and as a result, she has been assigned as a junior botanist under the tutelage of Florin Argro, Senior Botanical Engineer to the arboretum. Well done, Amley."

My father turned to shake her hand and then she returned to her seat.

"Next we have Mr. Anit Nossidam."

Anit rose eagerly and strode quickly to my father's side.

"Anit showed an interest in human mechanics from a young age, and despite his good health, insisted on spending hours, days, even weeks with Dr. Nyrmac in the infirmary," my father chuckled.

I looked at Felix, who, in turn, looked downward at his hands folded in his lap. Anit had spent more time with his father than Felix had, and his father was nowhere to be seen. The pain on his face was tangible.

"With an appreciation for oral appliances and big toothy grins, Anit is assigned as a dental apprentice in Orthodontics & Dentistry, located within the infirmary. Well done, Anit. Please be gentle when I have my next toothache."

Anit shook my father's hand enthusiastically, then hugged him, then turned toward the audience and bowed, before returning joyfully to his seat. There was a newfound wiggle in his step, and his delight and pride were palpable.

"Mr. Creedan Wylde, it's your turn," my father called.

Hoots and hollers escaped the audience, but from none more loudly than Felix and Etan, who whistled with ear-drum piercing intensity as Creedan stuck out his tongue and crossed the stage.

"Passionate about video games, Creedan has wasted, I mean, devoted himself to achieving the highest scores ever recorded in merstation gaming history. Dating back to Y1, Creedan chose to forgo trivial things like sleep and food to defeat every videogame challenger in the deep sea, including those aboard Sihai Longwang and Morskaia Derevnia. He is the undefeated champion in *Dragon's Cry*, *Combat Bait*, *Mariner's Quest*, and *Mermaid Savage*. His thesis involved the programming of a new game, *Badass Alpha Foxtrot*. I've played it and it's incredible; therefore, Creedan is assigned as a senior fungineer in Gaming & Amusement, working in collaboration with Charles Knarly. Together, we hope to support them in the creation of entertaining pastimes for all three merstations."

Despite the no-clapping rule, the audience went bananas as Creedan played an air guitar in the fingerless gloves he'd been given by Duanra before initiating a long, choreographed handshake with my father. It was something they'd obviously practiced beforehand. It was a cool assignment, and I was happy for him. He had a unique gift.

"Mr. Creighton Kress, I invite you to join me at the podium."

Creighton stood up, squared his broad shoulders, and walked across the stage with dignity. Never a misstep, never a falter, he was level-headed and calm, all of the time. He was never too loud or too soft, reliably correct, and notably nice.

"During his scholastic tenure on Aqueous, Mr. Kress has demonstrated sound judgement, fair-mindedness, athletic prowess, and calm leadership. He is helpful and insightful. Obtaining an academic standing of distinguished and exemplary trial scores, Creighton has been assigned as a lieutenant (junior grade) under the guidance of Commander Hark. It should be noted that this is the first time a graduate has been assigned directly to Command. You've done well, Creighton. Congratulations."

My father extended his hand to the new officer.

*Wow.*

The audience, educators, choir, and graduates stood to clap as Creighton smiled modestly in acknowledgement. He had not been defeated by Felix after all, and I wondered if he regretted his earlier actions. He turned to return to his chair, making eye contact with me as he did, and I gave him two thumbs up as we seated ourselves again.

"An admiral in the making," whispered Lilith. "You're a lucky one. Absolutely, positively, surrounded by admirals."

She was in fine form today. I certainly felt unlucky to be stuck next to her.

I zoned out as Crimson Menow crossed the stage in a colorful pair of knee-high socks, emblazoned with different types of fish, to be assigned as a junior aquatic species technician. I was still processing Creighton's assignment. I had exceeded his academic scores and arguably outperformed him during the trials. There was a high probability that I would be placed as a cuvier, and after rejecting all of the assurances from fellow trainees, I was finally starting to feel confident. The assignment might not be a longshot after all.

". . . so I am pleased to inform you that Elsby has been assigned as an early childhood caregiver. She will be working with Mrs. Keystone to ensure that our little ones have a caring start to each new day."

Elsby Fositter would become a super stinker, and that made sense. She loved little kids, and everybody knew it. Duanra had given her a soft, eight-page children's book denoting the most common animals of the deep sea.

"Etan Biggott," my father announced. "Etan has been a boisterous presence on Aqueous. I don't think I ever saw him walk as a child."

The audience murmured in agreement.

"He is a strapping young man. Strong. His physical development and staunch ideologies are unwavering," my father continued, trying to give Etan some sort of positive recognition for his poor academic standing and undisciplined behavior. "Etan has been suitably assigned as a junior custodian, working under the direct supervision of Jimmy Scrub."

Etan, wearing a pair of fuzzy slippers given to him by Duanra, grabbed and shook my father's hand violently, completely unaware that he had become the janitor.

Lilith raised a hand to her mouth, trying to stifle her laughter.

"My next introduction is someone special. Mr. Felix Nyrmac, will you please join me up here?"

Felix rose from his chair slowly and strolled across the stage. He had proudly wrapped his new scarf, made with twenty-one different colors, around his neck.

"Ever the cool one, aren't you, Mr. Nyrmac?" my father teased.

The audience chuckled.

"Slick swagger aside, many of you might be unaware that Felix has always been a sensitive and thoughtful young man."

Creedan and Etan laughed aloud, as Felix looked downward and shifted uneasily on his feet.

"As his father worked tirelessly in our infirmary, spending incredibly long hours ensuring the health and well-being of our community, Felix became a son to many of us. Certainly to me," my father confessed to Felix's surprise. "Hard-working and astute, he has achieved the highest academic scores ever recorded by MMLSSE, and his trial scores are frankly, out of this world. Felix, we know how talented you are and that you will be instrumental to this station."

Creedan and Etan were no longer laughing.

"I encourage you to let down your guard. Cast aside the sarcasm and shenanigans that you have unnecessarily shouldered because it is my absolute pleasure to announce that you've been assigned as an Aqueous diver. You will be joining the elite cuvier team as Lieutenant Nyrmac, under the direct supervision of Lieutenant Commander Keel in Sub-Command."

Felix looked shocked. He stood aghast, in total disbelief as my father pulled him in for a bromance hug.

"Congratulations, son. You deserve this."

There was a collective gasp, followed by unsettled whispers, as the audience processed the exceptional placement, and with momentary delay, they slowly remembered to clap.

"Well, this is a game-changer," Lilith purred. "But wait a second, isn't that the assignment you wanted?"

I didn't answer her. I was immobilized.

After thanking my father and nodding his appreciation toward a shocked audience, Felix pivoted and returned to his seat. Disbelief and anguish registered on his face as our eyes met. We did not need words to state the obvious. He had been awarded the assignment that I wanted, and I would be placed somewhere else.

I looked to my mother, but she looked away, letting her shoulders slump forward over hands that lay lifeless in her lap. It was a pose that was not indicative of her usual, graceful self. She was not discussing the cuvier assignment with those seated next to her, nor was she confirming or denying the attributes my father had mentioned, and she was not celebrating or balking at the achievement of Felix. There was no surprise in her posture. She had known this was coming.

I spotted Reggie near the kitchen hatch, holding a dishtowel. Graduation was a busy day for him and his team, and he was probably popping in and out during dinner prep to catch the few assignments he could. He looked bewildered. His mouth hung open, ready to refute, while his eyes darted left and right, trying to assess if the rest of the crowd was as confused as he was.

I closed my eyes. It was happening. What I had dreaded. I would not become a diver. They would never assign two cuviers in a single graduation.

Subconsciously, I registered that Felton Bytes was assigned as a programmer in Security & Intelligence, Joen Mastiv as a mobility marshal in Athletics Development, and when I opened my eyes, Julip Marble, wearing an apron embroidered with *Kiss the Cook,* was assigned as sous-chef to the kitchen.

"Now, I have a special surprise for all of you. As some of you may have noticed, there was a trainee missing," my father explained as he stepped off of the stage and walked toward the hatch connecting the bethel. "But missing he is no longer."

Utilizing crutches, Kyro Syberg emerged in the doorway. Wearing a modified jumpsuit we could see that his left leg was casted from hip to toe. Flanked on each side by his parents, who were physically supporting him, his head was bandaged and he was squinting.

"Now we know why the Aqueous trials are a closely guarded secret," said Mason.

Felix jumped to his feet and started to chant, "Kyro, Kyro, Kyro, Kyro . . ." and the rest of the Y10s joined him.

Kyro tried to smile, but the pain from the lights and the sound was visible.

"Okay. Okay. I know you are excited, but I don't think this much noise is a good idea. Reduce the lights, please," instructed my father, to no one in particular.

The lights dimmed immediately, and I, along with my peers, quietly sat down.

"Kyro had a bad fall . . ."

*That was an underwater understatement.*

". . . and as a result, spent some time in the infirmary, but we are assured by Dr. Nyrmac that he will make a full recovery, and as such, has been assigned as a robotics engineer in Robotics & Automation."

We couldn't contain our happiness and cheered wildly for Kyro, who we hadn't seen since the League Trial. He was shockingly battered, but alive.

"Shhhhhh," reminded my father, silencing us again.

"That was sweet, but can we hurry up? I look my best in limelight," whispered Lilith.

"Green is your color," replied Mason.

*Shut up!*

My father gingerly hugged Kyro before he was led away through the bethel, probably back to the infirmary. It was a brief, but beautiful reunion, and although I was relieved to learn that he would be alright, I questioned why our evaluators would have allowed such risk.

Making his way back to the stage, my father predictably assigned Leop Gneiss to Mining & Minerals, but I didn't catch his title because of Lilith's interruption.

"Finally," she said.

She rose from her seat before being called to flamboyantly straighten her jumpsuit and toss her hair.

"Miss Lilith Brizo, an accomplished artist, dancer, and songstress, will be performing for us at the Aqueous tenth anniversary."

Lilith glided toward my father as he announced her upcoming performance. Upon reaching the podium she grabbed both of his hands and planted a kiss on each of his cheeks. It was nauseatingly extra and shockingly awkward for the admiral.

"Lilith's passion for the arts made her assignment straightforward. She is assigned as a senior director to Visual Arts & Performance, and will be collaborating with our educators and Atelier to create events that entertain us and highlight the impressive talent onboard. Congratulations, Lilith."

Lilith gave a deep, dramatic curtsey before pirouetting back to her seat. It was my turn.

"This next assignment, as you would expect, is near and dear to my heart. Miss Marisol Blaise, can you please join me over here?"

I rose from my seat and walked toward him. Any rustle or disturbance from the fidgety crowd, eager to move onward to food and refreshments, stopped abruptly. There was intense interest in the admiral's daughter's assignment. Especially now that her dream job had been awarded to someone else.

"As you all now know, Marisol is not our biological daughter. She was a precious gift, received and cherished by her mother and me on the eve of the Aqueous launch. She is an accomplished girl who we have been blessed to care for. Multi-talented, she has achieved the highest academic and trial scores for a female trainee, ever, but her greatest strength is her kindness and appreciation for everyone and everything around her. She is courageous. She is honorable. She is strong."

And yet there I stood, struggling to harness the necessary strength to accept his next words.

"She wants to be a diver, and she'd be a great one, but I made a pledge to her biological mother that I would do my best to keep her safe . . ."

His words were choked out by his tears.

"Marisol, you would be an asset in any department, but your command of math and science, as evidenced in your thesis and academic scores, have identified you as someone needed to mentor the rest. You've been assigned as a professor and will work in conjunction with Professor Eseer in the offices of MMLSSE."

Through a neutral expression I looked at my father. There was a subtle tilt of his head to one side as if to say he was sorry. There was no cheering or excitement. I nodded my acknowledgement to him and he gave me an awkward hug that I stiffly accepted with arms hanging at my side. Standing raw and exposed, I looked toward the audience, trying to summon gratitude, only to find the remnants of my broken dream reflected in their blank expressions. Numb, I waded back to my seat through heavy silence, taking my undesirable place on the Aqueous graduated scale.

"Be thankful that Amley got the arboretum. We can't have everything that we want, Marisol," Lilith whispered.

"And thank you, Lilith, for the worst pep talk ever," I whispered back.

I sat in silent reflection. Instead of accomplishing something with my life, I had been sentenced to a lifetime of assisting others accomplish something with theirs. My existence would become mundane repetition, where I regurgitated the information I had already digested to feed it to others. In fact, this was exactly the opposite of graduation. It was never-ending purgatory where every year I would arrive at the exact same place.

I pondered this as the expected assignments for the remaining Y10s were announced and the ceremony came to a close. Mason Joiner was assigned to Quality Control & Predictive Maintenance, Murphy Stout became our poultry producer, Naviah Hark received her Atelier assignment, Purity Myre would work in Desalinization & Decontamination, Sugar Tao (who had extended her stay on Aqueous) would intern as a dietary analyst, and Yarrow Prunen would become the cultural curator to the grand pavilion.

Sensing my irritation at her earlier comment, Lilith leaned closer to me and conceded by saying, "It was the worst pep talk ever. Your assignment sucks, Blaise, and the only sensible thing to do now is to deploy the pods, open the airlocks, and let the entire station implode."

And in that moment I decided that I liked her and replied, "I'm in."

## CHAPTER TWENTY-FOUR

Following the most unsettling graduation ceremony since Aqueous inception, the choir, accompanied by our recreational jazz band, launched into an awkward rendition of Matchbox Twenty's, "How Far We've Come." Intended to mirror the jubilation of the crowd, the frenzied tempo was meant to inspire our audience to sing along and dance as we exited. Conversely, it enhanced the already cringeworthy atmosphere that had congealed our convocation. The crowd forced some disingenuous smiles and side stepped to discombobulated, mistimed claps as we exited ahead of them toward the grand pavilion.

The refreshments served in the grand pavilion would allow Reggie and his team to quickly flip the dining room for our formal dinner. The tables needed to be returned and set, but it wouldn't take them long, so I broke away from the line and proceeded toward the trees as soon as I passed through the hatch. I could not deploy the pods, open the airlocks, and let the entire station implode as Lilith had suggested, but I was tired of aquatic life, and I needed to escape and hide. I prayed to awaken from my nightmare and find myself at the surface, reunited with the sun.

I found a secluded spot to sit and collect my thoughts in an earthly alcove beneath some trees, where my disappointment could trickle away on the sound of an engineered stream, but I had barely sat before I was found.

"Marisol, are you okay?"

It was my father's "son," Felix. He knelt down and then sat beside me.

"Yes, I will be fine. Don't worry. I know it's not your fault, Felix, and that you'll be fantastic as a cuvier. I am intelligent enough to understand that."

"I had no idea this was being considered. If I had, I would have told them to give it to you."

"I should have predicted this. It made my parents so uncomfortable whenever I talked about being a diver, but Felix, my father was correct in saying that your talents extend far beyond how you see yourself. This is not a mistake. You earned it, and I don't want my own disappointment to detract from your achievement."

Felix had been my strongest competitor, but he was a good person. I had lost sight of that over the years and did not want to do so again.

"I think there's more to it, Marisol."

"Like what?"

"There's one major difference between us that you have overlooked."

"And what's that?"

I tried to tamp my defensiveness as I braced for another lecture on gender-based ability.

"I'm disposable."

"Disposable? What do you mean? No one is disposable, Felix. We're on the brink of extinction."

"Cuviers are tasked with dangerous operations. There's no room for error and things can go badly. If something were to happen to me there would be minimal impact on our community."

I was dumbfounded by his nonchalant attitude toward his own mortality.

"I have no parents, no siblings. If I die in the line of duty, they simply train a new diver."

"Felix, that is not true. You have all of us—your friends—and you have a father who loves you very much."

"Not sure about that, Marisol. Where was he today?"

It was true that I hadn't seen Dr. Nyrmac during the ceremony, not that he wasn't there, it was a large crowd, but it was difficult to argue positively on his behalf even though I could not accept that he did not love his son.

"He must have been in the audience."

"No, you're wrong. He told me this morning that he would be unable to attend. Something about reorganizing the apothecary cabinet to ensure that the medications had not expired. It's most important work, you know."

The sarcastic armor guarding Felix's heart had cracked.

"He loves you, Felix, but he doesn't know how to show you."

"You still think so? Because it sounds like he loves Anit."

I reached over and grabbed his hand. It was an involuntary, natural gesture, unplanned and sudden, that made neither of us uncomfortable. We needed comfort, but my newfound disappointment was far less painful than the lifetime of rejection Felix had endured.

"Hey! What's going on back here? Do I need to explain to you two how a party works?" It was Naviah. She had discovered us.

I let my hand fall from his. We had had a brief escape, an interlude from our aquatic life to allow our disappointments to wash away, and now it was over.

"We're taking a moment to understand what happened back there," Felix explained. "I mean, you being assigned in Atelier. That was a bit of a stretch."

"Funny. But in all seriousness, do you think Murphy had been dreaming to become Captain Chicken?"

Murphy walked up to us.

"Murph, be sure to save me every single feather that hits that floor, okay?"

"Every single one, Nav," he confirmed, draping his gift from Duanra, a large yellow blanket with the word *HAPPY* written across it in bold pink lettering, over his shoulders like a cape.

"And only geniuses get to be Malice, so get over it, Blaise. You're officially the smartest. And you, Felix," Naviah continued. "It is my opinion that you've been overly rewarded for years of unruly, bratty behavior that I, and many others, have had to endure. Both of you stand up right now, get happy, like Murphy's blanket says, and start thinking about residents who aren't named Marisol or Felix."

Felix and I shared a concerned glance for Naviah. All of the hours she had spent being a supportive friend must have worn her out. She was losing it.

"You're right, Naviah. I regret the way I mistreated my peers, and I won't be behaving that way any longer."

"Finally! You know how long I've waited to hear that?"

"Too long," he said.

"True, and ya know what else I want you to say?"

"I don't."

"Mercy!"

She leaned in and gave him a strong pinch on the arm.

"Ouch!" he wailed. "Mercy! What has gotten into you?"

"I've never had a brother, so I wanted to see what that felt like."

Rubbing his arm, he turned to Murphy and said, "I'd be careful with that one, if I were you. Man, that hurt."

Murphy looked at Naviah, dreamily.

"And congratulations on your assignment, buddy. It's the perfect match for you. Those chicks are cute, and you've always wanted a pet. You're going to enjoy it."

Refocusing on Felix, Murphy replied, "I know, right? So cute and fluffy. I already have ideas for a new coop."

Naviah rolled her eyes. She obviously liked him, but couldn't understand why.

I hadn't considered where Murphy would be assigned, but his

happy demeanor could not be chipped away by the pecking order of Aqueous. Egg and poultry production was important, and Murphy could find joy anywhere. Those were some lucky hens.

"Hey! Felix!"

It was Anit, rounding the corner. I had chosen a pathetic hiding spot.

"I'm glad I found you. Things got awkward back there, and I wanted to clarify that I didn't spend hours, days, weeks with your father in the infirmary. It wasn't like that at all."

"It's alright, Anit. I'm happy that the two of you have a shared passion."

"No, he wasn't there. I spent most of my time with Dr. Weksa. I hardly ever saw your dad."

"That's impossible. He had to be there. That's the only place he ever is."

"Here. There. I don't care. Can we get back to graduation now?" Naviah interrupted. "All this drama has made me hungry angry."

"It's hangry. You're hangry. Hangry was a thing," I said.

"Whatever, Blaise," she replied.

We stood, allowing her to lead us from the sanctity of the trees. We headed back toward the crowd clambering around light-blue jumpsuits, and I could hear the graduates recounting the emotions they felt as their assignments had been announced. It was time for me to embrace my future and be thankful for the honor bestowed upon me. It could have been much worse—a life sentence in Biosolids & Compost, the world's largest toilet.

I spotted Creighton chatting with his parents and my own.

"Pardon me everyone, but I should go and see my folks."

Excusing myself, I left Naviah, Murphy, Anit, and Felix to be congratulated by others and strode purposefully across the room as an important professor does.

"Hello, Officer. Should I salute?"

It was my best attempt at post-grad humor to put the others at ease.

"I don't know, Professor Blaise, you may outrank me."

*Professor Blaise . . .*

The sound of Creighton saying my new title made me nauseous, and an uneasy giggle escaped from my lips, giving my mother the false impression that I liked it. Her shoulders relaxed, and she smiled genuinely for the first time since my party.

"Well done, Marisol. I couldn't be happier for you," said Mrs. Kress.

"It's a remarkable day for everyone. Prestigious placements for an exceptional group," stated Captain Kress.

"I agree. I hope all of the graduates were pleased. It's not an easy job, you know. Looking into the hopeful eyes of an eager student and announcing their future to the entire station. It's a lot like jumping out of an airplane. If that chute doesn't open, you can't go back," my father said.

His comment was met with laughter from the captain and our mothers, but Creighton and I stared at him. There weren't any airplanes underwater.

"If you don't mind, Marisol and I should use this time to congratulate our friends. We'll join you at dinner?" Creighton suggested.

"Of course," replied my mother. "Enjoy yourselves. We'll save you some seats when we move through. I hear there's candied seaweed on the menu tonight."

*Seriously?*

I was no longer a child. This situation could not be remedied with sweets, but I reminded myself that my mother had been under duress too, and that it was better to smile with forced enthusiasm than create a scene.

Creighton guided me by my elbow away from the group, through the crowd, toward a vacant table near the glass. He did not seek out the other Y10s.

"Are you alright? I can't believe they gave your assignment to that sneaky little Felix," he seethed. "If my father had anything to do with this I will find out, Marisol, and I will fix it."

I had never seen Creighton upset.

"You look handsome in your new hat, and Felix isn't sneaky."

"What?"

"Your hat," I repeated. "It suits you."

"We're having a crisis here, Marisol, and you're thinking about my hat?"

"Listen, like you, I was initially upset that Felix became a diver and I did not, but I've decided to accept it. Felix is talented. His scores were astronomically high, and he didn't have the easiest childhood."

"Neither did you."

"True, but I have parents who tell me ad nauseam that I am wonderful. Felix has raised himself. I'm choosing to be happy for him, and to be grateful for the assignment I got. Besides, nobody argues with a professor. Not even a lieutenant."

"Alright then. If you're satisfied, I will not object."

"Thank you, Creighton. Your support means a lot to me, and educating trainees will be fun. I'm going to have a blast."

It was a lie. The biggest lie I had ever told, and I was assigned to it.

"You know what? Your parents are right, you are wonderful, and you deserve to hear it ad nauseum. You've been assigned for less than an hour and you're already teaching me things."

He moved uncomfortably close to me, causing me to wonder if he knew me at all. He was too easily convinced, and I did not appreciate his ill-timed, public advance. My heart had shattered, but he couldn't feel the shards beneath his shoes.

"We should join our friends," I chided.

"Ah. Okay," he said. Sensing my need for space, he stepped back, looking hurt. "Lead the way, Professor."

And lead I would. Quashing my disappointment, I would lead with lies and deception when those around me needed my untruths.

I would lead future trainees to believe that they could achieve their dreams. I would lead the girls onboard toward a shatterproof ceiling and the residents that cared about me to believe that I was satisfied. I would lead all of them with altruistic dishonesty, toward uninsured happiness. All but one, that is—Felix.

Felix would not be willingly led. He scrutinized Creighton and me as we approached the group, appraising our welfare and stripping away my falsehoods with each and every step. It was futile to be fake. He understood how I was feeling. After a decade under the sea, I had finally been crushed.

## CHAPTER TWENTY-FIVE

Life is a journey of reward and loss that swells and retreats with the tide. An infinite game of victory and defeat, it surges forward with bounty only to renege soon after, leaving vast beaches of emptiness as it recoils. I combed the empty sands of my aspiration to find that I had been left with insignificant treasures—a new title, an office. Sand dollar tokens left by the tide, after it swept away my dream.

It was the morning of the anniversary, and I was still adjusting to defeat. My time following grad had been spent preparing for my inescapable destiny. In addition to the salty sting of failure, my future contained an additional element of aggravation—trainees. There were shoals of pupils, circling, eager to feed on an inexperienced professor, and I had been informed by Professor Eseer that I would be instructing Y6s. They were the most voracious of them all.

Achieving independence from their parents, the Y6s were notoriously ungovernable. Their individual mini-pod allocations highlighted their newfound freedom, and this, in combination with the discovery that their refusal to participate and know-it-all attitudes were not easily counteracted, likened them to a battery of barracudas. I would be caught in their riptide, waiting to be bitten.

Reminiscent of our first week onboard, Aqueous students received a week long hiatus between the completion of their year and the Aqueous Anniversary. It was a time of celebration, recalibration, and relocation. We shuffled pods during this week, and as such, I had been moved into a propulsion-pod.

Situated in the MMLSSE corridor, my new pod was mobile capable with a cockpit that I would undoubtedly never utilize. Behind the cockpit was a small lounge with fixed seating and a low table. My bed was no longer above my desk. It was farther back, in a separate room, behind the lounge. The pod was considerably larger than my mini-pod, and in the event that I ever needed space for double occupancy, a future partner would fit. The bathroom was the same as MP124.

After receiving my new address, I had slipped away from the after-grad dinner to confirm that my beads and dress had been safely transferred. Then, showering off any last remnants of my adolescent hopes and dreams, I attempted to fall asleep.

I failed to sleep after graduation. My mind raced. I re-evaluated my thesis, relived the trials, and searched my memory for any fault to validate my circumstance. I stared outward through the glass until the exterior lighting became brighter, signaling the return of surface sunshine and the commencement of morning routines. I had found the view ironic. It was the same as MP124, but on the other side of the labs.

Following that restless night I spent the entire week in my office, preparing lectures and demonstrations for the Y6 sea monsters that would soon consume me. Professor Eseer had given me the former lesson plans of Professor Proem.

"Don't let them blow themselves up," Eseer had warned.

I was to corral them in menial lab one and focus on activities involving water, soil, and light. It would be their first departure into lab work, and I needed to keep it simple and safe. Anything noncombustible would suffice, although my own burnout was likely.

Underwhelmed and exasperated, my predecessor, Proem, had requested permanent reassignment to any department. An expert mathematician and chemist, he was seconded by Desalinization &

Decontamination until he deemed himself to be fit to return to educational development, working with the age group of his choice. His burnout rate? One hundred percent over ten years. Not good news, but I would undertake my assignment without prejudice. My title of professor had been instantly assigned, but the act of becoming one could take years.

When does learning end? It doesn't. It's an infinite quest through a universe of endless time and space. It's a voyage of discovery toward an unreachable horizon. Perhaps satisfying the inherent curiosity of children would become my passion, but that was unpredictable. There was no benchmark. I had no younger siblings. Either way, I needed to brace for the Y6 Charybdis that would whirl through the lab hatchway in my imminent future.

Jostled from thoughts of my unfortunate situation, there was movement beyond my transparent hatch. Naviah was banging frantically while Lilith stood beside her. I tapped the release, granting access.

"Ah ha! I knew we'd find you holed up in here," Naviah said.

"Nice digs," commented Lilith, surveying my small, but private office. A merstation rarity.

"Look at you," Naviah continued. "Unkempt hair, casual SIDs . . . Have you even had a shower?"

"Of course I've had a shower."

"Today?"

"Maybe not today."

Naviah looked incredible. Gone was her former youthful, whimsical style, having been replaced by the smart silhouette of a dressmaker. Her black, mid-length shift dress had three-quarter-length sleeves cuffed in white to match the white Peter Pan collar. She wore black Mary Janes, and her hair was piled high, tied in place with a black-and-white scarf.

"This is worse than you expected. I say we abandon her and go and enjoy ourselves," suggested Lilith.

"Grab her," ordered Naviah, lunging toward me. "This calls for emergency services. We'll swing by Malice Palace and grab her formal SIDs, then drag her over to my place for an atelier intervention."

Pushing me through the exit, I tried to explain that I only needed to wash my face and change into formals, but they would not listen. I resigned to follow behind them as they walked briskly in the direction of my pod, and as I did Lilith looked over her shoulder at me with disdain.

"If you make me late for my performance I will make it my mission to ensure that every Y6 arrives in your lab with a surging scalp of head lice," she threatened.

"Head lice was eradicated before we boarded. There is no more head lice," I informed. "It doesn't exist."

"Then I will bring it back so that you can get it. You can count on that, Marisol Blaise."

I had forgotten that it was her big night, and that the performance that would justify her assignment as the senior director to Visual Arts & Performance. She had spent countless hours preparing unique renditions of popular hit music with the accompaniment of the Aqueous choir and jazz band.

"I promise I won't make you late. I'm looking forward to your performance this evening. I think you'll do great," I said, attempting to convey encouragement through my tired tone.

"Do you think so? I mean, of course I will. It's not an easy medley, you know. The range is unachievable for even the most accomplished vocalists."

"Well, if anyone can pull this off, it's you," I stated truthfully.

Arriving at my airlock she turned to me and admitted, "I'm nervous."

Standing before me was the Lilith I liked the best—the real one—so I smiled at her, grabbed her hand, and offered encouragement.

"Don't be nervous. You could belt out those songs with laryngitis, and we'd still be impressed. We are well aware that your singing would sound better than ours, even if you were submerged under water. You can't ruin this. It's impossible. You are Lilith Brizo the Great, so enjoy yourself. Have fun showing off like you normally do."

"You're absolutely right, I am great. Thank you, Marisol. Unfortunately, you are not. We have a lot to do to improve your look in a short period of time."

*And just like that, snarky Lilith was back.*

We descended my airlock, so that I could take a quick shower and change into the black and white MMLSSE formal SIDs required for the evening. As part of the Aqueous ten year celebration, all residents were issued new formalwear, and I would be wearing an outfit to reflect my new assignment. It consisted of a black Nehru jacket with corded black, mandarin collar, matching straight-legged pants and black ballerina flats. It was the first reissue of formal SIDs since station inception, and a massive undertaking for Atelier which Naviah was now proudly part of.

Realizing too late that there was no time to dry my hair, the girls towel dried it before marcelling its natural waviness in aloe vera gel that Lilith ran and stole from the arboretum. They partially pinned it back in a vintage style that looked surprisingly good. There was no denying that they had skills.

Appearance rectified, we traversed the level toward Atelier where Naviah's pod was located. Naviah's pod contained a menagerie of handicrafts fashioned from abandoned objects intended for compost or combustion. It was her imagination brought to life to beautify the station.

Atelier pods had unique workspaces specific for textile work and storage. There was a large table in the center of the pod, littered with swatches, scissors, and measuring tapes. Hanging in a nook beyond her sewing table was the most incredible jumpsuit I had ever seen. Sleek and shiny, it had thin shoulder straps and a plunging back and neckline. Far racier than the conservative, gender neutral attire we were used to, it was bright, shimmering white, having been encrusted with thousands of crystals.

"What is that?"

"Don't touch that, Marisol. It's mine. Tonight I will outshine you all," Lilith stated, overconfidently.

"Wow! I've never seen anything like it before."

"It's a basic jumpsuit, but I used a silk, instead of the linen, jute, or cotton we usually get. Then I adorned it with polished salt crystals, courtesy of Desalinization & Decontamination. See, I did pay attention in science, but only when it applied to my true love of fashion and design," Naviah explained. "Sadly, most of my efforts will be recycled after this evening, so be sure to be photographed from all angles, Lilith."

"That won't be a problem," she replied, grabbing the garment and disappearing into the bedroom to change.

"As for you, Marisol, I do apologize that I don't have a glorious, glitzy garment for you to wear, but because you're my best friend I did make you something. You get a one-of-a-kind hair clip."

Naviah opened a drawer underneath her table and produced a thin bedazzled hair pin adorned with the same polished rock salt that covered Lilith's jumpsuit.

"Completely professional and unassuming, I think it's the perfect complement to your new MMLSSE formals, and it will blend effortlessly with the alluring hairdo you're sporting tonight."

*An alluring professor? Impossible.*

"If it's a hit, I plan to create one for each of the female faculty and cut smart-looking pocket squares for the men. Here, let me position it for you," she offered, walking toward me with clip in hand.

Naviah slid the clip into my hair, above my ear, in the concave of a slick, aloe wave, and curious to see my reflection, I crossed her work space toward the full length mirror that had been installed for resident fittings. Most pods, including my own, had one tiny mirror above the sink. I was unaccustomed to seeing my full self, and even more shocked when I looked toward my reflection and there was an adult starring back. A purposeful, nonsensical, complete adult, and I was pleased by her professor-esque appearance. I was appropriate and pretty.

"Isn't it incredible what clothing can do?"

Lilith emerged from the bedroom, in a flash of beaded light, and answered, "You mean what clothing can partially do. It takes some pretty fierce women to make any clothes sing. Now let's get going. I have a show to do."

## CHAPTER TWENTY-SIX

A party can be a group of people with a united purpose or a social gathering of invited guests amused by conversation, food, and entertainment. The Aqueous tenth anniversary was both. It was a celebration of life by a group united through death and a social moment to rejoice and remember what sparked their collaboration.

After ensuring that the costumes were in order, Naviah and I delivered Lilith to the bethel where she would warm up before taking the stage. As an assignee to Atelier, Naviah had backstage access to the grand pavilion, which had been closed for two days in preparation for the big event. It would be the setting for all performances and speeches, prior to the buffet and dance in the dining hall. A special night, the anniversary would not only commemorate our last year of achievement, it would recount a decade of tenure before forecasting our bright future.

Due to high attendance, tonight would be standing room only. Large screens had been erected to broadcast the events in the grand pavilion to the overflow seating in the dining hall, but with Naviah's backstage access, we claimed prime spots next to the stage where we would see Lilith clearly.

Over the last two days, the grand pavilion had been completely transformed. Thousands of fragments of borosilicate glass had been suspended from the ceiling to twinkle like stars in an unknown sky. Golden up-lighting, in memoriam of morning dawn, cast a warm radiance onto dormant life-walls. The rain wall had been turned off, and the observation ponds had been illuminated in vibrant pink. The usual fish had been replaced with thousands of tiny jellyfish, bobbing about in ignorant bliss. The trees in the discovery gardens had been wrapped in white, flowering clematis, and where there were no trees, ceiling-height spires had been erected and wound in the same flowering plant. An elevated, circular stage had been installed in the center of the room, and its edges mimicked a jagged, rocky mountaintop. We would be transported to the surface tonight.

Instruments were visible on stage, and a beautiful woman sat erect at the piano. It was Lilith's mother. An accomplished pianist, she would play continuously, effortlessly, as everyone arrived. Yarrow, who was nearby, tablet in hand and headset on head, would cue Lilith's mother to begin playing soon. I could only image the week that he had had as the newly assigned cultural curator.

"Naviah, this is incredible. How were you able to pull this off? The construction, the flowers, the jellyfish? It must have taken teams of residents and months of planning."

"A little magic, and the combined efforts of Manufacturing & Technology, Atelier, the arboretum, the kitchen, and mothers."

"Our mothers?"

"Yup. Duanra's creative eye combined with Empyreal's power of persuasion. They were a dream team. My mother is blowing my mind lately. She's such a siren. And your mom, as usual, flexed. This took an enormous amount of resources, and without her strong-arming the departments, we never would have been able to convince Command to allocate the necessary items. Fortunately, it's all recyclable. The flowers will remain growing in the discovery gardens, providing happiness and beauty; the glass fragments will be melted down and refabricated; the spires and stage are comprised of materials needed by both Manufacturing & Technology and Quality Control & Predictive Maintenance, so they will be dismantled and sent back tomorrow; the jellyfish, so sea-flipping cool, were Yarrow's idea, and they will become fertilizer, candies, green fluorescent protein for medical research, or diapers."

"Diapers?"

"Diapers."

I felt a tad guilty. Naviah and I had been so invested in ourselves that we hadn't noticed the incredible things our mothers had done to enhance our existence. I needed to commend everyone involved in this special day, especially my mom.

Alfrid, Naviah's mentor, was across from us, double- and triple-checking the room from the opposite side of the stage. He was such an elegant man—private and single.

"Have you enjoyed working with Alfrid?"

"I haven't seen him much."

"But this is such a huge undertaking."

"He gave me checklists, and I had a team, plus input from Lilith and Yarrow. He's been busy conducting cuvier-assisted scouts of the kelp forests."

"Why?"

"Because the botanists have sown hundreds of square nautical miles of it to suck up $CO_2$, but it could also be a game changer for textiles, depending on the variety. Wait until you see the new mycelium SIDs. They're mind blowing."

"But why now?"

"I don't know. I'd like to think it's because he wanted to get out of here. He finally has a capable assistant."

She was more than capable. She'd been born for this.

"And as long as the costumes hold together and the props remain in position, our work here is done."

"Then it's time to party."

"Hardy! Until the performers return everything to me in the morning, that is. That will be the opposite of a party, and speaking of which, they will be taking their places shortly, after the opening of the hatch."

Murphy arrived.

"How'd you get through?"

"Same as you. I'm the VIP guest of Naviah Hark," he answered. "But I can't stay long. I'll watch the performance then run back to my pod, change, put the chickens to bed, change again, and come back to eat," he explained, exasperated.

It was a hectic evening for many, but his new formal SIDs, consisting of an incredible bomber jacket, black polo, white chinos, and black shoes, hid his frantic state. He looked good.

"You'll probably miss the speeches, but they'll be boring anyway," Naviah said, forgetting that it was my father who gave them. "Be sure to lay your SIDs flat on the bed so that they don't wrinkle while you're with the chicks."

Somewhere between the trials and now they had transitioned into a little old couple.

"How's your assignment going?" I asked Murphy.

"It's messy, but the hatchlings have imprinted on me, and now they chirp whenever I arrive. I chirp back, and then we all chirp together. It's so fulfilling, Marisol. I love them."

We didn't often have hatchlings. The hens provided a few eggs, but were mainly kept as a contingency. Most meat and poultry, including eggs, were grown in Proteins & Cloning.

Naviah rolled her eyes and jealously admitted, "I think he likes them more than me."

It was a possibility. Captain Chicken was a proud poultry papa. Just another satisfied graduate, proving that the Aqueous Assignment Committee never gets it wrong. Except with me, of course. They ruined my life.

Yarrow signaled the piano and the hatch opened, allowing residents to pour in. Mason emerged from the crowd and approached us. It looked like he had lost weight.

"We finally get a break. I can't believe it. They've had me doing an inventory of manufactured items, and I can't find anything. Where is the so-called surplus everyone is talking about? It's like we've been robbed."

"Have you looked in Aux? There's oodles of space over there," suggested Naviah.

"I didn't think of that, but that's a good idea. Maybe I can pilot my pod over there and save some steps. I've nearly worn out my new shoes."

He held up his foot to prove that the tread on his soles was depleted.

"Did either of you see Felix or Creighton? I expected them to join us," I said.

Mason shook his head and Murphy stated, "If they don't have feathers, I haven't seen them."

It had been a busy week. New assignees had frantically scrambled to understand and assimilate to their new roles. We hadn't had time to connect, especially now that some of us were housed on different levels. Creighton had moved to the OP corridor, and Felix now lived near Sub-Command. It was doubtful that they would be able to squeeze through to stand with us now that the grand pavilion had filled up and the festivities were about to begin. We would have to reconnect with them later, in the dining hall.

The lighting in the room faded to black as the sound of the piano was replaced by the mournful chant of the emerging choir. They had circled up, in single file, from somewhere beneath the stage.

"Wait a second," I said. "How did they get under there?"

"They walked in with the crowd in black capes. You didn't notice? Lilith passed close by and winked at us."

"Lilith, discreet? No way."

Naviah elbowed me and laughed.

"There's an entrance to the underside of the stage at the back. They staggered their arrival and entered one by one, ditching the capes once inside. It gave them more time to warm up and less time to be squeezed together underneath. Impressed?"

"So impressed, and so aware that I could not have organized this. Magic is your department."

"I can't take all the credit. Yarrow came up with the overall theme which is a nod to Mother Earth's gifts: air, fire, and water. The show is spectacular."

And as the show started we stood, shoulder to shoulder in solidarity, in almost complete darkness as the choir continued to circle the outer perimeter of the stage. Their swaying silhouettes were illuminated minimally, unearthly, by exterior lighting permeating the glass walls, and the band, who I hadn't even noticed until they began to play, was being hoisted above the choir on a central, hydraulic platform.

The hoisting of the band caused Yarrow to cue an interior spotlight to focus our attention on Lilith, who was lifted even higher into the air and draped in an endlessly long, white smock. The choir, similarly clad, continued to sway below her as the glass fragments turned vibrant blue and the edges of the stage greened like the windward side of a mountain. The pools responded too, and swirled to aquamarine while the white clematis on the trees and spires yellowed. Then the life-walls were strummed into action, pixelating to powder blue perfection as white clouds formed upon them and drifted across the room.

The audience was mesmerized, barely noticing the little stinkers, each led by an older fleck, emerging from the kitchen. They had created colorful, bird-like creatures on extendable poles that they proudly waved above the audience. We were back on solid ground, terrestrial once more, but in this seemingly healthy world we knew that Lilith, our beacon of hope about to sing, was doomed.

Oh World, are you here my friend?
I need to know this is not the end
Cause I need you
I can heed you

Can you forgive, can you wait for me?
I'm doing better, and I want you to see
That I fear you
I'm dear to you

There was a time I was lost and alone
But I'm doing better, can I come back home?
There was a time when I was young
I was reckless and cruel having too much fun

Oh World! Can you believe in me?
Oh God, I just need you to be
My haven
My salvation

I miss the sun, the skies, the air
The grass so green, your kiss, your care
Please don't turn your back on me
Cause I've improved and you will see

Oh World! You'll be proud of me
Oh World, I know that we can be
Together
Forever . . .

The song continued, verse after verse, pleading for forgiveness and
pledging to change, but as it concluded the birds vanished and Lilith

was lowered to the stage. Dimming the lights once again we were returned to darkness as somber drums alluded to our misfortune ahead.

The dark interlude was an intentional pause for reflection on the incredible life we had enjoyed before human destruction thrust us into chaos. Residents in the audience began holding hands, clinging to each other as if they could cling to the past. Many wept. Some wept for lost families and familiar homes, some wept for animals big and small, some wept for wind and wild abandon, some wept for the horizon and what lay beyond, but together they wept for the sun and the life it had perpetuated. A sun that had not been forgiving.

The drums, beating us out of our solace, quickened, creating a violent transition to the next piece of our story. The lights came up at once, red, causing the stage to appear volcanic. Flames engulfed the life-walls, and the world burned as Lilith, now clothed in a garnet robe, swung on silks above the crowd to lyrics of "Burning Down The House," by The Talking Heads.

Soaring above us like a resident phoenix, she spectacularly delivered a painful message—we did this to ourselves. There had been ample, disregarded warning before we arrogantly chose greedy pursuits over the well-being of our planet. Images of luxury cars, closets of clothes, and the factories producing them, polluting the air and water, flashed upon the screens. We viewed wasted food being tossed into dumpsters while refugees of rising water starved. There were images of fires, floods, and melting ice. It was a shocking montage of the well-known events that inspired Aqueous. We, the audience, had burned down the planet. We had burned down our house.

Concluding the song at the center of the stage, Lilith fell dramatically to the ground. The red silks cascaded downward, around her, and the choir rushed to her aid feigning distress and disorder, but like a phoenix rising from the ash, she stood again, emerging from the choir in her silvery, shimmering jumpsuit.

A guitar introduced the next song, and with the first clap of the melody the lighting changed from red to blue. We were back under-water and safe once more, in our habitat below the ocean. Cheers and applause rang forth with the recognition of the song: David Bowie's and Queen's iconic collaboration, "Under Pressure." White circles of light were repeatedly cast up the spires and trees, disappearing into the ceiling of glass like bubbles rising to the surface. Here we were, ten years later, under the pressure to remember, the pressure to im-prove, the pressure to survive.

Lilith's sexy jumpsuit shimmered like water on her skin as she moved around the stage, belting out the lyrics. I was enchanted by her performance and her ability to morph, effortlessly, from one charac-ter to another. She captivated the audience through her music and her motion. She was a storyteller, a true artist, and the show seemed flawless until a panicked Yarrow approached us.

"Naviah, we have a crisis. The flecks forgot their props for their tribute—*Living the Sea Life*. They're still in the arts & crafts room, and Mrs. Brightly is ineffectively rehearsing without them. To make matters worse, Dr. Pryor forgot to bring the tablet with the admi-rals' speech, and now she's occupied entertaining our delegates from Morskaia Derevnia and Sihai Longwang. We need the props for the kids and the tablet for the teleprompter. Help me."

Lilith sang on, unaware that there could be hiccups in the eve-ning's scheduled events, which, by way of her new assignment, she was ultimately responsible for. The audience, engaged and enter-tained, was also ignorant to the potential disruption as the digital bubbles floating upwards filled with images of Duanra Hark's face, causing gut-wrenching laughter, most notably from the commander. Duanra's inability to handle pressure had been suitably synced with the lyrics of the song.

"Ha, ha, ha! That's so funny," laughed Naviah, before quickly re-membering that we had a crisis to solve. "Oh, sorry. But did you see my mom up there? It's like she's a celebrity."

Yarrow and I stared back at her without answering.

"Okay, I get it. Nobody panic. We can rectify this. I know exactly where the props are, so I will grab those while Marisol grabs the tablet. It's in Pryor's office, Yarrow?"

"Hopefully," he answered.

"It'll be there. Inform the admiral that he needs to stall for a bit. Let him do his stand-up, ad-lib, comedy act thing that he thinks is funny, but isn't, and everything will be fine."

"O-Okay," sputtered Yarrow.

"Marisol, you understand what you need to do?"

"I'm on it."

# CHAPTER TWENTY-SEVEN

Once I was out of sight I took the stairs two by two, thankful for flat shoes. Dr. Pryor's office was a level below, near my own. A word-smithing wizard, she had been the obvious choice to polish my father's prose. He had outward ease, and was a natural speaker, but his motivational speeches had been recycled too many times, so she had been asked to create something special for tonight's augmented audience that included foreign merstation diplomats.

Arriving at the MMLSSE offices, I was surprised to hear voices in the corridor, farther ahead. I thought everyone was upstairs, enjoying the show. There was no need for system supervision in my department, but whatever, it was not my concern. I needed to grab the tablet and deliver it to Yarrow before merstation merriment entered meltdown mode.

Ignoring the voices, I identified at the hatch and tapped the release to Pryor's office. Luckily, my new handy dandy security clearance got me right in, and the tablet was sitting neat and tidy on top of her desk. Wonderful. I would be back with time to spare.

I grabbed the tablet and exited the office, hearing the voices again. *Creighton? Why was he still down here?*

Deciding that I could spare a moment to investigate, I turned toward his voice, but as I got closer I instinctively stopped. The tone of the conversation was unusually harsh and threatening.

". . . because you took it away from her. The only thing she's ever wanted. What she worked so hard for and deserved."

It was Creighton's voice and he was upset.

"Stop trying to intimidate me, Mr. Wannabe Boyfriend. You're not the only one who cares about Marisol. I would never have purposely tried to hurt her. I didn't even want this!" replied a second voice.

It was Felix. Felix and Creighton were having an argument over me. They were around the corner, out of sight, and I should have approached to end their confrontation, but my feet held back, anchored in place. I wanted more information.

"You had to beat her in the trials, didn't you? Did that make you feel special? Did you finally get the attention you so desperately need?"

"What? We were supposed to try our best. It was a competition . . . Oh, wait a second. It's starting to make sense. You threw it. You let her beat you, which unfortunately allowed me to beat you too," Felix surmised. "That explains why you were so snarky at grad. Losing your cool for once."

"It was better than helping her. You treated her as though she wasn't capable of doing the tasks herself."

Creighton had thrown the trials. My mind was racing, trying to remember the details of each one.

"You think I didn't notice the silkworms or the oyster tank? She didn't want your help."

"Well, that's what you do when you care about someone. You help them. It's not all kisses, cuddles, and romantic slow dances, it's about shouldering them when it counts. I know why you're angry, Creighton, and it has nothing to do with me. It's your loyalty to your father. You're conflicted. I too have a security clearance, mine's actually higher than yours if we're splitting hairs, and during the week we've been assigned we've had more than enough time to learn what's transpired down here and what's going on above."

I was transfixed and had completely forgotten about delivering the tablet. I wanted to know more about Creighton's father and the surface.

"My father acts with integrity at the discretion of the admiral. He follows orders."

"As if. Everyone remembers his integrity when he broke you of your shyness. A crying little Creighton forced to stand for hours reciting the dinner menu to residents as they arrived at the dining hall. Standing there until you got it right. No bathroom breaks. No dinner. Night after night. It was top-notch parenting."

"This wasn't his decision! Lay off of my father, Nyrmac. You've never even had one."

"Well, you may want to find a way to paint him in a good light because she will find out that he was the one who sidelined her into MMLSSE. That conversation is coming, Creighton. I promise you. One day soon she will learn that the only reason she got stuck spoon-feeding the flecks is because your dad, the almighty captain, refuted the unanimous recommendation of the Assignment Committee to assign her as a cuvier."

My heart stopped. I had received the assignment I wanted. It didn't make any sense.

"It wasn't him! It was her mother, Empyreal. She calls the shots around here and you know it. She made him overrule."

I was beginning to feel unwell.

"Whether it was the brainchild of your father or her mother, we both know that it was a decision made to prevent her from reaching the surface. To stop her from discovering what they've known the entire time, and unlike you, I won't keep it from her."

"You'll lose your security clearance, and you'll be reassigned."

"I don't care! That doesn't matter. Don't you get it? What matters is that there are survivors up there. There are survivors at the surface and that's why they won't let her dive."

The tablet I was holding dropped to the ground, smashing loudly on the floor in unison with my heart. Screen shards pierced my fingers as I picked it up and started to bleed, but the cuts didn't hurt. What hurt were the lies. They caused rushing blood to fill my ears as my body reacted to the flood of unsettling information. It drowned the voices of the boys calling after me, washing away my desire to celebrate and dousing the urgency to deliver the tablet, but I turned from them and ran. I ran toward the answers I desperately needed.

## CHAPTER TWENTY-EIGHT

What is life? It's an activity of existence. It's the growth of a soul through the creation of a unique storyline. I had wanted my story to come full circle. That was our deal from day one. I would be their child until I could meet my mother again, but my story had no ending. It was an incomplete ring. I needed to know if she was alive.

I stared upward at my handsome father, who, with my mother, had taken to the stage to address the audience. Arm-in-arm, above the rest, the king and queen of our underwater castle. A show of health and harmony before their loyal subjects, they were charming and charismatic, effortlessly holding their residents captive while their princess remain locked in the tower.

My father began reading from the teleprompter.

"Ten years ago, when we abandoned the pedosphere, Empyreal and I could not have imagined the scientific success this merstation, Aqueous, would become. We had dreamt of a new, egalitarian world, void of weapons, currency, and illness. A simple life, where people were united by the preservation of humankind and living in harmonious coexistence with our planet. Basic survival was our goal, but we have greatly exceeded that. Today, we stand together in an abode embellished with ornamentation created from a surplus of resources. A feat made possible through our collective efforts and collaboration with our good friends from Sihai Longwang and Morskaia Derevnia."

He nodded his gratitude in the direction of the audience and then toward the visiting admirals now seated on the stage. My mother nodded and clapped in agreement, beside him. They looked angelic in their white attire. My father wore his newly sewn uniform, while my mother sported a bespoke garment. Created specifically for the admiral's wife, it was a sleeveless, midi, bodycon dress with jeweled neckline and matching box jacket. The jacket was adorned with epaulettes and buttons in similar fashion to my father's.

"To mark this special occasion, Empyreal and I have a big announcement."

I held my breath, waiting to hear him declare salvation for the survivors above.

"Command has approved our dietary analysts' requests to sow coffee beans."

*Coffee beans?*

The crowd went nuts. I had never heard so much noise.

"If there's one thing we've all dreamt about over the past ten years, it's been coffee. I don't know about all of you, but I'm dying for a soy latte," he added.

My mother giggled beside him, tickled, but I stood appalled as he started to speak again.

"Many of you know the story of our aquatic migration, but I believe that on a night like this we reconnect and refocus by retelling our past. Ten years ago, for ourselves and our children, who may have been too young to remember, we abandoned the only life we knew. With the terrestrial comforts of our childhood depleted, we needed a sound solution for their generation. The world was in collapse, a natural extermination of the species who had abused it for too long. Corruption and greed had fueled the individual agendas of the powerful, dividing us. There were great rewards for some, but modest means for most. It was the cruel and sad sickness of a self-serving society."

"The need for leadership was apparent. Leadership that could transcend national boundaries to unite the scientific minds capable of utilizing Earth's greatest gifts—the oceans. Previously deemed impossible, Admiral Bojing, Admiral Afanasy, and I united to research the possibility of inhabiting such a place. A place for life on a dying planet, and gathering experts from around the globe we launched Operation Nereids. It would be our last stand."

"Nereids was a covert mission unbeknownst to our heads of state. Their disbelief and inability to globally unite, rendered them useless, ineffective leaders, so we shut them out. A coup d'état for the survival of our species would see them perish in their grand white houses, along with the innocents they had bureaucratically suppressed."

His comments were met with somber whispers from the crowd. Their discord toward previous governments had inspired this aquatic life, but saving everyone had been impossible. They listened intently as my father's monologue continued.

"Nereids was launched at an ideal time, when shrinking populations reduced $CO_2$ output significantly, halting ocean acidification. Power failures, natural disasters, and death resulted in abandoned land resources well-suited for the construction of our conceptualized merstations. We united experts, collected materials, and began building sustainable, saltwater cities deep beneath the surface of the ocean."

Momentary applause escaped the audience.

"But we could not save everyone. During the harvest of humanity we sacrificed loved ones. Extended family members and good friends who could not be told of our operation, perished. We did the unthinkable, turned our backs on them to face the ocean, and embraced a new family—all of you. You are the souls who built this station so that we could descend together toward a greater cause."

My father paused and there was more applause.

I remembered the launch vividly for it was the most significant day of my life. They had not taken every soul who contributed to the station. That was a lie. Aqueous workers had been turned away at the dock, in front of us, and rumors that personnel with fever, illness, or disability had been denied embarkation had pestered since. The bureaucratic plague of previous political administrations had infected my father as well.

"Over the last decade, our commitment to each other has not faltered. Submerging together to where we began, we are as committed now as we were then. Exceeding benchmarks has become our wheelhouse because Aqueous provides an environment of absolute focus. A healthy vacuum of sustainable living, free from disease and hardship. Clear your mind and exceed the limit. It's a simple, shared experience without discrimination or corruption. We all contribute and we all receive. Our needs are met equally as they should be. Every department plays an instrumental role in this harmonious symphony at sea."

The crowd clapped wildly. They were buying what he was selling.

"And supporting us further are our aquatic neighbours at Sihai Longwang and Morskaia Derevnia. With departments that mirror our own, we've tripled our abilities. Information sharing has played a vital role in the expedition of station productivity, and with that said, I would like to invite Admiral Bojing and Admiral Afanasy to join me at the podium."

My mother sat as the visiting admirals rose from their chairs and crossed the stage to my father. They had remained on Aqueous since graduation to collaborate with our officers.

Admiral Bojing, a jolly faced man, would be the first to speak. He had a trustworthy demeanor, but I noticed that he was adorned with a large round watch. An item that I only knew from history and that we had no need for on Aqueous.

"It is with great honor that I celebrate this ten year milestone with all of you today. I have known Admiral Blaise for many, many years, and he is a man of great vision and integrity. He is a happy man. He is always willing to help us, and his funny disposition has made him a favorite at our station. Your admiral saved many lives that would have been lost. He is wise, and our station is grateful for the continued friendship and support he brings to us."

My father looked rather bashful after the admiral's remarks.

Admiral Afanasy would speak next. Residing on Morskaia Derevnia, she was a thin, stern woman who approached the podium like a wave crossing the sea—powerfully. Her presence was felt before her voice was heard. She was someone to be feared. Her formals, created for this occasion by the atelier on her station, consisted of a tightly laced corset in glossy black, over a crisply starched, white, collared shirt. The keyhole neckline encapsulated a large golden emblem tied around her neck. It was similar to the blue, double-ringed, circular crest that adorned our SIDs, but with what I presumed was the name of her station in the middle. Modest medallion it was not. Neither was her body-hugging skirt or her tall heeled boots that lacked practicality. Her lips and nails were notably varnished in red. Makeup was a forbidden extravagance on Aqueous, and something I had only seen when forced to peruse fashion articles with Naviah, but it looked good on her. She had not spoken at graduation, but tonight she was a spectacle of excess, ready to address the crowd.

I scanned the faces in in the audience, searching for recognition of the hypocrisy before us, but they were transfixed, motionless, eagerly waiting Afanasy's words.

"I can count on Admiral Blaise to do the right thing. He is a logical, strong man. He will never sacrifice our security for himself or anyone else who may try to jeopardise our collective safety. He is a loyal comrade, and my residents and I salute him for making tough decisions for the good of all people."

She signalled Admiral Bojing to follow her to their seats near my mother, and I watched them closely, trying to ascertain if they knew of the life on the surface.

"Thank you, friends," my father said.

Their complimentary remarks were a show of allegiance and possibly an act of deception. The admirals had omitted any mention of the survivors above, ignoring those who had been abandoned to struggle under the sun. There were potentially many residents with relatives up there, unaware that their loved ones lived on, awaiting rescue, with no apparent reason for them to be shut out and us locked in. We had Aux. I wanted answers.

"I think we saved the day. For a second there I thought Yarrow would have to be reassigned," said Naviah, returning from delivering props to the flecks.

The sea life tribute was up next.

"Are you okay, Marisol?"

I could feel her eyes surveying my appearance. It wouldn't take long before . . .

"You're bleeding!" she exclaimed softly, trying not to draw attention.

"I'm fine. I dropped the tablet, but it appears to be working."

"Dropped the tablet? That isn't like you."

"I overheard Creighton and Felix arguing. Naviah, there are survivors above."

"As in people? That's impossible."

"It's not. The boys have high-level clearance, and they've learned that there are people alive, above us."

Naviah was motionless. A rare act, nearly never witnessed.

"Is your birth mother among them?"

"I don't know. I need to talk to my parents, but based on the argument between Creighton and Felix exceptional measures have been taken to keep this information from me."

"Oh boy," Naviah said, shifting her gaze back toward my father. "This is going to get ugly."

Unaware of the storm brewing, my father, microphone in hand, continued the bravado by introducing the darlings of the ceremony.

"And without further ado, to the delight of parents across the station—in fact, it feels like only yesterday that our little Marisol was one herself—I give you our FUNdamental superstars, our scientists of tomorrow, and our future, the flecks, *Living the Sea Life!*"

The delegates left the stage and the lights dimmed as the flecks appeared, wearing pod costumes that were illuminated by handheld flashlights.

"It must be around here somewhere."

"They call it Aqueous."

"It's our new home."

"I can't wait to find it!"

The audience chuckled as the youngsters enacted a narrative of our decade onboard, which included our arrival, pods, new friends at schools, lots of science, and eating weird stuff. Naviah held my good hand as we watched in silence. The kids did a good job transitioning between their backdrops and props. It was a hit.

Lilith returned to the stage to close the show.

"Weren't they superb, ladies and gentlemen? Give me a huge round of applause for the flecks!" she yelled.

She had a mic and she was going to use it.

"I've been a lover of the arts my entire life, and it's my dream to give them a stronger presence here, at the bottom of the sea. We need more lights, more color, more song, so I'm inviting all of you to sing along with me now. Sing and dance for the ten glorious years we've been a family. Sing and dance to burn some calories before we feast on the culinary delights prepared by our handsome chef, Sergeant Eirome. We love that guy, don't we?"

The audience erupted in cheer and applause for Reggie. Lilith could work a crowd.

"They love her," remarked Naviah.

"She's so good," I agreed.

"And they love you too, Marisol. Everything will be alright. I know it will. You're surrounded by residents who care about you. Let's give your parents a chance to explain. I'm sure they've had their reasons to keep this information from you. Let's listen to them and pray that soon we'll be celebrating your mother's arrival. The two of you united on Aqueous," she said.

"Yes, let's hope so," I replied, but it was unlikely. To say there were survivors on the surface did not guarantee that my mother was alive, and if my father had planned to save any of them he would have done so already.

We shifted our attention back to Lilith.

"Reginald, where are you?" she purred. "You're supposed to come up here and dance with me."

The crowd began to chant, "Reggie, Reggie, Reggie . . ." as Lilith looked around for him, and without fail he emerged behind her, smiling and waving to the crowd with both of his extra large hands.

Draping her arm over his massive shoulder she said, "You're gonna save our stomachs tonight, right, Reg?"

Reggie looked slightly uneasy, but shrugged and nodded happily in agreement.

"You've been saving them for ten years already, my friend," she continued.

The band introduced the beat of the next song and Lilith started jumping in place as Reggie fist-pumped in the air. She was closing the show with Swedish House Mafia's, "Save the World."

As Lilith sang, the grand pavilion was illuminated like a disco. The trees, spires, ponds, and stage changed color to the beat of the song, in endless combination. Reggie twirled and hip-bumped with members of the choir and the audience danced along. We had achieved the unthinkable. We had saved the world, or at least some of it. The rest of it had managed to save themselves.

"She's almost finished. Do you mind if we go to the dining hall now?" I asked Naviah.

"That's a great idea. We can clean off your hand before we eat," she said, not realizing that I had lost my appetite completely.

I stayed close to Naviah as she zig-zagged her way through the dancing crowd. She was small, but mighty, and I was happy to let her lead. My mind wandered as I followed along.

*Would my mother have survived? She was capable, clever. She would have fought.*

We passed into the less crowded dining hall. The same glass fragments that adorned the grand pavilion had been strung here also, but in varying lengths with the lowest points found directly over the tables. Combined with clematis cascading from the ceiling, they created a canopy of inverted centrepieces above tables covered in pink cloth matching the jellyfish ponds. The walls were flooded with the same golden light that had initially illuminated the grand pavilion. It was a coherent look to unify the spaces.

Many of the tables were already full. Parents had positioned themselves close to the monitors so that they could see the show and feed their youngsters. It was a rolling buffet, followed by a dance, with small children fed first.

Sugar could be seen flailing her arms at us from a table near the kitchen. As Aqueous' newest dietary analyst, she had been heavily involved with the menu selection and portion allocation for the event. She was seated with Julip and Purity. Together, they needed to occupy a table where they could keep an eye on the food.

I pointed them out to Naviah.

"I see them. If they've plated tubeworms there's gonna be trouble," Naviah threatened while moving in their direction.

"Naviah! Marisol! Isn't this great?" asked Sugar as we neared. "There's so much color, so much fun. It's like being back on Sihai Longwang."

Julip looked surprised and stated, "Is Sihai Longwang better than Aqueous?"

"Hmmm . . . I love it here, but it's white and stiff. They could loosen things up a bit."

"But white shows the dirt, making it easier to clean," said Purity.

*Feels dirty to me.*

Crimson, who had just arrived, barked, "Purity, I'm too tired to hear about cleaning, so zip it."

*Thank you, Crimson.*

Etan, Felton, Joen, Amley, and eventually Felix and Creighton, joined us to linger near the monitor beside the table. It was almost time for dinner, but I would not be eating. My appetite had torpedoed.

As the performance ended with the completion of Lilith's set, Murphy emerged. Back in his formals, he looked flushed and upset.

"Did everything go smoothly?" Naviah asked. "Are your chicks tucked neatly into bed?"

"Some of them. The older ones were missing."

Confused, Naviah asked, "Did they escape?"

"Oh no," gasped Purity.

"Guess what's for dinner," said a disheartened Murphy.

"I'm so sorry, Murphy," said Sugar. "It's a celebration and everyone loves chicken. There wasn't enough cloned."

Naviah turned on her, asking angrily, "Still think the evening's colorful and fun now?"

Sugar looked intimidated, but as a dietary intern said, "We're bringing back coffee."

"What is coffee?" asked Joen.

"I don't know, but I'm never eating chicken again," said Murphy.

"Too bad you butchered your meat growth demo, Murph," said Etan, with a surprising amount of empathy.

Naviah put her arms around Murphy's sagging shoulders and said, "Today couldn't get any worse."

Creedan arrived and asked, "What's wrong with today? I hear there's booze."

"Well, I could use a drink," said Felix.

"Me too," said Creighton.

"Me three," murmured Murphy.

"Excuse me. Did I overhear you saying that you are planning to drink tonight?"

We turned in unison to see my mother and father walking toward us. My mother had her arm through his as they stepped together in unbreakable allegiance, but their gait was off, like he was supporting her. She hadn't seemed well lately.

"Let's hope it's champagne!" cried Lilith, waltzing in to stand too close to my father who stepped back from her. The teenage, man-eating vibe she was emitting made him noticeably uncomfortable.

Crimson glared at her and said, "What do you know about champagne?"

"I know it's the best, like me." Her hair was wet, slicked back, and she had changed into her new formal SIDs—an outfit consisting of a high-collared black blouse with billowing long sleeves and a high-waisted pencil skirt. Inexplicably, she had managed to make the dull uniform of a drama teacher provocative. "Besides, we need to toast to my first show. Did I kill it out there or what?"

She was still riding high on her performing arts horse.

"Yeah, you were good," Naviah stated flatly.

Naviah was too emotionally drained to support Lilith's ego. Something I could relate to. I looked from Creighton to Felix to my parents, trying to decide who I would accost first.

"Good? Lilith, you were magnificent," gushed my mother. "Absolutely captivating, my dear. We were blown away." She extended her arms to give Lilith a congratulatory hug. She was the mother everyone wanted. Praise alone from Empyreal Blaise could power the station indefinitely. "Where's your mother? Her piano playing was such a complement to the evening. She must be so proud of you."

"She's taken her meal in her room," said Lilith, looking disappointed.

I couldn't imagine that it was easy for Lilith's mom to share the spotlight with anyone.

"And your mother, Naviah?" my mother asked.

"She's gone to the nursery to supervise the little ones. She thinks their parents should get a night off."

"That's kind of her. I hope she got to see all the costumes and our formal SIDs before she left. You've done such an amazing job. We've never looked this good. You are the right woman for Atelier."

"Thank you, Mrs. Blaise."

"Marisol, do you have a second to chat?" Creighton asked, sidling up to me discreetly. "There's something important that I need to tell you."

"In a few minutes, Creighton. I'm speaking with my parents first."

He knew I had overheard his conversation with Felix, making it obvious what he was about to divulge, but the admission was not his responsibility. Neither Creighton nor Felix were accountable for my well-being. The circumstances determining my assignment were expunged through the deceit of our superiors—my parents. I would address them directly to protect the boys. I did not want either of them to disclose classified information on my account, so moving past Creighton I approached them.

"Mom. Dad. Can I speak with you for a moment?"

"Sure, sweetheart. What is it? Are you enjoying the evening?" my mother inquired.

"How was my speech? For some reason the visibility on the monitor was bad tonight, so I had to wing it."

"Can we go somewhere private?"

"I'm sorry, honey. We can't leave right now. We have to get back to the delegations from Sihai Longwang and Morskaia Derevnia, but tomorrow there should be . . ."

"This cannot wait," I snapped.

The tone of my voice was a surprise to myself and my friends, who halted their conversations to stare. My mother was quick to control the situation by putting her arm around me.

"Is everything alright?"

She smiled outwardly at my friends, but I would not be sidelined. I was no longer a child, as determined by the Aqueous Assignment Committee, and if my parents wouldn't give me a private audience, I would give them witnesses.

"Is it true that you derailed my assignment as a cuvier to prevent me from discovering that there are survivors above?"

My words drew strong reactions from my peers. Lilith put her hand to her chest, Creedan cursed loudly, Joen ran his hands through his hair, Amley sat down next to Sugar, and Creighton and Felix exchanged concerned looks as Naviah looked upward and crossed herself.

My father responded without falter.

"What are you talking about, princess? By the sound of things you've had a lot of excitement this evening."

He chuckled confidently while his eyes worryingly surveyed the havoc my words had wreaked. By my estimation, if there were survivors above, the information would shatter the apriorism Aqueous was anchored to, but I wanted the truth.

"Is my mother alive? And I don't mean this one," I said, casting my eyes toward his wife. "My biological mother. Have I been confined to this station to prevent me from finding her?"

I could feel the eyes of others, residents within earshot, turning to illuminate our discussion like the spotlights on the stage.

"Oh my God," said Empyreal, bending over to steady herself on the edge of a table.

"Marisol, please," said my father. "This is some sort of misunderstanding. You need to calm yourself. You are upsetting your mother."

"No! I want answers, and I want them now."

Dr. Pryor approached our group with the visiting Admirals, blissfully unaware that she was leading them toward calamity.

"Why don't we discuss this privately? Let's go back to AP1 for a drink. The three of us. We haven't spent any time together lately."

I would have agreed to my father's suggestion, but Empyreal, who had not been herself lately, snapped.

"I told you this would happen," she hissed at my father. "No matter what we did, or how hard we tried, the biological connection was always going to eclipse our efforts."

"Empyreal, don't do this," cautioned my father. "Not now."

But disregarding my father's warning she turned to me and said, "We promised to protect you, love you, but we never agreed to return you. You are *my* daughter, and I don't care who's up there. You are staying down here, safe, with us."

"Empyreal, I implore you. Stop," my father said.

The delegates from the other stations had closed in. Admiral Afanasy was the first to react.

"It's time to control your wife, Admiral. She does not have clearance to possess this information. You've allowed this problem to exist for too long, and I have tired of her antics."

Admiral Bojing attempted a diversion by yelling, "Everyone! It's a party! Let's dance!" But DJ Kade didn't drop a beat in time with his announcement, and he found himself side stepping in silence. To no one in particular he then said, "We need some music. Like, really, really loud music," and ran off toward the turntables.

Empyreal attempted an explanation.

"Yes, we lied, but it was for your own good."

Her eyes were wild, pleading, but also tired and strained. Keeping this secret must have caused her considerable anguish, tarnishing her polished exterior. She wiped her brow and shifted on her feet. Her torment was tangible, and she repeatedly pulled at the cuffs of her jacket, trying to straighten things out.

"You worked so hard, Marisol, defying the odds to become who are you are today and we've been awed by the little girl we raised, but I can't allow your dreams to derail this community. Our sanctuary. In a cozen, you would have returned to the surface and ruined everything."

"You're not a mother. You're a monster. A selfish monster. How many people are you knowingly allowing to suffer up there? Are there few or are there many?"

She attempted to take my hands, but I pulled away.

"Marisol, one day you'll forgive me and understand that my motives were good. This is what's best for you. Being here with us is your destiny. We saved you, but we couldn't save everyone. It wasn't possible. It isn't possible. You need to believe me."

I had never seen her like this. Grovelling. Begging for pity. Her love for me had destroyed her. It had clouded her judgement and impaired her sensibility. We were working to save humanity and they had declared a surplus, moments earlier, on the stage. I understood that ten years ago choices had to be made, but now, with abundant resources and ample lodging, we could invite the survivors to join us. There could be salvation for everyone.

The blaring background music stopped abruptly.

"ATTENTION. ATTENTION. Incoming object. Proceed to pods immediately," alerted the AI Assistant.

The residents stopped eating, stopped dancing, and looked around at each other in surprise. It was an unexpected announcement.

"Admiral Blaise, was this scheduled?" asked Creighton.

"Not to my knowledge."

A hush befell the crowd.

"ATTENTION. ATTENTION. Incoming object. Proceed to pods immediately," alerted the AI Assistance again.

"A malfunction, perhaps? It is highly unusual to test your system during a celebration," commented Admiral Afanasy, looking upward through the glass.

Admiral Bojing returned, concerned. It was not a drill.

"Ladies and gentlemen, there was no scheduled drill for this evening, and while this is probably a glitch, I advise all of you to calmly proceed to your pods as previously practiced. Please remain there until such time as we have rectified the situation," my father instructed loudly.

Groans could be heard from the residents as they began shuffling to the staircase. The interruption of their festivities was highly annoying.

"Attention all Aqueous residents, this is Captain Kress. I repeat, this is Captain Kress. All officers are requested in Command, immediately. All divers are requested to man their posts, immediately. We have an inbound ship on course to collide with the station. Proceed to your pods in preparation for station abandonment. I repeat, prepare for station abandonment."

Groans turned to gasps and gasps turned to panic as residents dashed in every direction. Parents screamed for their children. Many of which had wandered off to dance and play, enjoying their late night freedom. There was no indication of how much time we would have before impact, or if there was even time to get to our pods before the hatchways would seal.

"Marisol, I have to go. Follow your father to AP1. It's the safest pod," said Creighton, turning to run with the officers toward the officers' staircase.

"Admirals, take your delegates back to Mass Landing and ready your pods. Empyreal, Marisol, come with me," echoed my father.

Turning to lead us to safety, he would return to Command prior to piloting AP1 with his family. Empyreal was right behind him, but I did not move. I needed to return to my pod and rescue my beads. They were my only true possession and the link to my past.

I turned away from them, toward the kitchen. I would descend to my level in the supply lift and traverse to my pod from there. There would be time to collect my beads and get back to AP1.

*Clear your mind, forget what others expect of you, and exceed the limit.*

Empyreal didn't realize that I had not followed them until it was too late. Residents stampeded between us, creating an impassable divide, trying desperately to gather their children and force their way down the grand staircase to their pods. I could hear her screaming my name and struggling against my father's hold as I briskly walked away.

I did not know where my friends were, but they were well trained. We all knew what to do. There were many ways off of the station. The main thing was to remain calm.

"Marisol! Marisol!" someone called from behind me.

It was Felix.

"You should head to Command with your family."

"I will, but I have to get something from my pod."

I was icy cool and laser-focused. There was no fear. The events of the evening had exhausted my emotions, so my hands were steady and my thoughts were clear. I was going to do what I wanted to do for a change.

"You may not have time. This is urgent."

"I can always pilot my own pod, Felix."

"But your parents will wait, compromising their safety."

*Why would I care about their safety? They cared about coffee beans.*

"Where are you supposed to go, Felix?"

"I'm supposed to report to Sub-Command and await further instructions, but I'll go with you to get your beads and then see you safely to Command."

I stopped. Felix knew about my beads. I couldn't recall mentioning them to him before.

"Marisol, please. We need to keep moving. This situation could be dire."

"Alright."

We descended in the supply lift together, moving briskly past Comestible Silos & Refrigeration, through the arboretum, and toward the corridor housing the MMLSSE offices. It didn't take us long. The station had emptied significantly since Captain Kress' announcement.

I descended my airlock, grabbed my beads, and returned to Felix expeditiously with an enormous sense of relief. I did not know if my mother was at the surface, but I had my story beads. Her tiny legacy would survive with me whatever the future may hold.

"Come on," Felix motioned. "If we ascend the grand staircase we can ensure that the kids are sorted on the way by."

"I can do that on my own, Felix."

"I insist."

There was no time to argue, so we headed through the labs.

"Where is your father?"

"In his pod near the infirmary, I assume. I will check on him once this is over."

"ATTENTION. ATTENTION. Hatchways closing. Stand clear," alerted the AI Assistant.

I had never seen the hatchways close involuntarily. The hatchway connecting the labs to the MP corridor was before us.

"ATTENTION. ATTENTION. Hatchways closing. Stand clear," alerted the AI Assistant again.

The hatchway began to close.

"Marisol, run!"

The urgency needed no explanation. There were no pods in the labs. To be enclosed there would to be without escape. We needed to be in the corridor.

Sprinting toward the hatchway we dove beneath it, barely sliding through the diminishing opening in time. I stood up, relieved, and looked to my right where Felix should have been, but I was alone. The hatchway had sealed with Felix on the other side.

"Felix!"

I banged on the glass as hard as I could, but it would not budge. I tapped the release, repeatedly, but the hatch did not respond.

"ATTENTION. ATTENTION. Prepare for impact. Repeat. Prepare for impact," alerted the AI Assistant.

Felix tapped the intercom.

"Marisol, you need to ascend into a mini-pod."

"Felix!"

I kicked the seal in vain, trying to dislodge the hatch and free him.

"Help! Somebody! I need help!"

My screams echoed along the abandoned corridor. Residents with children would have disengaged in propulsion pods already, awaiting further instruction from a safe distance. I expected no answer, but then a mild voice replied to my cry.

"Is somebody there? Who is that?"

I could not see who it was around the curved corridor.

"It's Marisol, and I need help. Please! I need to release this hatch."

A figure came into sight. It was Duanra. Her expression fell when she saw Felix trapped on the other side.

"Marisol, you need to ascend in an airlock," he instructed again.

"I can't. I can't leave you."

"Marisol," soothed Duanra, putting her arms on my shoulders. "I've loaded some flecks and stinkers into the mini-pods. Starren and her friends were down here playing, and now they're separated from their parents. They're terrified. In the event the pods detach, I could really use your help up there."

"Up there? I'm not going up there. I can't," I said frantically. "I have to free Felix!"

"Marisol, I cannot override the lab hatch, but the mini-pod airlocks released automatically. It is imperative that you ascend quickly."

She pulled me from Felix toward the nearest airlock as I continued to look at him. The memories of our childhood, the years spent together, came flooding back, and now I could see that the former lonely boy had been replaced by a remarkable young man. A man that I cared about.

"Disposable, remember?" he reminded with a sad smile. "Not like you. You are the girl who is loved by many mothers. Someone far too precious to lose."

"I-I caused this. I was too slow. I should have left the beads. These silly, worthless pine needles. We could have escaped together in my pod," I stammered, but there was no way to amend my mistake. I could only hope that a station breach would not compromise the labs. "I'm sorry, Felix. I'm so sorry."

My words were stifled by loud moaning coming from above. It was the hull of the approaching ship, collapsing under the weight of the sea. It had arrived.

We looked up to see its growing shape as it absorbed the lights of the station. It was huge. A dark hulled vessel on a collision course with Aqueous, and there was no way the station would remain intact.

"Go, Marisol!" screamed Felix.

Duanra pushed me into the nearest airlock and tapped the release, sending me upward as she ran to the next one. I ascended safely, hopeful that she would have time to do the same.

"ATTENTION. ATTENTION. Prepare for pod disengagement. Repeat. Prepare for pod disengagement," alerted the AI Assistant.

"No! No! No!" I yelled in childish refusal.

The pod had no propulsion. I would be relinquished to the sea like a wayward charge, set adrift on the current of its whim. I was a diver, a should-be cuvier, and I was needed down here.

An escalating rumble shook my pod like the vibrations of an avalanche chasing down its victims. Grinding, popping sounds could be heard as an eruption of bubbles temporarily obstructed my view. The pod lurched forward as it released, throwing me onto the glass and giving me a direct view of the sub level and seafloor. The ship had made contact, hurtling scraps of debris across the seascape like asteroids scattering through space. The sub level of the station was dark, inevitably compromised by the boat's unforgiving assault, and with its structural integrity gone, Felix would be gone also. My true friend and protector would be the ocean's champion now. Taken too soon by a renegade ship that I could clearly see. The large rusty tanker was illuminated by still-functioning exterior lighting, and it ripped through the shafts near the turbines before colliding with the earth. Plumes of silt shot upward as it began to list, revealing crudely painted letters on the hull—CADRE.

I struggled for comprehension as the force of impact created upward pressure, righting my pod and sending it skyward. I was prevented from surveying the ship further, but I knew what I had seen. It was not a random ghost ship downed by inclement weather. It was a vessel voyaged with announcement. My mother was alive and waiting for me above.

# Acknowledgments

That voice inside of me, the writer, sat dormant, waiting, for years, decades, steadfast. My love of reading developed during my childhood, on our farm, on the prairies. With no cable television and a party-line telephone, reading was a great escape. Visiting worlds beyond my small town, I would often think: *I could write a book*. I would dream and dream, lost in my thoughts, inventing my own stories effortlessly, but the act of writing was sidelined by studies, career, and household responsibilities until my teenage daughters encouraged me to start. Camryn, Emorie, and Reese are my greatest motivators, my besties, and the inspiration for all that I do.

So with the encouragement of my children, *Aqueous* took shape. I wrote the first few chapters, then I wrote the end, and I filled in the middle as it revealed itself. I typed out conversations when they sprang into my head, finding suitable locations within the text to insert them afterward. I'd daydream while driving (driving alone without the radio on is the best way to write) and pull over to create notes on my phone. Little by little, the chapters took shape, until, finally, my rough draft was complete, but I'd told no one what I was doing. It was one thing to write it, but another thing entirely to share it with others. It was time to divulge my secret.

Risking embarrassment, I selected a talented group of caring women (and a couple of men) whom I admired and trusted. Eventually dubbed my Beta Babes (at the time I didn't know what beta readers were), they were the first to peruse my pages, and, not unexpectedly, they expected my manuscript to be horrible, discreetly discussing how they would break that to me. In no specific order they are: Yasmine Khan, Tara Pencak, Heather Spero, Kayla Spero, Karen Chun, Tina Wilson, Nadja Davis, Camryn Anderson, Emorie Anderson, Reese Anderson, Claudia Eichhorn, Mark Eichhorn, and Arnaud Lelouvier. They found mistake after mistake after countless, ugly mistake, and gave genuine, heartfelt feedback. They nosed out the boring bits and pointed out the preachy parts. Did I make all of their suggested corrections? Absolutely not. But every comment was honest and valuable, and, surprisingly, they liked it. I will never forget the conversations I had with each of them about the emotions they experienced as they read *Aqueous*. They are indelible words etched onto my heart.

Gina Knox changed the course of my life. A friendship created on the Adriatic, we became fast friends on a ship. She's real, she's kind, she's witty, she's understated.

She's basically everything without knowing it, and that's what makes her gorgeous. Gina and I, eventually, discovered that we shared a love of reading and writing, and then she introduced me to her close friend, Kate Gale, who is now my editor. It was not a typical pathway to publication. It was a stroke of luck. I queried a gazillion times, like every other unknown author, to no avail.

Kate Gale, my editor, was quick to read my manuscript cover-to-cover, parallel it to other famous works (goosebumps), and explain that of the hundreds of manuscripts she received each year, Red Hen Press would publish mine (goosebumps upon goosebumps). It was a surreal experience. I had no idea how publishing worked, but Kate, a respected poet and industry veteran, spoke to me as though I was an accredited writer, not a newbie stricken with imposter syndrome. She has been delightful to work with, suggesting changes that enriched *Aqueous* without stripping it of its soul. She's available, grounded (in her yard, surrounded by her dogs and the veggies that she grows), and brimming with imagination, making her eternally youthful. Kate's a good egg.

Red Hen has many good eggs. Mark E. Cull, for example, makes great sushi and pies, and he's excellent at explaining the publishing process. I needed his explanation.

In addition to Kate and Mark, my Red Hen team has consisted of Tobi Harper, Rebeccah Sanhueza, Monica Fernandez, Shelby Wallace, Tansica Sunkamaneevongse, Ariadne Makridakis Arroyo, and Amanda De Vries—the literary sprites parlaying the passion of each Red Hen author into the professional world of words. Thanks to each of you.

Warren J. Sheffer, of Hebb & Sheffer, gave invaluable guidance. I'm grateful for his wisdom on an industry that can be challenging to navigate.

Kathleen Carter, my incredible publicist, shined her sunlight onto Marisol and Aqueous, illuminating them for the masses. Kathleen is kind, connected, and lovely to work with.

I'd thank my agent, but I don't have one.

Richard Mull, husband to Gina, welcomed me into their home when I flew to California to meet the Red Hen team. That trip marked the official debut of my author identity, making it not only enjoyable, but meaningful. Thank you for putting up with Gina, myself, and our giggles; thank you for riding your bike often, so that Gina and I could do other things; and thank you for that breakfast concoction where you piled weird, healthy stuff sky-high onto pancakes. It was good.

My author photos (where I look younger and smarter) were shot by the talented Brian Reilly of West Studios. He's hysterical, but warning: laughing that much during a photo shoot hurts. And it didn't help that during the pandemic lockdowns I had repeatedly bleached my hair with kitchen-found chemicals (not recommended, but hilarious) to the brink of baldness. Thankfully, Brian's lens, with Danielle

Grad's expertise in hair and makeup, magically balanced it out. Sadly, my day-to-day life does not include either of them, so there's a vast disparity between my author pics and how I usually look—also known as reality.

Capturing moments, for posterity and social media, is critical, and Claudia Eichhorn (neighborhood friend and photographer extraordinaire) donated her time, camera, and fierce skills to frame my Beta Babes (which is no small feat as they don't stop nattering) in gorgeous group photos that I will cherish forever.

Brenda Beltran of Vibrant Beauty was responsible for my makeup during the shoot with Claudia. Thanks, gal.

My glam squad also includes Andrea Berrie, who can throw in hair extensions faster than a drywaller with a nail gun. It's necessary. My hair refuses to grow.

June Fontaine, lover of racquet sports and mother to Cherie, confirmed that my sea dragon, Sihai Longwang, was spelled correctly. Then she helped me to pronounce it, which was more difficult than walloping her at tennis, but easier than defeating her at pickleball.

Lara and Elizabeth Provost (Lara is an incredible painter) are the mother/daughter duo who told me that the original name I used for the merstation located in the Kuril-Kamchatka Trench made no sense. I had used a feminine word with a masculine word, messing it up badly enough that they intervened with alternatives. I ultimately changed the name to Morskaia Derevnia. Thanks for the save, ladies.

I'd also like to thank the University of Calgary for closing all educational doors except the one that led to the Department of English. My marks were terrible, I partied too much, but it paid off.

And then there's the readers, the dreamers, the fictional world adventurers who sank with Marisol and myself into the darkest depths of the ocean. It is to you that I owe the biggest THANK YOU of all. This story is for girls and boys who have endured hardship, felt misunderstood, awkward and/or unsure of themselves. You are perfection as you are. You are worthy, you are strong, and you are smart. Most importantly, your unique journey enables you to be empathetic and make our world a better place. You have all the right stuff, right now, already. Now, read that again.

So that's my village, and it took all of them to raise *Aqueous*—a story for my children—to the surface. And like Marisol, who arrived in a place never meant for her, I am grateful to be with these people.

# About the Author

Jade Shyback was born in Red Deer, Alberta on June 24, 1973. A nature lover, she spent five glorious years with her parents and brother in Nanaimo, British Columbia, riding her bike and scavenging for sea life on the rocky beaches of the Pacific coast. At age nine she returned to Alberta to live on a farm nicknamed Mosquito Flats until she obtained a degree in English, the only faculty that would have her, from the University of Calgary. A career in financial services led her to Toronto and onward to Abu Dhabi where she raised three daughters amidst sand and camels while working in Dubai as a financial regulator. She now lives in Oakville with her greyhounds and cat. Jade's hobbies include beekeeping, boating, playing tennis, and gardening. *Aqueous* is her debut novel, and despite her love of the ocean, she would never descend two and a half kilometers to live beneath it.